Say It Ain't So

By: Christopher Clark

Say It Ain't So

ISBN: 978-1-68564-536-6
Copyright © 2021 by Christopher Clark

Published by: C'Cliché LLC
Email: cclicheme@yahoo.com

Acknowledgments

First off I have to give thanks to God. He has given me the strength to be where I'm at right now. I want to thank brother Randel for helping me get on my job and Ms. Sheree because without them this could've not happened, I would still be at square one. I want to thank my mother for doing an amazing job of raising me and molding me into the man I am today.

My two sisters Kara & Ashley for being there when it was tough.

My best friend Nzomiwu for holding it down. She has been loyal to me from day one.

My baby brother Johnny, Rip, and I'm going to rep you forever.

Rip my brother Nard who walked that 10 years down with me and kept it100 with me when he touched down.

My HP dogs. YOO!

Much love to my Solah brothers who stayed on me about getting my priorities intact.

My brothers from another Larry Oriol., Deon Thompson., Kejuan Davis., Eric Woods., Geezy, Pa Karl, Kevin Ampey, My Brody Calieb Tillman.

Lastly my brothers that's doing time. My Tru brothers holding their heads trying to get home. I love y'all and it's gone forever be Truuuuu!

To my readers and supporters, I want to thank you for rocking with me. Even when I was down y'all was with me helping me when I thought it was over. Never give up and keep fighting for what you believe in. You control your own destiny.

Love is Love
Loyalty is Law

CHAPTER 1

July 12th, 2000

I stepped up out the joint thinkin' to myself how it was gonna be a hot summer. I had on a Dickie outfit and some hoe-ass state shoes. *I gotta get the fuck up out this bullshit*, I thought to myself.

I was born and raised in Highland Park, Michigan. Which is a small city in the middle of Detroit, but I'm not from the "D", I'm from Highland Park. A lot of people consider Highland Park, Detroit, but if you said that to a real H.P. nigga, you would of got yo' head split. I grew up with four sisters, two brothers, and mom dukes. My dad was a deadbeat; he only came around when he needed something. He ended up in prison for armed robbery. We all took over our dad's last name. I was the youngest and spoiled like some milk that sat out for weeks. Things changed once I jumped off the porch. I started smellin' my ass. Mom dukes ended up workin' for General Motors, so we never wanted for nothing. We stayed in the latest shit. A lot of times my moms would look like who shot john, but she made sure we had food on the table, a roof over our heads, and clothes on our backs. Sometimes I would be embarrassed because she would come inside my school dressed like anywho. But I didn't really care cause I loved her to death. I always wanted to make my moms proud of me, so me graduating from high school and going to college was my goal. None of my other siblings went to college except Amber, but she dropped out to go to nursing school.

Everything had changed when I was fifteen. My twin sisters, Lisa and Leslie were killed in a car accident. They spoiled me the most out of all my other siblings. They were on their way to UCLA, they had just graduated from

Highland Park High School. My heart was crushed and my moms was depressed. She ended up losing her job and her mind. I was sick after the funeral. The fucked up part about it was that neither one of my brothers did anything to the niggas that caused the accident. I wasn't thinkin' the same. I was ready to "**MURK**" a nigga after the two niggas took the plea for lifetime probation. I was heated. I didn't know how God could let this happen, but I never questioned Him. What I did do was grab a burner. It wasn't shit to get a pistol. I had a few dollas saved up for working with my Uncle Deven. I brought a .38 revolver for $150.00 from this ol'school named Red that lived around the corner from me. The two niggas that killed my sisters stayed right in the Park, so it wasn't shit to catch em'. The next month I saw both of em' I Coney Island fast food restaurant flirting with these two young females I went to school with. These niggas get to enjoy life while my sisters were gone? When I walked in they never noticed, but the cameras did, but I didn't give a fuck! As soon as I pulled out the .38, the two females screamed. I let off the first shot striking one of them in the shoulder. He fell while the two females hit the floor. The other nigga ran out of Coney Island yellin', "What I do!" I took off right behind him squeezing the trigger. I didn't see where the bullet struck, all I knew was he was down on the ground. After I saw everybody looking at me, I ran. I ran until I had no wind left. I couldn't go home because I knew the two females were gonna tell the hook where I lived, so I ran to my best friend's house. Daron was always there for me. The summer was here so it wasn't no school. I told Daron what happened and nobody else. Aunty Vicki was cool and so was Uncle Phil. Uncle Phil wasn't Daron's pops, but he's been around since Daron's dad committed suicide. Daron told his moms I was stayin' over for the weekend. I stayed for a couple days until my sisters had called Aunty Vicki to tell her that I was wanted for two counts of attempted murder and two counts

of felonious assault. Aunty Vicki was my second mom, so anything she said, I listened. She told me I needed to turn myself in, so I did. The judge looked out for me on the strength of me turning myself in. My family and the niggas I shot family didn't wanna send me to prison because of my age, but the prosecutor wanted me in the system. I ended up takin' a plea for five years. They dropped the two attempted murder charges and the two felonious assaults, and charged me with great bodily harm less than murder. Five-ten years for the two counts of great bodily harm less than murder. You can't beat that! All I thought about was Lisa and Leslie. I asked myself, "Was it worth it?" Well, fuck yeah! Even though I wasn't goin' to see none of my teenage years, I still had to look at it in a good way, I was coming home...

I ended up in Alpha Youth Facility. It was a prison for juveniles. There were so many young niggas there it was a shame. Wasn't nobody there from H.P., so I stayed to myself. Niggas there were from cities I never even heard of: Kalamazoo, Muskegon, Saginaw, and Holland just to name a few. I thought everybody was from Detroit. All I did was read, workout, and sometimes I would play chess or cards. I never got visits because Alpha was so far, but my family stayed writing me, even Daron would write. A couple of people would write from high school, but they didn't stay in to have for long. My girl stayed writing though. My first year being locked up, my moms passed away. I was sick, I felt like my life was over. I had so much on my mind cause' my family didn't have enough money for me to go to the funeral, so I missed it. I knew that at anytime I would snap, so I stayed off the card table, the basketball court, and out the C/O's face, because I didn't have time to be catching no petty tickets. I ended up having an altercation with this Inkster nigga. Every time he came around I went the other way because I knew he was trouble. I heard him say "Yeah bitch ass nigga, you better leave." I

just kept walking until I looked back and saw him walking with his crew towards me. I turned around cause I wasn't trying to get stuck. We were finally face to face. He kept yellin' all this Ink-town rah-rah all in my face. I guess by me not responding to his remarks he was heated. I could care less what he said, I had a family to get home to. He ended up pushing me and that's when I "lost it." I blew his shit out so quick, he fell to the ground holding his jaw. His homeboys didn't do nothing, but watch their boy on the ground scream. I stood there with my fists up waiting for anyone of them clowns to try me. All I felt was the C/O's rush me to the ground. That's when I realized he was still on the ground pointing at me. I went to the hole for assault on an inmate and Man-Man stayed in GP. I did 30 days in the hole. Those 30 days made a nigga really open his eyes. I had people who loved me and wanted me home. My girl Zaria stayed writing me. Her mom would put a letter with hers sometimes. Everybody else had stopped writing me going on my third year. I thought about what I was gonna do when I got out. I was supposed to see the board in two more years. Everybody kept tellin' me Zaria was goin' leave me, but I ignored everybody. She was so beautiful, caramel complexion, 5'3' with the roundest ass I've ever seen, hazel brown eyes, and nice C-cup titties, not too big and not too small. She just didn't have the looks, fast-food brains. She wasn't like the rest of these dumb broads, schemin' on niggas that had money.

I ended up getting out the hole, ready to go back to the hole, but it wasn't even that type of party. Man-Man ain't want no smoke. He walked right pass me with his head down and his homeboys was tryna' be cool with me, but I wasn't fuckin' with em', but I still had to play Man-Man close. When I turned 20 years old, they rode me out of Alpha because of my age. I ended up in T.C.F. It was a laid back joint, so I didn't have no problems.

I ended up at the board on May 6th, 2000. I only caught three tickets, so I was good. The only thing they tripped about was me not getting a trade and catchin' that assault ticket on Man-Man's bitch ass. I had my G.E.D. and my A.D.P. finished. The Counselor vouched for me too, so that was a plus, wasn't any cash shit, but I just took it in. They ended up letting a nigga go and here I am downtown at the Greyhound Station waiting for Zaria. I couldn't believe that Zaria rode the whole five years. I saw a 1999 Monte Carlo pull up, and Zaria jumped out lookin' so good with her black shades, her tight jeans, and her polo shirt on. My jaw dropped.

"Heyyy baby!" She yelled.

"You ain't goin' say nothing?"

"Oh hey baby," I finally choked up the words.

We hugged each other so tight, she was my first. I would've been hers, well I was here because dude she was fuckin' didn't really pop her cherry like he was supposed to. We kissed but it wasn't no tongue. I haven't saw her in five years. She never sent pictures because she said she was insecure about how her pictures turned out.

"So what were you doing while you were waiting on me, Mr. Clark?" She called me Mr. Clark when she was being funny.

"Just thinkin…."

"That's it? Thinking about what?"

"Thinking about if you were going to show up."

"Boy shut up and get in the car," she said punchin' me in the arm. I grabbed my bag and hopped in her car.

"So where we headed Ms. Jones?" I said, being funny.

"We bout to go home boo." That shit sounded so good…home! I couldn't stop lookin' at her thighs. She was so thick and her waist was so small. I knew she saw me cut the corner of her eyes. She still had her black shades on so I never saw her eyes. She had to see the dick print in these

tight ass Dhavekie pants. You couldn't miss it. She said, "You mighty happy to see me huh?" I just smiled and put my hand on her thigh. My hand eased between her thick thighs. I was now rubbin' her pussy through her jeans.

"Boy you better go on somewhere," she said giggling. I started unbuttoning her jeans and started to stick my hand inside her jeans passing her trimmed up hairs, to her hot spot. Damn she was warm as hell.

"Dre, let's stop this, I want this to be special." Her jeans were pulled down just enough so I could move my fingers in and out. She let out a low moan.

"Dre I'm serious, I can't drive and do this at the same time," she said taking my hand out. I put my fingers up in my nose and smelt her sweetness then sucked her juices off my index and middle finger.

"You so nasty boy," she said pulling up her pants and buttoning em' back up at the red light.

It didn't take us long to get to Oak Park. That's where Zaria lived.

"How yo' moms doing?" I asked.

"Oh she moved to Atlanta a couple of years ago." We were in front of her crib. It was small but nice. I had to admit Zaria was doin' her thang. She had her own car, crib, and money, and didn't have any kids running around. You couldn't ask for more. Plus she had a job. Twenty-two years old, the average chick her age would be on her second if not third child by 22. When we got in the house, she had her shit plushed out. A big flat screen in the front room, carpet, and the house smelled so good.

"You can take them ugly clothes off if you want to," she said still trying to be funny.

"You got jokes huh?"

"Okay, the bathroom straight down the hallway and the bedrooms are on the right side of the hallway. Next to the bedroom is the room where your clothes are at."

"Clothes?"

11

"Yeah, I bought you a couple new outfits and shoes until you get back on your feet. You never asked for money so when I thought about sending some, I put it up and saved it, cause' I knew my baby was coming home. Why you think I used to ask what size shoe you wore? You don't remember all the fast-food I asked about your pants size?"

"Yes, I remember. I thought you were trying to be funny or freaky when you asked those questions."

"Boy you so crazy," Zaria said slapping me on the arm. I knew she was the one, but how could I even pay her back? I ain't have no income. Zaria hopped in the shower while I walked around inspecting the house. She had my pictures all over her mirror in her room. I saw candles and the only thing that flashed through my mind was to light them and wine and dine her. I knew Zaria was out here fucking, but I didn't care because what I was about to give her was going to be special.

When Zaria came in the room with her towel wrapped around her beautiful body, I was laid out in my boxers with the candles lit all around the room.

"Damn baby you still know how to spark up the moment," she said.

"Yap, but I'm not a teenager no more," I said.

"And I'm not either," she said dropping the towel, revealing her perky C-cup breasts, her flat stomach, and her pussy hairs were trimmed just right. I could actually see her ass from the front. I made love to her for hours, expl ofoding in her every time I came. She told me she was on birth control, so I took advantage of that.

It had to be at least two o'clock when I woke up. Zaria was still sleep, looking like the sleeping beauty. I hopped in the shower to get the sex smell off. I couldn't go see my family smelling like that. It felt kind of awkward getting into the tub, cause I had to take showers for 5 years. When I got out, I went to the room where Zaria said my clothes were. I opened the closet door and saw a closet full

of clothes. I had put two and two together, so I knew Zaria worked at a clothing store. I had three pair of white on white air force ones, and enough Pelle Pelle and Guess outfits to last me a month straight, not to mention, a bunch of socks, boxers, and white t-shirts on the top shelf. I had like $163.00 in my pocket from saving my last months of being in prison. I grabbed some jeans and a plain white t-shirt. I threw my forces on and was on my way out the door.

"Damn, I almost forgot that state shit," I said. I grabbed a trash bag and threw the Dickie outfit and them hoe ass state shoes in there, and was out of there with Zaria's keys and cell phone. I had to go see my family. I got in the car, threw the trash bag in the passenger's seat, and pulled off. It felt odd driving, but I got back use to it. I just had to get the hell out of the Oak Park. Oak Park was like a middle-class city, but the hook was reckless, so as I got to Detroit, I threw the bag out the window.

Doing my first couple months in prison, Jevon, my 2nd oldest brother was telling me my oldest brother Kevin was down south getting major dough. "anything fuckin' with the weed and from what Von was telling me, Kev was fuckin' with the "White." I had to get put on, but, was Kev really going to let his baby brother get involved with drugs on parole or even period? I can imagine that nigga right now.

"You going to school, you goin' be better than everybody in the family." But fuck that, I needed some dough.

"I need some music," I said to myself. I searched through Zaria's Cd case at the red light because the radio wasn't talking about shit. I came across "The Eastside Chedda Boys." Zaria was telling me about these niggas. Soon as I put it in that shit was pounding. Shit done really changed since "95." Niggas riding on big rims, hoes access is ridiculous, and everybody wearing glasses. I remember if

you wore glasses, you was a lame. Everybody wearing platinum chains and shit, but everybody was wearing gold when I was out. I took the long way to get to Highland Park riding down West 7-Mile, banging Eastside Chedda Boys. As I'm riding, I see a small ground billboard saying, 'FREE HP DRE' T-shirts so I hit a u-turn to see what was up. When I parked and walked up to the store, I saw my picture on the shirts. It was a mugshot photo of me when I first came down. There was a young female passing out flyers for a party. I couldn't believe a nigga was making money off my face. I guess the female that was passing out the flyers didn't recognize that it was me that was on the flyers. The t-shirts were hanging on hangers outside of the store. The young girl handed me a flyer.

"Thank you," I said.

"Your welcome," the young girl said blushing fast-food still be in school, maybe a junior or senior in high school.

Her whole facial expression changed once I asked her who was throwing his party. She rolled her eyes and said, "the owner of the clothing store." She said it like I was supposed to know already. I looked up and the clothing store was called, "Money Talk$."

"Alright, thank you." I said entering the clothing store. When I walked in, it was designer everything: Timberlands, suits, Air-Force ones, Kenneth Coles, Fubu, Everything you wanted it was here. Soon I got halfway in, guess who I see?... My bro Daron. He was fresh as hell, had a cold ass chain on, some wood glasses that looked expensive, and a iced out watch.

"Daron!" I said, trying to get his attention. He looked up with is cell phone to his ear. Soon as he saw me he dropped the cell phone. He was froze wasn't any

"Yeah nigga," I said. Daron almost tripped trying to get to me.

14

"Man, when you get home?" He asked while hugging me.

"Nigga if you was writing more you would've known."

"Get off dat bullshit nigga," he said letting go and hugging me again.

"This yo shit?"

"Hell yeah, I own this shit legit, legal, you name it."

"What's up with this party you throwing?"

"Oh, I throw a party every year around this time 'cause it's close to your birthday. Speaking of birthdays, happy belated birthday nigga. Twenty-one years old, you legal now," he said laughing.

"How long have you had this place and how long you been makin' money off my face with yo' petty ass?" I asked.

"Man, this building been in the family for the longest, but I opened up the store like 3 ½ years ago. I been grindin' ever since. Zaria's the one that came up with the idea of putting your face on t-shirts. Zaria was Daron's lil cousin.

"Man that girl love the hell out of you bro," Daron said going back to pick up his cell phone up off the floor.

"Yeah I know, I love her too."

"So where you headed?"

"I gotta go see my family."

"Here write this number down. This my cell phone number. You can call anytime you need something." I wrote down the number and put it in my pocket.

"Love you nigga, make sure you let me know if you need something."

"Love you too nigga," I said walking out the store like damn that nigga doing his thang, and he was only 24 years old.

CHAPTER 2

Damn that nigga Daron changed. I thought that nigga would have been in the dope game hard. Not trying to sound like a hater, but he was worst than me. Everybody swore up and down he was on his way to prison. I got in the car and drove off. I dug in my pocket to get his number out. When I was out niggas had pagers, and if you had a cell phone you was that nigga.

I was finally in Highland Park. The air still smelt the same. Everything done changed: new barbershop, grocery stores, banks, liquor stores, and mini malls. I turned down my old street. Man, riding down my block brought back so many memories. My first fight, learning how to ride a bike, and sitting on my moms' lap steering her truck while she drove down the street. When I drove up in the driveway I noticed a Tahoe and a Lincoln LS. The Tahoe had to be Amber's because she was a straight up tomboy. She had fought every dude on our block and won! If she didn't win she had brothers that would woop yo' shit. The crazy part was she was beautiful. Not on no perverted shit, but my sisters were thick as hell and all of em' were pretty. I had to keep all of my friends outside the house. Carla and Amber moved back in the house when moms got sick. They sent pictures my first two years of being locked up, but it ended after that, and I had no idea how they looked now. I also knew I had a nephew, who warts four years old. Carla was the prissy type, so I was confused because I thought Carla was going to be the first one pregnant, but it was Amber. Carla was something else. She stayed with two or three boyfriends. One time moms caught a boy in the house, mom beat the hell out of Carla and pushed the boy down the steps. Amber was twenty-five and Carla was twenty-six. Jevon was thirty and Kevin was thirty-four, so we didn't have anything in common, because I was fifteen when I got locked up.

Soon as I walked up the porch steps, I saw a couple of toys and shit. Must've been my nephew's. Damn, I'm an uncle. I rang the doorbell twice. Soon as I heard someone say "hold on," I knew off bell who it was. Amber always had a raspy voice.

"Who is it?" Amber asked.

"U.P.S" I said cracking a smile.

"Carla what the hell you done ordered now?" Amber asked while opening up the front door. Her frown easily turned into a huge smile.

"Carlass, Carla come downstairs, hurry up!" Amber yelled. She jumped on me and hugged me so tight that I could barely breathe. Carla came running downstairs like it was a fire.

"Girl why in the hell you making all that noise?" Her jaw dropped soon as she saw me.

"Oh my God, you got so big, look at you! Give yo' sister a hug nigga!" She said pushing Amber out the way.

"When you get out?" Amber asked.

"I got out today. Zaria picked me up at the Greyhound," I said. Carla's nose flared up after hearing that. Carla couldn't stand Zaria. Zaria never showed any fear towards Carla and all the other girls I fucked with was scared as hell of Carla.

"Why you ain't call me to come get you?" Carla asked.

"Cause that's my girl," I said defending my baby.

"Boy whatever," Carla said throwing her hands up.

"Boy you hungry?" Amber asked. All I thought about was how I was eating Zaria's pussy earlier.

"Naw, I'm good, I ate already. Where Von and Kevin at?" I asked.

"Kev somewhere down south I think and Von somewhere around here riding on his motorcycle. Let me call him right quick," Amber said going to go get the phone.

"Where my nephew at?" I asked.

"He somewhere upstairs playing with his toys. Chrissss!" Carla yelled up the stairs. I heard little footsteps above my head.

"What Aunty Carla?" The little voice asked.

"Get down here boy," Carla demanded. When he came down the steps using one leg to step down it was so funny, because he looked like me. Kev, and Von rolled into one.

"What I tell you about answering me like that?" Carla said poppin him in the head.

"Damn Carla, he only four!" I said defending my nephew, who I never met.

"Stay out of this, you probably would've been here to see him born if you would've had the same treatment," Carla said sarcastically.

"This ain't got nothing to do with me," I cut in.

"I'm sorry Dre, come here. I missed you so much," she said hugging me.

Me and Chris talked for a while. He was so small and so smart.

"Dre somebody on the phone for you," Amber yelled. It gotta be Von or Kev calling me.

"Who is it Amber?" I asked.

"I don't know, just pick up the phone!" She yelled back.

"Hello?" I said.

"Boy bring me my damn car and my cell phone. You ain't even answering the damn thing, "Zaria demanded.

"You just goin' hold my car hostage huh?" She said laughing after she finished her sentence. I looked at the clock on the microwave. It was little pass four. Time flew by.

"Girl, I been over here playing with my nephew," I said.

"How he doing?" She asked.

"He alright. I ran into your cousin Daron. We kicked it and he told me about the party," I said.

"Damn that nigga talk too much. Did he give you some money?" Zaria asked.

"Naw, I ain't ask," I said.

"If you would've waited, yo' butt would've seen that $300 that I left you. It was sitting on the counter. Anyway, I need you to pick me up and take me to work and pick me up when the mall closes," Zaria said.

"Girl, I ain't bout to picking up no money laying around the house," I said.

"Boy, shut up and come and get me," Zaria said laughing.

"I'm on my way baby, love you," I said.

"Love you too bookey," Zaria said hanging up.

"Eh! Amber, can I take Chris with me for a minute?" I asked.

"Yeah, he needs to get to know you anyway. Make sure you grab his car seat out my truck," Amber said.

"Come on lil'man, we bout to ride out."

CHAPTER 3

Jevon was a little older than Dre and grew up real quick. He was known in Inkster cause that's where he was slangin'. Amber had just called him to tell him that Dre was out of prison. Von had called Kevin to tell him that lil' bro was out of jail.

"What should I tell em'?" Von asked. Kev told him to find him and keep him around until he gets there.

"Where you at now?" Von asked. Kev told me' he was in Benton Harbor.

"Well I gotta find em' first," Von explained. Kev told him don't fuck this one up like the last time.

"Alright, one," Von hung up. Von hopped on his ninja and sped off. He floated all the way to Highland Park to find his little brother. Thinkin' about how he was gonna tell him about all the bad news that's been happening since he been gone.

Von finally pulled up in front of his old house. Carla was outside watering the grass.

"Where Amber at?" Von asked.

"Damn nigga, you can't say hey little sis, how are you?"

"Hey, where Amber at?"

"She inside," Carla said with an attitude. She couldn't stand Kevin or Jevon. She hated the whole family. She wanted to tell Dre so bad that they got over two million dollars from Mary's death. Kevin didn't give Dre a dime, and it was all Kevin's idea. Dre was supposed to inherit everything, but Dre ended up signing over the money to Kevin until he got out. I wish I could've told Dre what he was getting himself into. Von walked right pass Carla, soon as he opened the door he yelled Amber's name.

"Damn boy, why the hell you so loud?" Amber said. Amber came out the kitchen, looking mad as hell.

"Where Dre at?"

"He took Chris somewhere, he a be back soon, Why you askin'?" She said in a snotty way.

"I ain't askin' Kev is." When Von said Kev, his name sent chills up her spine.

"Is he goin give him some of that money?" Amber asked stuttering.

"I want to, but Kev be trippin, he so evil Amber. I don't know what's wrong with him."

"I hope so cause that ain't right," Amber said.

Von knew his little brother was a hothead, so he wasn't goin take all this bad news easy.

"Well I'm goin be in the hood, just call me when he gets back."

"Alright," Amber said, going back to the kitchen.

Me and Chris drove back to Oak Park to pick Zaria up for work. I blew the horn a couple times to let her know I was outside waiting for her. She finally came out, lookin good as ever. Soon as she got in, she had a funny look on her face.

"Why you blowin the horn like you crazy?" She didn't even notice the little boy in the backseat.

"Oh, hello lil' man, what's your name?" Zaria asked in a baby voice.

"Chris."

"How old are you?"

"I four."

"Awwww, look at you, I'm Zaria," she shook his baby hands.

"Boy, why you ain't tell me you were bringing company? That must be your nephew."

"Yeah, that's my nephew Chris," I said. Chris ended up falling to sleep while me and Zaria talked. It took us almost thirty minutes to get to Fairlane Mall. Zaria let

me hold her cell phone so she could call me when she was ready for me to come pick her up.

I dropped Chris off, so I could find Von and see what was up. As soon as I walked in, Amber told me Von was looking for me.

"Where he at?" I asked.

"He somewhere on his bike riding around. He close, cause he just left."

"He got a cell phone number?"

"Yeah, here it go right here." She gave me his number and I was on my way out the door. I caught a glimpse of Chris's face and thought, *damn I see me all over again.*

"Alright lil' man, give me some dap." He shook my hand I headed out the door. I gave both of my sisters' hugs and dipped out. It felt good driving. I wasn't worried about shit, just cruising. Let me call this nigga Von.

"Hello?"

"Yeah who dis?"

"This your brother Dre, nigga."

"What's poppin' lil' bro?"

"Shit, looking for you."

"Where you at?"

"I'm ridin down Woodward in a blue Monte Carlo."

"Woodward and what?"

"Woodward and Davison at the KFC."

"Alright, I'm bout to be up there in a minute," I told em.

"Alright, one," Von said rushing to put his helmet on and speed up there. It only took Von a couple of minutes to get up there. I knew it was him cause Amber was tellin me about that bright ass bike. When he pulled up, the chrome on the bike was blinding me. The chrome wheels matched the chrome engine on the bike. He got off the bike and took his helmet off. His hair was long as hell. This

nigga done grew some dreads. I remember when we first grew our fro's out, but I got tired of getting it braided, so I cut my shit off. He still had that same scar on his lower cheek that he got for helping me in my first fight in high school.

"What's poppin' bro?" I said.

"Shit, just tryna maintain."

"I hear that."

"Man what the hell you been eating, elephant meat?" We busted out laughing and hugged each other.

"I see you out here riding good," I had to sneak that in to hear my brother's response.

"Yeah, I had to cop one, shit follow me so I can drop the bike and the Monte off, so we can hop in da' Vette," Von told me. We drove back to Carla and Amber's and pulled up in the driveway. Von parked his bike in the garage and I pulled up behind him. Next thing I know, Von was pullin out in a yellow 2001 Corvette, with five-star rims.

"Damn that bitch cold," I said still sitting in the Monte. He got out with a big grin on his face.

"You goin get in or you goin stay froze?" I couldn't even speak. I cut the Monte off and got out. I headed towards the passenger's seat of the Vette.

"Where you going nigga?" Von asked me.

"You going on the wrong side," he said.

"What you talkin bout?" I asked.

"Nigga, you goin drive the Vette or what?" Von asked. I was geeked.

"Hell yeah." Von dropped the top and got out.

"Give me the keys to the Monte and you follow me. We bout to go get some pussy." Von hopped in the Monte and I hopped in the Vette. He flagged me to pull up on the side of him, when we pulled out the driveway.

"We goin ride to my crib and drop something off," Von said and scurted off. I scurted off too, trailing the

Monte. I felt good as fuck, first day out, in a Vette. Von was floatin up I-75, dodging through traffic. We was somewhere in Hazel Park when we got off the freeway. It was a quiet neighborhood. The houses were real small. We pulled up to a red brick house. Von went in with a small trash bag. He came out a couple minutes later and waved his hand telling me to come on. It was almost six o'clock. We hopped back on the freeway and headed back west. When we got off the freeway we were on Fenkell. We had stopped at a light and I pulled up on the side of him.

"Where we going nigga?"

"Nigga, just keep following me," Von said. He pulled off when the light turned green. I just followed him. We was in Brightmo' somewhere cause I could tell how the houses looked. Von pulled up in front of this raggedy ass house.

"Park right here and I'm going to put the Monte in the backyard." I thought this was a spot. The block was quiet as hell. We got out and went in from the side of the house. When we got in he told me this was his crib.

"Dre you can fuck these hoes, but don't be eating the pussy. I mean if you do, that's you, I'm not. They clean bro, they just freaks." When we walked up the stairs, the house was plushed out. There were flat screens in the kitchen and in the living room. The new furniture had the house smellin' like Art Van. When we got in the den, there were seven bad ass bitches in there with different costumes on. A white chick in a police officer uniform, a sista' in a nurse outfit, a Latino chick dressed as a slutty college student, a brown skinned sista in a cheerleader outfit, another white chick dressed as a teacher, and the other two were in boy shorts and matchin color bras. They looked good too! They were twins, but the two black chicks looked young as hell.

"Pick anyone you want nigga, pick all seven if you like," Von said. Lookin at these hoes had my dick harder

than a steel weight. I had so much to give, me and Zaria only went two rounds, and that was earlier this morning. I pointed to the police officer with the short blonde hair, cheerleader, and the Latino chick. My brother took the other four. I wanted the twins, but I wasn't tryna catch a case. When we got in the room there was a big ass queen size bed, and a 47" TV in the room. Soon as they walked in with me, the police officer bitch threw me on the bed. She pulled out the cuffs.

"Oh naw baby doll, I can't do the cuff thang." She looked at me and smiled.

"Okay whatever you say," she said seductively. They tugged at my jeans and the rest of my clothes. I was naked in seconds. The Latino chick jumped on top of me. She didn't have any panties on under her cheerleader outfit. She kissed my neck, making her way down to my muscular chest.

"Damn baby you must like to work out," she said kissing my navel area. My dick was hard as hell. As she made her way down to my dick, she grabbed it and squoze it. I tensed up a little bit cause it hurted, but it felt good. She took me in her mouth, takin the whole 8 inches. She spoke in Spanish while she slurped my dick.

"You like this papi?" I couldn't even speak. I just bit my bottom lip.

"Damn I love prison dick," the Latino chick said pausing and lickin my dick head. The white chick and the black chick held my arms down while the Latino chick bobbed her head faster.

"Are you ready to come baby?" The white chick whispered in my ear. I looked at her and tounged her down. They let my arms go and they started to mess around. The white chick laid right beside me was naked while the sista ate her pussy. I couldn't believe this shit was happening my first day out.

"Oh….Oh…Oh…Yessssss!" The white chick yelled out. She was looking me in the eyes while she was coming. If she wasn't coming, then she was a good actress. After she came, she got up and massaged my balls. The Latino chick still stroke and sucked my dick. I felt myself bout' to come, but I tried to hold it as long as I could, but I couldn't.

"I'm finna come girl."

"That's what we want daddy!" The white girl said taking my dick and stroking it. She put her whole mouth over my dick lookin me dead in the eyes. My cum was so strong. She swallowed everything. My dick went limp, but it started to jump when I saw the Latino chick get behind the white chick and started eatin' her ass. The black chick played with her pussy, sucking and sticking her fingers back in her pussy. When my dick got back hard, the white chick was moaning loud. She was coming again from all the lickin from the Latino chick. Now she was grindin her ass into her face.

"I'm goin get this dick, daddy," the white chick said. She got on top of my dick and started ridin'. Her pussy was so warm. She rode me like never before.

"Oh…yes daddy, I feel it all in my stomach." The black chick was playin with her pussy. She put her fingers to my mouth and I sucked em. She kept mouthin, "eat my pussy." I didn't care what my brother said, I wanted to eat some pussy. I told her to sit on my face and she did. The black chick rode my face backwards, so she could face the white chick. My tongue twisted and turned in her pussy. I made sure my tongue did every trick in the book.

"Right there, yeah, don't stop," the black chick moaned. She rode my face like it was a small dick. I felt the Latino chick lickin my balls, while the white chick pounced on my dick. Her pussy tasted so good. I felt the white chick's juices flowin down my dick. She got up from my

dick and the Latino bitch mounted me. The white chick just kept squirmin on the side of me.

"I hope you make me feel like that papi," the Latino chick said. She eased her pussy on my dick slowly. The black chick came so hard in my mouth, it was like her shit wouldn't stop. I knew the Latino chick was coming cause her pussy muscles got loose and her shit got wetter. The black chick stood up over me, her pussy was still drippin. The black chick went on the other side of the bed to the white chick who was still panting. I gripped the Latino chick's ass so tight, that when she got off, I could see my hand print on her ass. My dick was hurting so bad. I looked over and saw the black chick eating the white chick's pussy. She was on all fours. Her ass was up in the air. I got up and got behind her. She didn't even know I was back there. Her ass was so round it looked like a beach ball. I rammed my dick inside her pussy and she let out one of the loudest moans I've ever heard. "Ohhhh!" She yelled out. She finally started throwin it back. Swerving her ass in a circular motion. Her pussy wasn't like the others. It was like her walls were contracting my dick. She yelled out again, but the white chick stuffed her face back in her pussy. I knew I wasn't capable of lasting any longer. I just kept pumpin.

"Yeah baby come," the Latino said playin with her pussy.

"Did you come nigga, cause my pussy can't take no more?" The black chick managed to say still eating the white chick's pussy. The white chick was making the sexiest faces I've ever seen. I just exploded inside of her. My hands were on her hips still thrusting every drop inside of her. I fell off the bed, come still drippin from my dick. The black chick got on the floor with me lickin my dick clean, saying thank you. She laid next to me still thanking me, rubbing my chest. I ended up dozing off.

Von woke me up. "Get up nigga, you let these hoes fuck you to death?" Von said laughing.

"What time is it bro?" I said yawning, looking at the three bitches that were still sleep. Von checked his phone...

"Um...6:15 nigga." I got up and checked Zaria's cell phone and there were eight missed calls. I ain't been out a week yet and I was fuckin' up with the one I loved.

"Eh, bro, I gotta go get Zaria from work."

"Take the Vette, and call me and let me know if you stayin with her tonight."

"I can't do that man."

"Go ahead nigga just let me know what's up, you got my cell phone number," he said throwing me the keys.

"If I ain't here the keys to the Monte goin be in the glove compartment."

"Alright bro, I'm goin call you and let you know."

CHAPTER 4

I was doin eighty on the Southfield Freeway to get to my girl. I had a long way to go. The mall was probably just closing, when I pulled up in the parking lot. I drove around the parking lot a couple times. I jumped when the cell phone vibrated in my pocket. It was Zaria.

"Hello, yeah I'm on my way… I was with Von… I love you too." Thank God I showered before I left. I didn't have the top off cause I didn't want her to see me. I saw her come out the mall with a redbone chick looking around.

"There go my baby." I had to turn the music down cause she was callin again.

"Yeah, I'm in the parking lot right now." She hung up, and I knew she was sad by the way she asked where I was. I pulled up on her, tinted windows, and the sounds bumpin'.

"Eh' girl, what's your name? You fine as hell, what's your name?" Zaria just kept walking away with the redbone.

"Where is this fool at? This nigga a be mad as hell if I started talking to this nigga in this Corvette," Zaria said.

"Girl he wouldn't be mad, he a woop his ass and yours," the redbone said laughing.

All eyes were on me. Security was tellin me to leave, so I came back around with the top dropped.

"Eh' girl, I was tryna call you but you ignored me," I said laughing, looking at Zaria's confused facial look.

"Dre, I'm goin kill you," Zaria said, mad as hell, giving the redbone back her phone.

"I'll see you next week Tiffany."They hugged and the redbone went the opposite way.

"I'm not getting into this car, until you tell me where my car is and whose car this is," she said with her "

"Girl, get in the car, you see security keep flashing them hoe ass flashlights." She got in and asked me again.

29

"Calm down baby, this Von whip, he let me use it for tonight," I explained.

"Where were you, I hope you weren't with none of those nasty freaks Von be with." I gave her the look like, come on now, I'm better than that.

"So Ms. Hicks, what do you wanna do?"

"I don't know."

"It's Friday night, I know you wanna do something."

"Well, I'm not hungry cause I had a big Cinnabon."

"You sure?"

"Yeah baby, let's just cruise downtown."

"You look tired."

"Yeah I am, I been standing up all day in these heels, you know Daron throwin you a party tomorrow. I wasn't supposed to tell you, but I wanted to buy these shoes for you."

"Yeah I know he supposed to be throwing a party, but not tomorrow, and what shoes?"

"Some Gators,"

"I ain't bout to be caught in no dress shoes, what the hell wrong with you?"

"They got gym shoes silly, I know you been gone for a minute, but you gotta trust me."

"I trust you baby, I know you ain't goin have your man lookin' like a clown at his own party."

"Naw, you know damn well I got you, nobody goin have what you goin have on." We got downtown and just cruised. Everything was lit up. I still haven't seen Kevin all day. Speaking of family I gotta call Von. He didn't pick up so I left a message. When I hung up, Zaria was lookin at me with those big almond shaped eyes.

"What's going in your head baby?" Zaria asked.

"My life and how I'm gonna pay you back for those five years you stuck with a nigga. I love you Zaria fo' real." Her eyes were watering.

"Dre, since you been gone it hasn't been a nigga who could satisfy me and treat me like you did, you understand me like no nigga could."

"Damn baby I don't know what I'll do if I lose you." Zaria cut me off quick.

"Don't say that Dre, you scaring me."

"I'm sorry baby," I said. Zaria grabbed my hand and squoze it.

"I love the shit outta you nigga." We drove home and slept good.

Kevin was in the city ridin around in his Bentley. Kev was the first nigga to have a Bentley in the hood.

"Come on nigga, pick up the phone," Kev said impatiently.

"Hello... Nigga what yo' punk ass up to?... I'm on the Lodge freeway... leave the door open, I'm on my way. Dre still there?....Aight." Kev hung up his cell phone heated. Kev pulled up to the spot. It was early in the morning. Kev grabbed his .357 Magnum from under his seat. Soon as he walked in the spot, it smelled like sex. He walked in the bedroom where Von was stretched out layin with one of the hoes he paid for. Von woke up to a bloody mouth.

"What was that shit for?" Von said spittin blood out of his mouth from Kev hittin him in his mouth with the pistol. The white chick woke up screamin, Lev shot her twice in the chest. She laid on her back choking on her own blood.

"Nigga didn't I tell you to have that nigga here. Didn't I?" Kev smacked him again.

"I couldn't stop him, Zaria called him and I let him take the Vette to go pick her up. He was goin come back, he left a message on my phone sayin..."

"Shut the fuck up nigga, I guess I gotta go get this nigga myself. You think I wasted $25,000 on them hoes for

31

you to fuck? I wanted that nigga tied up when I got here, why you keep fucking up?" Kev asked.

"I'm sorry Kev, we better then that man."

"Yeah I know," Kev said chuckling in an evil way. Von almost pissed on himself when he heard him laugh.

"You fucked up too many times," Kev shot his brother three times in the chest. "I loved you nigga, but you had to go and if Carla or Amber think different they'll be next." Von's eyes rolled to the back of his head after Kev got his last words out. Kev called his peoples to come clean the house up. Kev had so much money it was ridiculous.

Kev left out the house with a Kango covering his face. He didn't care if anybody saw him, but it was always good to be cautious. He hopped in his Bentley and drove off. Kev owned all type of shit: two carwashes, one barbershop, and three detail shops. He didn't give his family shit. All he did was buy those whips for his sisters, paid the taxes, and all the bills in the house they lived in. He couldn't stand his youngest brother for killin his moms. Mary spoiled the hell out of him until Dre was born. He loved his youngest brother, but couldn't stand em'. If Dre ever found out about the money, Dre would inherit everything Kev owned. Kev was a cold-hearted nigga; he hated everybody, he let the money corrupt his mind.

Dre woke up sweating, he knew something was wrong.

"What's wrong baby?" Zaria asked me. Zaria had woke up from all the moving I was doin.

"I don't know, I don't feel right."

"You hungry?" She asked.

"Naw I'm good baby, but I gotta take Von back his car."

"Want me to come with you?"

"Naw I'm straight baby, just get ready for the party, do you gotta work today?"

"Nope, but I gotta go to the mall and pick a few things up," she said getting out the bed, showing off her Apple logo green boy shorts and her tight wife beater.

"I'm goin be back with your car before nine o'clock." I was still waking up real early cause that's what I was use to in prison. A nigga might not want to take home a lot of habits, but sometimes a nigga might not have a choice.

"I'm goin drive the Taurus that's in the garage, just make sure you hurry up. I'm goin give you my cell phone so I cn call you. The Taurus don't have no tags boy, so you gotta hurry up fo'real." Dre got up, put his jeans and Nikes on and left out. He slept in his wife beater and hoop shorts. I told Zaria I loved her and closed the door. Forty minutes later, I was in Brightmo' lookin for the houses my brother took me to yesterday. I found the block and drove down it slow. I pulled up in front of the house and I saw some niggas carrying something wrapped up in some sheets. I rolled down my window to see what going on.

"Everything good?" I asked. It was three of em' with bald heads. The heavy set one pulled out a mag and told me to keep it movin'. The first person who came to my mind was Kevin. We always got Kevin when it was somebody older tryna fuck with us. I needed to find Kevin. I was froze.

"You heard me nigga keep it movin." I sped off. I didn't have a pistol and I didn't stand a chance against three niggas with pistols. I needed Kevin. "Amber," I whispered. I sped to H.P. to talk to Amber. Soon as I got there, I hopped out with the car still running. I knocked on the door, it took a minute for them to open it, but Carla ended up answering.

"What's wrong Dre?" Carla asked.

"I think somebody killed Von," I said loudly breathing hard.

"Wha what chu talkin bout Dre?" Carla said lookin confused.

"I had a bad dream that something happen to Von, so I got up and drove to Von's spot and I saw three bald head niggas carrying something wrapped up in some sheets. I know it was a body in there. I asked what was up and one of em pulled out a mag and told me to ride out. Carla broke out in tears huggin me tight as hell in the doorway. Amber came down yellin what happened. I told her somebody killed Von. But Amber refused to believe me. She told me to stop playin.

"This ain't shit to play about, where's Kevin, somebody killed Von." Amber almost fell on the floor after I told her, but I caught her.

"Where's Kevin Amber?" I asked again. She told me she didn't know. I was heated. I had to find Kevin A.S.A.P. Nobody had his number so the next person to turn to was Daron. I told my sisters I had to make sure it was him, but I had to leave and go see Daron. I left and jumped in the Vette and drove off. I called the number that Daron gave me yesterday to tell him what happened. After I hung up from Daron, he told me to slide by the shop.

Zaria was stressing because Carla had called her and told her what happened. Even though they didn't get along, they had no choice but to be around each other. Zaria was crying cause Dre wouldn't answer the phone. Zaria hurried up and called Daron.

"Where is Dre and you better not lie to me?" Zaria cried into the phone. Daron told her he was on his way to the shop. Zaria told Daron she was on her way and he'd better be there with Dre."

CHAPTER 5

I pulled up in front of Daron's clothing store "Money Talk$." Daron was sittin in a lawn chair waiting for me, surrounded by a clearance rack full of clothes outside. Soon as I hopped out, he knew most of the story, but not all of it. My eyes were red as hell. Daron called Suga to come out and watch the clothes. Suga had been with Daron since they were younger. She was three years older than Daron, but she loved the shit out of that nigga. Daron peoples always had money, stupid money. All Daron had to do was finish high school and his people would buy him anything he wanted.

"Hey Dre, Daron told me you was out, why you ain't come say hi to me?" I told her hi and I was sorry. Before we went in, Daron handed Suga a pistol. It looked like a .380. He told her to hold it down. Daron had so much shit in his store it didn't make no sense. When we headed to the back, Daron told me Zaria had called him and told him everything. I didn't respond, I just followed behind him. We passed by two big niggas with braids that worked in the store. They both nodded when I walked past.

"How did she know?" I finally asked Daron.

"I don't know, but she called me and told me. Dre that's my little cousin, my only cousin I got. She like my sister and you my brother, so she had no choice but to tell me," Daron said. We stopped at a backdoor, when Daron opened it with his key, it was shit stocked up all over the room. I saw Daron standing in front of a mirror like 6 feet tall. Next thing I know he was opening the mirror like it was a door.

"Nobody has ever been back here but you and Suga." We both walked into a cave like closet. It was so many guns it looked like Rambo's basement. He tossed me a lemon squeeze .45 with two loaded clips.

"That's for you, I know you on parole, but it's better caught with one then without one, fuckin around in the city." He told me to hold the two .38 revolvers he grabbed out the chest.

"Hold these too." He tried to hand me a .380 but I had to pick thc .45 up and put it on my side and sit the revolvers down so I could throw the pocket pistol in my pocket. Daron wasn't done yet. He lifted his shirt up and he was wearing a blue vest.

"You want one?" Before I could answer he threw me one. While I was putting it on I asked him, "Where the fuck did you get all this shit?"

"When pops committed suicide, my moms gave me a key to his chest box. She told me when I turned 18 I could have it. She never knew what was inside. She probably thought it was a bunch of porno books or something. Pops was in the Army so you know he stocked up on as much shit as he could. But that Army shit fucked his head up." When we left out the room I was loaded with pistols.

"Man, I love you like a brother nigga, I'd hate to kill a nigga but whatever happens fuck it, I'm ridin," Daron said looking at me with a serious look.

"I almost forgot something." Daron went back into the dark closet and came back out with a long ass revolver. It had to be a .44.

"I couldn't leave my baby, this my second wife Betsy, Betsy-Dre, Dre-Betsy," Daron said being funny. We left out the back room, Daron had to make sure everything looked normal with the mirror so he sprayed it with Windex to get his fingerprints off of where he opened it and wiped it off. Soon as we came out the room Zaria was standing right there with Suga crying. She looked at me and she knew I was up to something.

"Dre where are you going?"

"Nowhere baby, I'm here with you."

"Dre don't lie to me," she said crying even harder.

"Me and Daron gotta go take care of some business, plus I gotta go get your car."

"Fuck that car, I can get another one, but I can't get another Dre."

"Baby, don't talk like that, I love you, I'm coming back." I gave Zaria a kiss and Daron did the same.

"Give those .38's to Big Boy and Lil' Lou," Daron told me. I didn't know why they called him Lil'Lou, shit he was almost bigger than his older brother Big Boy. I gave them the revolvers and before we left, Daron told Zaria to close the shop early and meet him at the crib. When we left out the shop I noticed Zaria's car window was down. When I looked inside I saw her purse. I grabbed it out the passenger side. I remembered Daron giving Suga a .380, so I dropped the .380 in her purse.

"Hold on Daron, let me give Zaria her purse. I ran inside and gave it to her and told her I loved her and ran back out.. Big Boy came out behind me. Daron told him what was up. Big Boy went back inside. Me and Daron hopped in his burgundy 500 Benz and we drove off. As we drove to Brightmo' he told me how he got on by selling a little weed and saving every dime he made.

"What's up with Kev Daron?"

"Last thing I heard, he was down south getting major dough. It's a lot of shit you don't know fam."

"What chu talkin' bout Daron?"

"Man your family been acting real strange since your moms died."

"Like what nigga?" I asked getting irritated.

"That nigga Kev just moved out the hood, then like a month later he bought a Bentley, a phat ass crib, bought Von a crib, a bike, and that yellow Vette. Your sisters on the other hand, he just got them two cars. I ain't seen him in a grip, all I do is hear his name in every investment, every drug deal, anything that consists of making money." I

ain't know how to respond. All I could say was how did he get a Bentley.

"Yeah nigga a Bentley," Daron said shakin' his head. Damn something ain't right. I gotta find out what's going on cause a nigga is lost.

We pulled up at the spot where I saw the three dudes carrying the sheets out the front door. I got out the car with the mag in my hand while Daron parked. I headed towards the backyard. I heard Daron shut his door and seconds later he was on the side of me with his .44 out.

"We gotta go inside Daron."

"Let's go," he said. We checked the side door and it just so happened to be unlocked. We went in making sure we didn't touch anything. The house was clean, it smelled like bleach and pine-sol. We walked through the kitchen to the living room. I checked the back room and Daron went down the steps to the basement. Wasn't nothing wrong, everything was clean as hell. It looked like nobody even lived here, even the room I was in fuckin' them three hoes. Something was wrong, everything was wrong.

"Aye Dre, you gotta see this," Daron yelled upstairs. Daron scared the shit out of me cause the house was quiet as hell. I ran downstairs to see what was up.

"What the fuck?" Daron was standing next to the white chick dressed in the police uniform, the one I was fucking earlier. She was tied up in a chair like a shoelace. Whoever did this didn't have a heart.

"She had bruises on her face, her throat was slit, and there were two holes in her chest.

"Damn I had just fucked this bitch," I said so low Daron couldn't hear me.

"What you say bro?" Daron asked.

"Nothing man, this shit is crazy."

"Dre we gotta go foreal." All I thought about was my semen in that bitch cause I didn't use a condom. Soon as we headed out the side door, I saw a green Tahoe, four

niggas with pistols hopped out. Daron started shooting before me. His .44 almost made me go deaf. He hit one in the neck, he fell out holdin his neck. I let off the lemon squeeze. This shit was like a movie. It was daylight having a shootout. They were shooting back hiding behind the riddled Tahoe. I saw one hit the ground. Daron was reloading behind me. The brick was whipping from the shots that were coming in our direction. Daron went into the backyard so he could hop the fence to get a better aim at the niggas. There were two left. I heard a loud shot go off, it had to be Daron with the .44. I let off a couple more shots. I had to put another clip in cause I was empty. It was quiet so I ran out shooting. I felt something hit me in the chest. It was a hard impact. I fell on the ground holding my chest. I saw somebody walking up, but my eyesight was blurry. It was a shiny object pointed in my face. I heard another shot go off. I thought I was dead. My eyes were closed. When I opened em' I saw a nigga lying next to me with blood coming out his mouth.

"Nigga get up, we gotta go," Daron said helping me up. The vest had caught the bullet. My chest was red as hell when I lifted the shirt then the vest up.

"We gotta go," Daron kept saying. I finally got out the daze and ran to the backyard to get the Monte. Daron was already gone. I backed out the driveway and got the fuck on leaving the crime scene.

Damn I done almost died right there. I hurried up and sped back to Daron's shop. How the fuck was I goin' still go to a party with this shit on my chest. Wasn't no way in hell. I was sweatin and shit, I had to stop lookin so suspicious, but how, we just murked some niggas in broad daylight.

CHAPTER 6

Kev drove around H.P. all day searching for his little brother. He had a few words with the little nigga. He drove around in his black DTS with tinted windows and his chrome six star rims. Kev had just found out his niggas was killed, so he called his k-zoo niggas to go clean the shit up. Kev dialed Amber up to find Dre.

"Eh' sis what's going on?"

She wanted to say 'bitch you know what happened', "Von got killed I think," Amber said dry as hell.

"What?" Kev said loud as hell, tryin to act like he cared, but really he was trying not to let Amber hear him snickering. Amber couldn't believe how Kevin was actin' like he had nothing to do with Von getting killed.

"Dre came over here earlier and told me he had nothing to do with Von getting killed.

"Dre came over here earlier and told me he saw three niggas carrying a sheet wrapped around something that looked like a body."

"You damn right he did and yo ass a be wrapped up with em' if you tell Dre anything. Try me and I'll come over there right now and off you and that little motherfucker Chris. I'm tired of your smart ass mouth." Amber couldn't believe what he just said. She knew he wasn't playin. She had to figure out how she could keep Chris out of this shit.

"Kevin please keep Chris outta this," Amber said crying.

"Fuck with me if you want to, and I'll be planning funerals for all you motherfuckers."

"Why you gotta be like this?"

"Bitch, you ain't say that when I gave you that money and bought you that car, and bitch don't make me mention all them fixes you needed for your fucking crack addiction."

"You don't have to talk to me like that Kevin."

"I'll talk to you how I want to, cause you're my custo." Amber hung up in his face. Amber cried her heart out. She wasn't strung out like most fiends, she was thick, beautiful, had a son, and took good care of him. Amber snapped out of her daze when she heard the phone ring.

"Hello?" She said scared as hell.

"Bitch, I'm going to kill you!" Click. That's all she heard. Amber cried as she wrote her little brother a letter. She gave it to Chris.

"Give this to Uncle Dre okay Chris?" She said in a baby voice. She called Zaria to tell her she needed to talk to Dre and that it was urgent. After she hung up, she went downstairs and locked the door.

Me and Daron made it back to the shop.

"Baby, Amber called and said she wanted you to stop by and that it was urgent," Zaria said after I hugged her. I was confused cause if something ever happened to Amber she would always take care of it herself.

"You want me to come with you?" Daron asked me while I was walking out the front door.

"Naw bro, I'm good."

"Nigga I'm coming," Daron said but Dre didn't hear him. I left Zaria her keys to the Monte and hopped in the Vete and scurted off.

Daron went to the back and grabbed his Mac 11 and told Big Boy he'd be back.

"Lil'Lou, grab the pump and let's go," Daron said. Daron and Lil'Lou hopped in the black Tahoe and sped off.

I only had half of a clip left. Hopefully there wasn't nobody there with her tryna kill her. It took fifteen minutes to get to HP. I pulled up to the front of the house and hopped out, leaving the car running. As soon as I ran up to the porch, I saw a Tahoe hittin the corner. I had almost pulled the burner out, but I saw Daron hoppin out the passenger side.

"I thought I told you not to come," I said while entering the front door.

"Nigga you my brother," Daron said coming in behind me. Lil'Lou stayed outside with the pump. I saw Chris sleepin' on the couch. I hurried up, woke him up, and asked where his mom was.

"Momma went to sleep," Chris said in a tired voice. Chris handed me the note Amber wrote.

"Dre, I love you so much, Kevin has turned into a monster. He killed Von and threatened to kill me and your nephew. Get Carla and my son out of this house Dre. Take care of him, he needs a father figure in his life, and I know Zaria would make a perfect mother. I love you!

Love Amber, your sister. Here's Carla number (313)-372-2652

I ran upstairs to see what the fuck was going on. I tried to open the door but it was locked. Daron was right behind me, he had the Mac 11 at his side. I busted down the door and saw Amber laid out on the floor with a belt around her arm and a needle beside her.

"Nooooo!" I screamed. My sister was as stiff as an old rug in the winter time. My nephew came up the stairs. I hurried to cover his eyes.

"Damn Dre, we gotta do something, call an ambulance!" Daron said. I called the ambulance still holding Chris from seeing his mother. I handed Daron the note after hangin' up the cell phone. We left out the room and stood outside the door.

"I knew something was up with that clown," Daron said.

I called Carla and left her a message cause she didn't pick up. The ambulance and the police showed up minutes later. They asked me a few questions, but I couldn't answer any. I was fucked up. Amber was pronounced dead. The coroner had came and picked her up.

"Why the fuck hasn't this crackhead bitch answered the phone. I'm goin kill all they bitch asses then," Kev mumbled to himself. Kev was in Highland Park quick. Kev rode down Massachusetts, and noticed an ambulance leaving. There was a police car outside of his moms' house. He crept real slow.

"Look at this bitch ass nigga." Kev finally saw his lil' brother, but he wasn't little no more, he had to go.

"And look at this bitch ass nigga Daron, I never liked that nigga," Kev thought to himself. Daron had pull, but not as much as Kevin. Kev called his k-zoo niggas to come take care of some business.

"Niggas bout' to drop," Kev said bangin' his hand against the dashboard. "Come on pick up the phone," Kev said getting sad. They finally picked up. "Yeah, bring ya' best, it's bout that time." Kev hung up and hit the corner scurtin' off. Kev lit the blunt and puffed while he unzipped his pants. He let the white chick finish the rest. The model bitch took every inch and swallowed every drop of come that came out. Kev had a thang for white bitches. He hated he had to kill his white bitch for his brother's mistakes.

We stood and talked to the police for a minute. When they pulled off, I noticed a black DTS creeping up the street. The car slowed down even more when it got to front of my house. I couldn't see inside because of the tinted windows. Whoever it was, they peeled out hitting the corner.

"Damn, who the fuck was that?" Lil'Lou asked.

"Shit you got me," I said.

I headed back to the shop after dropping Chris off at Aunty Vicki's house. I parked the Vette in front of the shop and Daron and Lil'Lou parked in the back. When I walked in, Zaria wasn't there anymore. I called Zaria again and she picked up. When I told her what happened she flipped. She was cussin' people out in the shop and everything.

"Dre what the fuck is going on?" She yelled in the phone.

"Just drive to Daron's shop and we'll talk."

"Nigga, I can't drive, I'm goin' kill somebody!"

"Alright, I'm goin' have somebody come and get you."

"I don't want nobody to do shit," she said hanging up in my face. I had called from Daron's phone. Seconds later she called back and told me to send somebody to pick her up.

"Alright, yeah….. I need you' right now…. All is well." Daron hung up the phone and called Carla back to get the location. I went to the back where the kitchen was at to get something to drink. Daron came back there with me. I didn't wanna talk to nobody but Zaria, but she wasn't nowhere to be found, so I had no choice.

"My niggas on they way, I'm goin have them pick her up." I just nodded my head.

Thirty minutes later a dude came in the shop with a bunch of red on. I had forgot Daron was into all that gangbangin shit. I wasn't feelin that shit doe.

"Come outside with me," Daron said tapping me and the dude in the red. We got outside and I saw a red Monte with tee-tops. It didn't have no rims on it but it sat up high and sounds was ridiculous. It was a big black nigga in the passenger seat bangin Chedda Boys loud as hell. I thought to myself like I done seen this nigga before.

"Nigga next time get cho' fat ass out nigga," Daron told the nigga in the car with the red Cleveland hat.

"Nigga I ain't feel like gettin out." The big black dude said. Him and Daron shook up. I had to admit them niggas held the shit down.

"Oh this my brother Dre," Daron said introducing me to his gangbangin homies.

"This Freaky Rell," Daron said pointing to the frail black nigga, "and this K-Dawg," pointing to the heavyset

44

black nigga. I said what up doe to both of them. K-Dawg looked so familiar it didn't make no sense.

"Aye fam' you look familiar', you was in the joint a couple of years ago?" K-Dawg finally asked me.

"Yeah I was in Alpha," I told him.

"Yeah you was the nigga that blew Man-Man shit out and he ain't do nothing about it." I just smiled. Now I know who this nigga is, he had two flat. He stayed in some shit and stayed in the hole.

"You good doe?" K-Dawg asked me.

"Yeah I guess."

"Alright enough of the chit-chat," Daron said. We all laughed at his smart remark.

"Yes doa, I need you to go pick my sister up. Her name is Carla, nigga you know Carla." Freaky Rell had a confused look on his face.

"Man Carla, the one that use to do yo' baby mama hair," Daron said.

"Oh, aight I know who you talkin' bout' now," Freaky rell said.

"You talking bout' the lil' place on 6 Mile and Greenfield," K-Dawg said.

"I got chu," Freaky Rell said. They hopped in the Monte and drove off. Me and Daron went back into the store.

"We still closing early baby?" Suga asked Daron. Daron looked straight at me. I guess he was looking for an answer. Before I could respond Daron cut right in. "I ain't buy all this shit for nothing," Daron said while looking at me. So much shit done happened in two days. My brother and fuckin' sister is gone. I'm supposed to be chillin' with my family not burying them. "What chu goin' do bro? I already done rented out Club 2000. Do you how much cash I put in on this damn party? Huh?" Daron said getting pissed off. This wasn't about no damn money, fuck money, you can get that back. You can't get your family back once

45

their gone. I didn't tell Daron that though. My eyes was watering when they finally came down. Suga wiped them off and gave me a hug.

"We goin' get them muthafuckas Dre," Suga whispered in my ear. Zaria came in the front entrance. Her eyes were bloodshot red. I know something was wrong. She walked up to me.

"What happened to the car? I seen the, the bullet holes in it." I was froze for a minute until she repeated the question. I had to tell her the truth. I owed that to her.

"Baby all I did was protect myself. Some guys shot at me so I shot back."

"Where in the hell did you get a gun from? Did you shoot or kill anybody?" Zaria asked.

"Yes I did bay." I was tired of lying to her.

"I can't do this no more Dre." Zaria turned around and started walking toward the exit door. I grabbed her arm before she reached the door.

"I can't do or be without you. Why do you continue to put me through this bullshit? You can't answer me?" Zaria said looking me in my eyes. I didn't want everybody in our business so I took Zaria to Daron's personal bathroom in the back. The bathroom had a nice small shower for two. I closed the door and looked in her eyes.

"I love you Zaria," I said.

"Why the hell you keep doing stupid shit? You wanna go back to prison? I ain't sure if I could ride with you bay if you go back. It seem like you ain't goin' change nigga." I am goin' change baby. I'm pretty sure you tired of my bullshit, but you have to understand where I'm coming from. My brother and my sister just left me within 24 hours." Soon as I was finished Zaria kissed me passionately. Tears were now coming down. I locked her salty tears off her face. Zaria wrapped her arms around me while I cuffed her ass. Zaria's plaid polo skirt was so tight around her curvaceous body. My dick got hard instantly.

Now I was the aggressor and I was now tonguing her back. I started backing her up until she was against the sink. I let my left hand find her back zipper while my other hand gripped her ass.

"Dre hurry up, I'm horny as hell," Zaria managed to moan out. I finally unzipped her skirt, letting it fall to the floor, revealing her pink Victoria Secret panties with her matching bra. I had to step back and look at my baby. Damn she was beautiful. She stood there feeling on herself dipping her hand inside of her panties. Her head fell back when she noticed I was getting turned on. She giggled while pulling out her wet fingers, telling me to come here. I took off my shirt, I still had the vest on. It showed the bullet hole. I took it off and the spot was still red and swollen. She touched the red spot and I hissed. She jumped back when I did. She kissed the spot.

"Does it feel better now baby?" Zaria asked while kissing my abs.

"Yes," I said sucking the juices off her index and middle fingers. Zaria worked my zipper with her other hand. She finally had my dick in a vice grip lock with her small hands. She started stroking my shit slow. I pumped into her hands moving my waist slowly. I undid her bra while looking into her eyes. Her perky titties popped right out staring me right in the face. Zaria made funny noises while I licked her neck and moved down to her beast.

"Keep going down baby, my pussy is aching." I kissed down to her perfect navel making circular motions with my tongue and then kissing it. She now had her hand on my head. She pushed my head down between her legs. I was now on one knee. I licked her inner thighs teasing her. I had looked up to see her face but she was looking at the ceiling. I slowly stuck my fingers in the waistline of her panties, slowly pulling them down. Her trimmed up pussy looked so good. I always loved how she kept her pussy hairs. Not to much and not to little.

47

"On both knees," Zaria said smiling. I did as she said and soon as I did she pushed my face into her sweet spot. My tongue traveled up and down her slit.

"Ohh Dre, you do it so right, don't stop." I got turned on even more tasting her sweet juices. She now had one leg over my shoulder. Damn baby you taste so good," I said.

"Uhh, uhh, uhh, ooh shit," I tasted her nut. I let it run down my chin. When I stood up she wiped her cum off my chin and put her fingers in my mouth.

"Make sure you get every drip," Zaria said. I turned her around and bent her over the sink. I pulled my pants down along with my hoop shorts and boxers.

"Put it in Dre," Zaria demanded. She reached behind to try and find my dick and she did. She rubbed my dickhead up and down her clit. I finally stuck it in slowly. She let out a loud gasp.

"No Dre, stop!" Zaria said turning around and facing me. She kissed my chest then my abs. She was now on her knees. She kissed my dick, licking her juices off. She finally stuck my dick in her mouth. I was surprised. She would always tell me that she'll never put that nasty thing by her mouth. I couldn't control myself. When I felt a twitch, I pulled her up.

"What's wrong baby, you don't like that?" Zaria asked looking confused.

"Naw baby I loved that, but I wanna please you," I told her. She smiled.

"Now bend that fat ass over," I demanded.

"Okay daddy," Zaria said bending over and smiling. Seconds later I was pounding her back in.

"Arrghh," Zaria yelled. I started going faster getting more excited by looking at her pretty light brown ass smack up against my body. Her ass looked like a bowl of jello with not one stretch mark. She was looking in the mirror back at me while I worked her insides. She started grinding

her ass into my dick. I felt myself getting weak. I came so hard, I thought I wouldn't stop. We both fell to the floor breathing hard as hell.

"We done fucked this bathroom up girl," I said laughing. I'm glad that Daron had a personal shower. We got into the shower together with our underwear on hand and hand washed them. I washed my baby's back and she washed mines. Seeing the soap run down her flat stomach turned me on, getting me ready for round 2. Minutes later I was between her legs tasting her sweet nectar. We got out and dried off. We put our clothes on and threw our underwear in the dryer in the back.

"Baby I'm going through so much right now. I don't wanna have this party, but I know Daron goin' be highly upset because all of the time and money spent."

"Dre he's not going to be mad, well he might be a lil' mad but he'll get over it. I know you're going through a lot, that's why I'm here for you. Maybe you should have the party. It might get some stress off that big chest of yours," she said rubbing my chest. She always knew how to keep me smiling.

"Alright baby, we goin see how this is going to play out. Come on bay for me," Zaria said giving me the sad puppy dog look.

"I guess, I might as well, ain't no sense of me crying about it and sitting around. Amber and Von' wouldn't wanna see me like that."

"It's goin' be okay, we goin' get through this horrible storm."

CHAPTER 7

"We having the party or what?" I asked coming back with Zaria. Daron looked confused at first like I was joking or something.

"Shit let's get this shit poppin' then," Daron said after he saw that I was serious.

"Well baby I'm 'bout to take Zaria to the mall with me to get a few things," Suga cut in.

"Aight baby." Daron gave Suga a knot full of fifties. I wish I could've gave Zaria some money. I kind of felt embarrassed. Daron gave Zaria a similar knot, but it was a little smaller.

"Boy you know I don't need no money," Zaria said trying to give the money back, but Daron wouldn't take it back so Suga took it and put it in her bra. I hugged Zaria and told her I loved her before she left and Daron did the same with Suga. Suga and Zaria hopped in the CTS and drove off.

"I'm thinking about proposing bro'," I told Daron.

"Shit nigga you better put a ring on her finger nigga," Daron said laughing.

"Naw but on some real shit Dre I ain't ready for that now," Daron said getting serious.

"Me and Suga been together for almost ten years, we just been off and on. I know I ain't ready, she might be ready doe," Daron said. I thought they would've been married. I remember when Daron first met her, we was stealing Sega games. Man we were bad as hell. I guess she had a thing for bad guys. Somehow they ended up in the same school, after that they were stuck like glue.

"But do what your heart tells you, 'cause it might not ever talk to you again if you don't listen," Daron said. I kept thinking about what if something happened to me or Zaria and she didn't know that I wanted to marry her.

"Aye man, so what we bout' to do?" Lil'Lou asked Daron.

"Yeah, cause I'm hungry," Big Boy cut in. I couldn't believe how big these niggas was. Big Boy was older then Lil'Lou by two years and Lil'Lou was still bigger.

"Nigga you always hungry hungry," Daron said laughing. Before Zaria left she parked the Monte Carlo in the back. Me and Daron hopped in the Benz and Big Boy and Lil'Lou hopped in the Tahoe. I left the Corvette there along with the Monte.

Daron was from HP, but they loved that nigga on 7 Mile. He helped HP by donating money to schools and shit. He had a little program for kids and recreational parties.

"Man, I'm ready to roll this blunt up," Daron said.

"Man you know I'm on papers," I said.

"Oh my bad," Daron said putting the blunt back. We drove through HP and went to Miley & Miley Shrimp Shack. Everybody ate except me. I was good, I ain't have no appetite anyway.

"Hold on yaw, this Rell....Hello...Alright." Daron started laughing hard as hell.

"Alright meet me at the crib," Daron said hanging up his cell phone.

"Yeah Rell got Carla and K-Dawg mad as hell 'cause he had to drive her small Lincoln LS." We all busted out laughing in Miley & Miley. People was looking at us, but we didn't care.

"We gotta get ready for this party yaw," Daron said. I wasn't as geeked as everyone else, I still was thinking about Amber and Von. We got back in the whip and followed Big Boy and Lil'Lou to Daron's crib in Eastpointe. I didn't understand why he lived all the way in Eastpointe and Aunty Vicki still stayed in Highland Park.

When we got to Daron's crib, I couldn't believe how big his crib was. It had to have a pool inside the house, if it didn't then it had to be one in the backyard.

"Man how much this shit cost you?" I asked pulling up in the driveway.

"A lil' bit of nothing. Grams helped me buy it. He parked in the driveway and Big Boy parked in the four car garage. The garage was almost as big as a regular house in Detroit. We all got out and headed towards the front door. Big Boy went in first and Lil'Lou followed right behind him. They lived with Daron. They were like some all day bodyguards. Soon as we got in I called Zaria but she didn't answer. Maybe she didn't recognize the number, but she had to cause this was her cousin's number. I thought about having Daron call Suga, but I said fuck it. I didn't want to bug her. It was like walking through a baby mansion.

"Make yourself at home bro, 'cause I'm tired as hell bro. I'm bout' to find something to lay down on," Daron said taking off his shoes.

"The back got a futon back there, I'm going upstairs, I'll holla at you later."

Zaria and Suga shopped to they dropped. Zaria had to go to Fairlane Mall, so they could get a discount at the store she worked at. Sonny would be highly upset if she shopped anywhere else. The Broadway just got a new shipment of Mauris in. Soon as we walked in he had limited edition Motown Mauris on display.

"These cold right here," Suga said out loud.

"I like the black ones," I told her.

"I'm goin buy Daron the white ones then," Suga said.

"Alright, I'll get Dre the black ones."

"So you like these Motowns?" Sonny asked while walking up to us.

"Heyyy Sonny," I said hugging him.

"How are you?" He asked

52

"I'm good Sonny, just trying to find some shoes for Dres, but I found em' now," Zaria said looking at the Mauris.

"Hello Ms. Fashion," Sonny said to Suga.

"If you don't quit it out," Suga said playfully hitting him in his arm. The shoes were $385.00 a piece with the discount. Sonny looked out and knocked off $120.00.

"So what now?" Suga asked.

"We gotta go get the outfits," Zaria said. The Broadway didn't have a good variety of clothing so we went into 4Mens. Volouris jogging outfits was popping. Only niggas who had money had Volouris. Suga bought Daron a cream one to match the white Mauris.

"Pelle Pelle or Sean John?" Zaria asked.

"Well I got Daron the Pelle Pelle for $250.00. I think the Sean John is a lil' cheaper," Suga said.

"Well I guess I'm goin get the Pelle," I said. We got our bags and we were headed to get our things now.

"The things we do for our men," Suga said laughing. Soon as we got out of 4Mens, it was a gang of niggas walking past.

"Damn baby you got a fat ass," one of the guys yelled out to Zaria and Suga. Zaria didn't even look back.

"Bitch fuck you then," somebody in the crowd said.

"Girl don't even worry 'bout them broke ass niggas. You and I both know we got good men at home waiting on us," Suga said. The group of niggas ended up going in Footlocker and we ended up leaving the mall to go to Somerset Mall to pick up some loafers. Soon as we started to leave out I heard, there they go."

"You think yaw doing something cause you got a lil' money?" One of the niggas said. Now Zaria was heated. These niggas been following us for almost fifteen minutes taunting and degrading us.

"Look we got men at home and plus I'm married," Zaria lied but it did sound good.

"Bitch shut up. Nobody give a fuck about you or your husband," one of the older guys said. His friends were now laughing at Zaria.

"Mike Tyson could be your husband, but you watch how you talk to me," the fat dark-skinned guy yelled out. By that time we were close to the car. It wasn't no security around when you needed them. When we got to the car, Zaria reached in her purse to look for her cell phone but instead it was a small pistol inside. Dre had to put it there. Dre had some damn nerves putting a gun in her purse. Zaria just played it cool, maybe she wouldn't have to even pull it out.

"Who that 4Mens bag for?" The fat nigga said. Zaria just ignored him trying to put the clothes in the trunk.

"You driving real good, that's your husband car?" One of the niggas said trying to be funny. Zaria shut the trunk and she was headed to the passenger side. Suga was already inside.

"Aye girl," the fat one said.

Zaria turned around and screamed, "what?!"

"Damn baby, all I wanted was your number?" The fat nigga said laughing. Zaria just turned around.

"You goin' let that bitch play you like that Man-Man?" One of his homeboys asked. When Zaria opened the car door she felt him grab her arm, that's when she pulled the pistol out. He finally let Zaria go and started to bag up.

"Whoa' baby girl," Man-Man said.

"Naw, you tuff as hell, touch me again hoe," Zaria said gritting my teeth. By now the other four guys had took off. Suga had got out the car looking at me like I was crazy.

"Z, get in the car, fuck that nigga," Suga said. Zaria got in the car still pointing the gun at Man-Man. Zaria slammed the door and Suga pulled off.

"Ink-Town bitch! This shit ain't over!" Man-Man yelled out loud enough for them to hear him. Suga tried to call Daron but he didn't answer.

"You wanna call Dre 'cause Daron not picking up none of the phones?" Suga asked.

"Yeah." Zaria called her cell phone but all she got was the voicemail so she tried again.

"Come on Dre, pick up the phone," Zaria said under her breath. Zaria hung up and gave Suga back her phone.

"Girl where the hell you get that gun from?" Suga asked.

"Girl Dre probably put it in there. I don't know why he would do some crazy shit like that. How that saying go niggas be saying? Better caught with it then without it." Zaria and Suga both busted out cracking up. They drove to Somerset Mall to get their outfits. They bought their shit and left. Zaria fell asleep while Suga drove back to their house.

They pulled in the driveway. It seemed like it took forever to get there.

"How long I been sleep?" Zaria asked Suga getting out the car.

"Prolly like forty-five minutes," Suga said helping her get the bags out the trunk. Soon as they got in, Zaria yelled Dre's name.

"Dre where you at?" I woke up soon as I heard my name. Daron was in the den blowing with Big Boy and Lil'Lou'.

"Boy what I tell you about smoking in here?" Suga asked getting angrier at the weed smell.

"Stop trippin' girl," Daron said sounding drozy.

"What's wrong with you?" Daron asked Suga.

"You didn't pick up the phone when I called. Somebody tried to grab Zaria, well they did. I think the guy's name was Man-Man if I'm not mistaken. We didn't provoke them at all babe. Zaria pulled out a gun and he back up," Suga told him.

"Hold on, hold on, start over. You said what now?" Daron asked looking confused. Before Suga could repeat herself, I came out the back room yawning.

"What's wrong baby?" I asked Zaria. She wasn't crying, but I could tell she was upset.

"Somebody grabbed me and tried to take my shopping bags while we was in the parking lot," Zaria said. I hugged her before she could get the last words out.

"Who the fuck was it, did you know em'?" I asked getting more agitated by just thinking about it.

"I think his name was Man-Man and he kept saying something about Ink-Town," Zaria said with her head down.

"Yeah, that's what he was saying Inkster," Suga put her two cents in.

"I pulled out a gun and he left me alone," she said. I was glad as hell I put that pistol in her purse. I'll probably be at the hospital by now. My mind shifted, all I thought about was blowing that nigga shit out in the joint.

"Dre where you going?" Zaria asked me.

"To find Man-Man."

"Dre leave that shit alone, fuck him, you still got me." If Zaria didn't say that, I would be headed to Inkster right now.

Kevin knew Zaria had worked in Fairlane, so he sent Man-Man to see if he could game her.

"Did you get her nigga?....She pulled out what?...Where you at?...Let me speak to J.Money...What's up lil'nigga?....Nigga quit callin' me Joe," Kev said through the cell phone. J.Money was a stone cold killer but the coolest nigga to be around and have on your team, but when it involved a lot of money, everybody was his enemy.

"I need a favor... You know Man-Man gotta go?... I got fifty stacks on his head. Man-Man was supposed to off Dre in the joint but he bitched up. I ended up giving him a second chance and he let a bitch pull a heater out on em'. We don't need niggas like that in the family...I'm goin' be at my crib, bring something to let me know it's done...One." Kev hung his phone up and got the fifty stacks ready.

"Hello....Naw she pulled out a toaster...I'm in K-Zoo with J.Money and his lil' brother Pee-Wee... Kev' wanna talk to you," Man-Man said giving the phone to J.Money.

"What up Joe?...Nigga quit trippin'," J-Money said. Man-Man was all in J.Money's mouth.

"I hear you," J.Money said while looking at Man-Man with greed in his eyes.

"Alright one," J.Money said hanging up.

J.Money had something different on his mind, he knew Kev wasn't going to pay him no fifty stacks so he told Man-Man what was up. Man-Man looked like J.Money just lifted a thousand pounds off his chest.

"Grab the .40," J.Money told Man-Man.

"Now listen, we goin' kill this nigga Kev, don't be on no bullshit and we can get ya' mans Dre later on down the road 'cause I know you still heated about what happened in the joint," J.Money said while loading the clip

up. Man-Man couldn't be more satisfied. He hated Kev cause he killed his mans 'Von.

On their way there, they both popped a pill. Man-Man had turned J.Money out on pills and J.Money had everybody in Kalamazoo popping pills. By the time they got to his mansion they were amped. Kev' lived two miles from Benton Harbor. The houses were nice and te neighborhood was quiet. While pulling up to the house something changed J.Money's mind. "Fuck it, I might as well kill both of them," J.Money thought about all the shit Man-Man had done for him. If it wasn't for Man-Man, he would of never had a Monte Carlo on daytons or his crib where him and his little brother stayed. Man-Man introduced him to Kev' and Kev' paid him good to put in work. J.Money knew Man-Man had a big mouth so it was a big chance that he was going to brag about killing Kevin and J.Money wasn't having that. If Kev' was offering fifty racks then it wasn't no telling what he had in his safe. He probably had triple of that. Not counting all his jewelry and shit.

"Come on Man-Man, you gotta look scared. Nigga you done put on plenty of acts so try and earn you a Oscar nigga," J.Money told him. They parked in Kev's backyard next to Kev's gold Lexus. They both got out and J.Money had the .40cal with the silencer to Man-Man's back.

"Just go with the play, we goin' be good nigga," J.Money said shoving the pistol into his lower back. Man-Man tapped on the patio glass door. Kev' opened it right up. He was smoking on a Cuban cigar. J.Money nodded his head to Kevin, but Man-Man didn't see it. Man-Man was scared as hell 'cause he didn't know what was going on. Man-Man didn't feel a thing. J.Money shot him in the back of his head. It sounded like a loud whistle.

"You did good lil' homie. The bag right there in the kitchen," Kev said. J.Money was so money hungry he didn't even pay attention to Kevin.

58

"Who goin' clean up this mess?" Kev' asked him.

"Shit I'll clean it up," J.Money said while opening up the bag and seeing a bunch of chopped up newspapers wrapped in rubber bands. When J.Money looked up he saw Kev' pointing a .22 semi automatic at his face. Before J.Money could up the .40cal, Kev' let him hold the whole clip. Two in the face and the other six in the chest.

"Now let me ask you again, who goin' clean up this mess?" Kevin said laughing at his own joke.

It was 8:00pm and the party was about to start. Everybody was there except us. Rell and K-Dawg got lost trying to find Daron's crib, but he ended up getting there.

"Man you need to give some better directions," Rell said. Carla came in cursing everybody out.

"Where the hell my nephew at?" Carla asked. I told her he was over Aunty Vicki's house. She hugged me so tight I could barely breathe. Me and Carla needed to talk asap. I wanted to know everything that happened while I was gone that five years. Me and Carla went to the backroom where nobody was at.

"Dre I'm sorry I didn't write you and tell you what happened. I was scared of Kevin. He threatened the whole family Dre. He was goin' have you killed in prison but something went wrong. He used to walk around and say, 'get ready to bury yaw lil' brother. He went crazy after momma died." I couldn't believe what I was hearing.

"Slow down Carla, start over," I told her.

"Alright, when momma heard you were on the run she wrote a will giving you everything, but you got locked dup. You had two million dollars Dre. Momma was never broke. She was saving every since she had Kevin. Kevin signed the papers because he was the oldest. He also sent something to you to sign and you did 'cause you thought it was goin' help the family."

"All this for two million dollars?" I couldn't go to the funeral 'cause you claimed you didn't have enough

money, are you serious? I missed momma's funeral. My sister and my brother gone!" I yelled. I thought for a long time. That's why Man-Man got into it with Zaria, he probably would've killed if she didn't pull out first. It fucked my head up even more.

"Where he at?' I asked her.

"Somewhere in Benton Harbor." I hugged her and told her to go over Aunt Vicki's house. She knows you on your way. Before she left out she told me she'll be at the party. I hugged her one more time and she left.

We all started getting dressed for the party. I hopped out the shower drying myself. I went to the backroom where my outfit and Zaria was.

"Damn baby, you look good enough to eat," Zaria said while looking at my ripped body. I just laughed, while putting on my clothes.

"You like it?" Zaria asked.

"I like anything you do for me," I said.

"I can't tell, you don't seem happy." I didn't know what was wrong with Zaria. She knew I just lost my sister and my brother. I didn't give a fuck about none of this material bullshit but I didn't want to see her mad.

"Baby I am happy, I'm with you. Why you not dressed?" I said in a sarcastic way. She smiled and got up and went to the bathroom. Thirty minutes later everybody was dressed. Zaria looked so good in her Gucci outfit.

"We goin' go pick up Carla on the way there, so we'll meet you there," Suga told Daron. Rell and K-Dawg hopped in the Monte, Suga and Zaria drove the CTS, and me, Daron, Big Boy, and Lil Lou' rode in the Benz. The party was all over the radio. WJLB was hosting it, so everybody knew about it.

"Free from all haters. HP Dre has made it home. Come down to Club 2000, we ain't closing til' 3am," DJ Ready said over the music. I was geeked hearing that shit on the radio. I could't ask for nothing else. I had a bad ass

female, my brother Daron, Carla, and my nephew Chris. All I thought about was Kevin. I said a quick prayer in my head. Lord forgive me for my sins. I know I haven't been doing what's right, but I know you will help me along this journey. Help me clean my life up from all the evil. Let my family have a good time tonight. Thank you Lord for waking me and my family up today, amen.

Downtown was packed. Limos, cold ass cars, niggas riding good. Niggas was fresh but not as fresh as me.

"You ready Dre?" Daron asked me.

"Fa sho'," I said. We had V.I.P parking and a V.I.P. lounge. The line was so long and filled with bad bitches. Soon as I stepped in it felt like all eyes were on me. Daron walked off on me to go to the DJ booth.

"HP Dre is in the building.21 and over, come down to Club 2000 and party with them HP boys," DJ Ready yelled through the speakers. Everybody was geared up. But me and Daron killed them off the jogging outfits. I danced with Zaria a few times, but we parted after a few minutes.

"I on't give a fuck," the speakers blasted the Eastside Chedda Boys. "Oboy, nigga I on't be playin' nem games. Oboy, I'll come sprayin' nem thangs." That shit was loud as hell. Everybody in the club was rapping the song. I ain't even been here for a hour and this bitch was bangin'. Hoes was flocking around me like flies on shit. Zaria didn't never get mad 'cause she knew who I loved and she knew who I was coming home to. I couldn't believe how thick this chick was. She had me on rock mode. If I didn't throw these boxer briefs on I would've been hit cause my shit would've been sticking straight up. After the song was over she slid her number in my pocket and walked off. Zaria walked up to me grinning and shit.

"Why you fucking with them K-Swiss hoes and you got a Gucci chick standing right in front of you," she

whispered in my ear. She grabbed my dick and let her tongue swirl in my ear.

"What am I going to do with you?" I asked her.

"Whatever you want," she said with arms wrapped around my neck. I looked to the left and I saw Suga guarding her man like a watchdog. Big Boy and Lil' Lou was walking around looking like two big linebackers from the NFL. Freaky Rell and K-Dawg was on the dance floor buggin'. It was a Detroit song. Some niggas called it footwork, jittin, or hittin'. Don't get me wrong I could hit like a mothafucka, but Rell was fucking the floor up. It was to hot for that, plus I had on $400.00 gators. I wasn't about to do shit. Me, Zaria, Daron, and Suga ended up in V.I.P. We popped a few bottles of Cristal. I couldn't believe it. Niggas was barely popping Moet.

"To my brother Dre," Daron said giving a toast to me. We all drunk like it was no tomorrow. We left the V.I.P. and headed back towards the dance floor. Half of the party had on 'Free At Last' shirts with my face on it. I was loving this shit. Looking at Carla having a good time, all I could think about was Amber and 'Von. Damn I wish they were here. If Daron wasn't my bro', I'll probably be headed back to prison. Daron had so much damn money it was ridiculous. I know he wasn't all the way legit. I didn't care I was riding regardless. Right or wrong.

Only thing that ran through my mind was seeing Kevin's face. I ran almost every light trying to get to my parole officer.

When I got there the place was closed but it had a few names and numbers on a small piece of paper taped on the inside of the window. I wrote down one of the numbers to see if they could forward me to my parole officer. When I called they told me I was assigned to a Ms. Brooks. *Ms. Brooks huh?* I said to myself after hanging up the phone. I pictured this old ass miserable widow with a bunch of cats talking cash shit an
d was going to be ready to book me. I dialed the number to the parole officer I was referred to. When she picked up the phone she didn't sound old.

"Hello, yes may I speak to Ms. Brooks?...This is Dre Clark... Yes ma'am….Alright, thank you." I closed the phone mad as hell.

"Fuck!" I yelled loud as hell. This bitch done put a warrant out for my arrest. She gave me her address and told me to stop by. Something was up, I never heard of anything like this. She told me she'll drop the charges if I came and talked to her about what happened at the party last week. I knew she was going to have the sheriffs, state police, and the Ferndale police waiting for me. I couldn't stand Oakland because they were nothing, but racist ass white folks. It didn't take long for me to get there. When I pulled up to her house I didn't see anything suspicious so I kept going and I ended up coming back down the block. I ain't see no hook cars. I parked the Vette right in front of her house. I waited for a minute until I got out just in case. The block was nice and peaceful and everything looked normal. I still couldn't believe this bitch gave me her home address. I saw a red BMW in the driveway. I couldn't tell the model because it was backed in. All I knew was that it was a new

model. When I walked up the steps I made sure I looked good, dusting my Guess outfit off. Everything was ironed properly and made sure there were no wrinkles in my Air-Force ones. I knocked on the door and I heard a dog barking. Damn I couldn't stand small dogs. I guess I was wrong on the cat tip.

"Watch out Peaches," the voice behind the door said. Soon as she opened the door my mouth dropped. She was bad as hell. Her titties were about to fall out of her button down dress shirt. Her hips were out there. I knew she had ass.

"Hi, I'm Ms. Brooks, your parole officer," she said reaching her hands towards mines to shake them.

"I'm Dre Clark," I said shaking her hand.

"Well come on in Mr. Clark." Soon as I walked in the little mut was looking at me like I was a piece of bacon.

"Little shit, I wish you would," I said under my breath. The chick's house was out cold. It looked like a house that could have been on one of those house makeover shows.

"Have a seat Mr. Clark," she said. We both sat down at a small coffee table.

"Would you like a glass of lemonade, soda, or a cup of coffee?" She asked.

"Naw I'm good. Appreciate it though."

"So is that your car Mr. Clark?" She asked.

What the fuck is this about? Is this bitch going to drop the charges or flirt.

"Well it is now. It was my brother's car, but he's deceased now," I said while looking down.

"What is your brother's name?" She asked.

"Jevon, Jevon Clark," I said feeling uncomfortable. Her eyes suddenly lit up.

"Amber and Jevon are your siblings?" She asked in shock.

"Yes, how did you know that?" I asked starting to look more confused.

"I went to school with Amber and me and 'Von used to be high school sweethearts," she said before taking a sip of her lemonade.

"Damn it's a small world," I said.

"Who you tellin'?" She said cracking a little smile.

"So your Dre huh? You cuter then Amber described you as," Ms. Brooks said while uncrossing her legs. I didn't know what to say. Something wasn't right. The bitch knew exactly who I was. She probably knew my family. I guess this was a good thing. Maybe this could go in my favor. I made sure I was going to take full advantage of this situation. Hopefully big bro' didn't fuck her over.

"Why didn't you come to the funeral?" I asked.

"I was busy, matter of fact I was issuing the warrant out for your arrest," she said trying to be funny.

"So why didn't you report to me soon as you were released Dre?" She asked, calling me by my first name like she knew me. It kind of felt weird.

"I ain't goin' lie, it was so much on my mind especially with my family," I said.

"Slipped your mind, that party didn't slip your mind did it?" She said cutting me off.

"When are men going to stop acting like little boys?" She asked herself because she didn't give me any eye contact. She started writing something down in her notepad. She looked sexy as hell. I couldn't stop looking at her thick thighs and her pedicured feet in her Louis Vutton open toe heels. She had a green skirt on with her matching jacket. Her jacket was unbuttoned to show her double d cups. Her glasses had the letter C in the lenses, something like the ones Zaria wore. Damn I was feeling her even more. Big bro' always had taste. He stayed with the baddest hoes.

"What are you looking at Mr. Clark?" She asked lifting her head up. Damn I was embarrassed. She had caught me looking at her titties.

"Nut, nothing Ms. Brooks," I said getting frustrated.

"Damn all you niggas just alike," she said under her breath, but loud enough for me to hear her.

"What the hell you mean by that?" I said getting frustrated. I was offended and I hope she wasn't bringing 'Von in this conversation because he wasn't here to defend himself so I had to. She took her glasses off and rubbed both of her eyes with her index and thumb.

"Yaw lie over the pettiest shit, if you were checking me out, all you had to say was I was checking you out and I'm feeling you, even though I can't date you but I would of accepted the compliment," she said. I couldn't believe what I was hearing.

"Now do you have something to say to me Mr. Clark?" She asked. I wondered why she started calling Mr. Clark now.

"Aight Ms. Brooks, you bad as hell, I couldn't stop lookin' at you. I don't know what you're doing but you got my head gone." I was scared as hell because I never cut into a chick like that because I didn't have to especially a chick like this.

"Excuse me," she said. I repeated myself and before I could get it all out she slapped the hell out of me.

"You don't talk to me like that, I'm not one of these little tricks or hoes. You got a real foul mouth little boy." I just held my jaw while she still was snapping.

"You ain't nothing but another convict on his way back to prison," she told me. I jumped up quick as hell.

"Don't you ever tell me I ain't shit and put yo' hands on me again then you goin' have a real reason to send me back to prison 'cause I'ma whoop yo' ass," I said getting up and heading towards the door. She just sat there looking crazy. I opened the front door and all I heard was

the fucking dog barking. I was on my way out the door and I heard Ms. Brooks say "wait," When I turned around I saw her with her shirt unbuttoned and her breast were falling out her bra.

"Wait, I'm sorry. I just been so stressed," she said while heading towards me closer and closer. I knew she felt my dick rising. That's how close she was. I looked into her china doll eyes and lust just took its course.

"Do you forgive me Mr. Clark?" She said in a baby voice. Before I could respond, she grabbed my dick.

"If you don't then he do," she said laughing. She started working my zipper while she kissed on my neck. She had my pants down in seconds. She stroked my dick until pre-cum came out. I started to suck and lick on her neck now. My tongue traveled down to her large breasts. I pulled her shirt off and unstrapped her bra to expose them titties. I sucked and licked on them titties like it was no tomorrow. She didn't deserve no lovemaking she needed to get fucked. About time I got done it was red marks all over her titties. My dick was hurting it was so hard. It was time for me to dick this bitch. After I pushed her on the couch, she started pulling down her skirt. She never took her eyes off of me while doing it and that shit really had me going crazy. I got on top of her before she pulled her panties down. Her tittties were so fat I couldn't keep my hands off. I worked my way down to her navel smelling the bath and body works on her. When I pulled her panties off, it surprised me because she was completely waxed.

"Eat it mothafucka," she demanded grabbing the back of my head and shoving me into her sweetness. I kind of liked being submissive. She was making crazy ass noises I never heard. On top of that that little mut kept barking so the noises combined really sounded strange. She wouldn't even let me up. I had to squeeze her nipples for her to let me up. She finally let me up after about twenty minutes. I yanked her up by one of her arms off the couch so she

could stand straight up. I turned her around over the edge of the couch.

"Bend that ass over." She did as I told her. I teased her by rubbing the head of my dick up and down her clit.

"Please put it in, I promise I'll behave,' she said. I drove my dick in and she tried to get away but I had her waist in a grip lock.

"I can't...ta...take it anymore," she said panting.

"Shut up!" I yelled. I was gritting and grinding my teeth until it felt like they were going to break. She looked back at me biting her bottom lip. It was something about a female biting her lips and looking back watching me pound they ass in. I felt my knees giving out on me, but I kept going until I nutted all on her back and on her ass cheeks. The nut ran down the crack of her ass while I stroke the rest out on her thighs. She fell out on the couch breathing like she just ran a marathon.

"Get the fuck out now!" She yelled at me. I thought she was bullshitting, but she was dead serious. This bitch had to be bipolar. I grabbed my shit and got the fuck on leaving that crazy ass hoe laying on her stomach hoping she would drop that warrant. I smelt like sex all over. I couldn't believe I just fucked my parole officer. I never even thought about using a condom, not even on them hoes 'Von introduced me to. I felt nasty going home fucking Zaria. That shit wasn't cool at all. It wasn't going to happen again. I had to get in the shower and get ready to go downtown to Wayne County Jail to see about this warrant.

I hopped on Woodward and took it straight to Highland Park. When I got on Aunty Vicki block the little kids were playing street football. I saw Aunty Vicki's BMW in the driveway so I knew she was home. I pulled up right behind her car. She was sitting on the porch reading a newspaper.

"Boy why you ain't called me or came to come see me?" She said while taking the newspaper from her eyes.

"You almost been out for a month and you haven't sent a letter or nothing. Did you get that money I was sending to you?" She asked looking a little upset.

"Yes ma'. That's my fault. It's been a lot of things going on in the family so I been real busy," I said putting my head down.

"I know what's going on. As long as you don't forget where you came from," she said picking her newspaper up. She was right because she sent me money every month so I didn't want for to much. She also kept me on that religious tip.

"You've gotten so big. Last time I remember, you were at my kitchen table eating a bowl of Apple Jacks. So how's it going?" Aunty Vicki asked.

"Nothing much, surprised they let me go," I told her.

"Why you say that? Were you in there doing stuff you had no business doing?" She asked.

"Naw ma' I stayed out the way of everything," I said.

"You better stay out of trouble," she said turning her newspaper over.

"Aye ma', I wanted to know if I could get in the shower?"

"Boy you know damn well you can do anything in that house as long as it isn't anything illegal," she said.

"All-right ma," I said.

"I think Daron should have some boxers, tee shirts, socks, and some basketball shorts up in that chest. All that stuff is brand new," she said. I went and grabbed everything I needed. All I thought about was what was going to happen. I wasn't no snitch so I didn't have nothing to worry about. Bitch ass detective was probably going to play good cop bad cop. I knew Daron was going to be mad at me but it was time for me to man up. I got out and dried off and threw my clothes on. Soon as I got out I asked

Aunty Vicki where was Chris. She told me he was in the den with Uncle Phil. Uncle Phil was a cool ass old nigga. That nigga had dough too. Him and Aunty Vicki had been together for a minute. After Daron's dad passed away, he came right in and started taking care of Daron.

"What's good unk?" He was in the backroom watching sports center.

"What's happenin' nephew, when you come home?" He asked. I told him I been home for a couple of weeks.

"Chris you not goin' say nothing to your Uncle Dre?" Uncle Phil asked Chris. Man that little nigga looked just like me.

"What up lil'man?" I held out my hand and told him to give me a five.

"I gotta go take care of some business lil'man," I told him.

"Why you don't never take this boy with you nephew?" Uncle Phil asked.

"Man I been so busy, a lot of stuff hitting the fan right now. I'll let you know when everything cools down," I explained to him.

"You know he about to have a birthday in two months," Aunty Vicki said while coming in the room.

"I thought it was in two weeks," Uncle Phil said rubbing his head. Uncle Phil stayed getting high so he stayed forgetting something. "Well I gotta go, so I'm goin' call yaw and let you know what's up." I hugged Aunty Vicki then I picked Chris up and hugged him.

"All-right unk." Me and Uncle Phil shook up and I was out....

CHAPTER 10

I drove to Wayne County Jail and found a parking spot. I put a gang of quarters in the water because ain't no telling how long I was going to be in there. I called Zaria to let her know I was turning myself in. She was mad as hell. I told her to meet me at Big Boys on Jefferson so we could talk and told her to take a cab. I know somebody was going to be happy as hell about that meter. I drove straight to Big Boys. Zaria didn't have her cell phone because I had it so I couldn't call her to see where she was. I waited for almost a hour. I saw the old purple cab pull up and Zaria got out with her skin tight blue jeans on and her red polo shirt. Her Air-Forces were so small I knew she had to have bought them from Kids Footlocker. I hopped out the Vette to hug her and before I touched her she snapped.

"Dre why the hell you have me take a cab up here. Now you got me smelling like Chanel perfume and anti-freeze," she said. I broke out laughing. She looked so cute mad.

"It's not funny Dre," she said in a baby's voice.

"How much was it?" I asked. She gave me that look, like nigga are you serious.

"I already paid for it," she said.

"I didn't ask you all that. I asked how much was it," she smacked her lips and told me how much it was. I pulled out a crispy hundred dollar bill and gave it to her.

"Where in the hell you get that from?" She asked.

"Daron gave me some cash until I could get on my feet." We went inside and ordered our food and talked about what was going to happen. After we were finished with our food Zaria drove me to the Wayne County Jail. I told her I was going to write her soon as I got my commissary. We kissed and I told her I loved her. I got out and went in the building.

"May I help you?/" The funky ass deputy asked.

"Yeah, I'm turning myself in."

"What is your name sir?" I told him my name.

"Smart man," the fat ass deputy said under his breath. He typed for a couple of minutes then he called the sheriffs from the back to arrest me. They cuffed me and took me to the back. They put me in this stankin' ass bull pin with a bunch of niggas complaining and lying.

"Clark!" One of the deputies yelled my name. I went out and they fingerprinted me.

"You know what you're in here for boy?" A tall, racist sergeant asked me. I ignored him and that pissed him off even more.

"Oh so you one of those bad ass 7 Mile boys huh? Well let me inform you Mr. 7 Mile, your wanted for four murders and you're being investigated about the shooting that happened July 13. You've been on the run for almost a month. You would have been better off runnin' and hidin'." Kind of glad Ms. Brooks dropped that parole violation.

"Go to cell seven Mr. Clark." I was confused. Four murders? I just played it cool. When I walked in everybody that was in there was looking at me. I didn't see nobody I knew so I had to watch my surroundings. We sat in the bullpen for about another two hours until we changed into our greens. When we got upstairs it was probably two in the morning. Everybody had to sit in another bullpen. They started calling our names off. They finally called my name. I grabbed my bedroll and headed to my rock. Quarantine was packed. I stood in front of my rock and waited until they opened up my door. I was glad as hell it was a extra mat and a bed to put the mat on. Soon as I made my bed I stretched out and dozed off. It felt like soon as I closed my eyes they called chow. I opened my eyes just a little bit and I saw niggas scattering like roaches to the door. I sat there on my bunk until everybody was gone. Soon as everybody left I got up and every single breakfast was gone.

"Aye trustee, you short a breakfast," I yelled through the tray slot. He told me he put fourteen breakfasts' in here and it's only thirteen. I was mad as hell. "Ain't nobody grab a extra breakfast?" I asked. Nobody responded, all I heard was wrappers tearing and juice shaking. I just got back in my bunk. A, light skinned nigga tapped my bunk because he was under me on the lower bunk. I looked down and he was handing me a whole breakfast. I ain't want shit from nobody. Being in the joint for five years taught me never to accept nothing from nobody. This was my first time in the county too so I really had to play it different.

"Is that my shit/" I asked him.

"Naw, I won this from playing spades. Here you go take it. I got like five more coming later on." I took it because the little nigga didn't pose a threat, but I never judged a book by the cover though.

"My name Wes'," the short nigga said.

"They call me Dre," I told him. Me and Wes' kicked it until he moved off quarantine. They moved me three days later.

"New side, Clark, Jenkins, Franklin, and Thomas, your going to 9th floor." The deputy yelled out. We sat in another bullpen until our rooms were opened. I was the last one to go to a room. They put me on 9 northeast small rock. When the doors opened I saw Wes' watching TV.

"What's up pilla?" Wes' said while hopping up to shake m hand. Wes' started calling me pilla because it was short for H.P.

"Shit, glad as hell to get away from them crackhead ass niggas," I said while putting my bedroll on the table.

"What cell you going to?" I told him I was going to cell 6.

"All man yo' bunky stank man. See if you could get in the room with me. I'm in 5." I ain't even ask. His cell was already open so I just went right in his ell. I came out

73

and Wes' was glued to the TV. I was on quarantine for eight days bird bathing so I had to get in the shower. The showers on quarantine were horrible. I grabbed my shit and jumped in the shower. Soon as I got out the social worker was on the rock. Wes' told me to grab my phone list, visitors' list, and phone request so I could have the social worker call my peoples.

"What chu' need big fellow?" The big black social worker asked. I told him what I needed, but I asked for two phone request slips.

"I can only do one man. You new?" I told him yeah.

"Alright give me the numbers." I gave him Zaria's number first, then I gave him Daron's number. I wrote down what I wanted him to say to them.

"Good looking fam'. I really appreciate it," I said.

"No problem," the social worker said. I filled out my phone and visitors' list and gave it to him. I put Daron, Zaria, Carla, Uncle Phil, and Aunty Vicki on my visitors' list. I only had put Zaria's and Aunty Vicki's number on the list because everybody else probably had cell phones.

"Aye social worker, how long is it going to take for you to process this?" I asked.

"Call me Rob and it'll probably be on in four business days," he said.

"Alright, good looking," I said.

"Anybody need the social worker/" After he left I went to my cell, made my bunk, and laid it down. Thinking about Zaria had me stressing.

"Attorney visit Clark!" The dep yelled through the glass. I grabbed my shirt and came out. They opened the automatic doors and I headed towards the vistors' booth. When I got in there I sat down. It was a fat black guy with dreadlocks in there.

"How are you Mr. Clark?" He asked.

"I'm good."

"Do you have money in your account?" I remembered I gave all my money to Zaria before she dropped me off. She was supposed to send it to me, but I knew the social worker didn't give her my message yet.

"No sir."

"Alright, I'll take care of it when I leave. Well the good thing is you turned yourself in so that shows a sign of innocence. Do you have anything to tell?"

"No sir."

"Alright you'll be arraigned tomorrow. I don't know how you pulled that off. But usually you go to the precinct first, but guess that's a good thing. I'll have your family put some money in your account. I'll put a few dollars in your account for now," he said while packing his things.

"Thank you."

"No problem, I'll be at your court date tomorrow. The lead detective should be up here soon to talk to you about the club situation, but don't worry about that."

"Alright, anything else Mr. Clark?"

"Yeah, I didn't get your name," I said.

"Mr. Simmons," he said.

"Alright Mr. Simmons."

"Have a nice day Mr. Clark." I told him the same. When I got back to the rock everybody was looking at me like I was crazy. Wes' called me to the cell. When I got in there he shut the door behind me.

"What up doe?" I asked. Something was up but nobody was telling me nothing. I was heated.

"What up Wes'?" I repeated myself.

"Man they got you all on the news sayin' you raped some broad," Wes' said.

"What nigga? I ain't raped nobody. I get to much pussy," I said mad as hell.

"I believe you fam'," Wes' said. I was sick. I ain't do no shit like that. I didn't even want to look at nobody. I

was wondering why Mr. Simmons didn't tell me what the fuck was going on. I stayed in the room until they called chow.

"Road kill on the rock!" I heard niggas yelling.

"Road kill, what the fuck is that?" I asked Wes'.

"It's everything we had this week. Pork, chicken, beef, turkey, mixed with rice and vegetables," Wes' said. I almost threw up at the smell of it.

"You ain't goin' eat that?" A fat old school asked me.

"Wes' you want this shit?" Because that's what it was.

"Naw I'm good," Wes' said. I gave the whole tray to school and went back to my cell. I stayed in the room until lockdown. Soon as they called lockdown, the quiet storm came on WJLB. I listened to a couple of slow jams until they cut it off from the booth. I heard Wes' down there praying so I just said one in my head and dozed off.

"Clark, court!" The deputy yelled. They had cut my light on in my cell. It was bright as hell. Damn it was early as hell.

"What time is it?" I asked Wes'.

"Nigga it's prolly three o'clock in the morning," he said in a groogy voice.

"Take that brown paper bag with you 'cause you goin' be starvin' in them bullpens," Wes' said.

"Good looking Wes'," I said.

"It ain't shit," he said while turning towards the wall. I got up, brushed my teeth, and washed my face. I couldn't go nowhere with that horse on my back. I brushed my hair a couple of times then left out the door. I waited for the dep' to call me off the rock. They finally called me and four other dudes off the big rock next door. We waited in the bullpen for thirty minutes then they came and put us on the elevator. They gave us one small cereal and one small

76

milk when we got off the elevator. They told us what bullpen to go to after we went through the metal detector.

"Clark, 5!" The corporal said. We sat in the bullpen for a minute until they called us to get fingerprinted. Another two hours elapsed.

"Clark! Where's Clark?" One of the sheriffs said.

"Right here!" I said. I came to the front of the bullpen and they opened the bullpen's cell door. When I came out there were two Oakland County sheriffs standing there with shackles. They shackled the hell out of me; my ankles, waist, and my wrist. I got on the bus and there were only two young white chicks on the bus. They kept looking back at me smiling.

We got off the bus and went into the county jail. The two females went the opposite way I was going. I sat down on a bench and waited for the process. They put me in a another bullpen by myself. I was so damn tired of bullpens. This shit could break a nigga. I just laid on the bench and went to sleep.

"Clark, you alive in there?" A young, white deputy asked me.

"Yeah, yeah I'm good," I said while stretching.

"Must be tired huh?" The deputy asked.

"Yeah man, it's bullpen to bullpen," I said. We just laughed. We kicked it for a hot second while on the elevator. He was cool as hell.

"So what's this all about Clark?" He asked.

"Man this is all a big misunderstanding, you'll see." I played my shit right because he still was the hook so I wasn't telling him nothing.

"This is just arraignment, the court is empty. The judge doesn't like anyone looking back," he stated giving me some advice.

"So nobody is in the courtroom?" I asked looking confused.

"Nope."

"Not even my lawyer?" I asked.

"Nope, not even your lawyer." I was mad as hell. When I went into the courtroom it was empty like he said. I didn't even have to sit down. The judge told me I was charged with 1st degree criminal sexual conduct and habitual charge. She told me my bond was five hundred thousand. Ten percent of that was fifty-thousand. After I left out I was sick. How could this bitch do this to me. I was facing some bullshit ass charges.

I was now back on the bus headed back to Wayne County. It took us a minute because we had dropped a few guys off in Macomb County.

We got back like around nine o'clock at night. I ate the cakes and chips Wes' gave me because I was hungry as hell. I didn't get upstairs until like ten o'clock. I was tired and exhausted. Everybody was locked down in their cell when I came back. When I got in the cell, Wes' was finishing up a letter.

"Good looking on that food," I said.

"Man I told you I ain't care about that shit," Wes' said with his back to me. He was still writing when he asked did I hear any good news. I paused for a minute because I was so tired.

"There wasn't any good news. Nobody was at my court date. They charged me with some straight bullshit. Man Wes' on some real shit, I'm ready to get the fuck on, I'm tired Wes'. I just did five years. I can't go back Wes' especially for some shit I didn't play a part in."

"You good pilla, don't let that shit get to you. Uh, I would of bought some hygiene for you, but my money was low," Wes said.

"When the next time the store coming, 'cause it seem like they only come when I'm at court," I said. Wes' started laughing.

"Yeah it be like that sometimes. They'll be back in two days." I just laid down looking at the ceiling wishing I had some stamps so I could write Zaria.

The following morning I was wide awake. I got my breakfast, stayed up, and watched TV while everybody else went back to sleep. I turned to Channel 4 News to see if I could see if this bitch was on there. I was about to go back to sleep, but I heard breaking news up next. I finally saw the bitch saying she was raped by me. I couldn't believe this shit. This bitch done set me up. I tried the phones, but it was to early for the phones to be on. I paced up and down the rock until my legs were ready to fall off. I had to lay down. I went to the cell and laid it down until they called lunch. I got up, grabbed Daron's number, and tried to call it, but it was a block on the phone. I tried Zaria's phone, but it said the same thing. My last number was Aunty Vicki. Her number went right through. I told the operator my name and they put me right through.

"Hello…. Hey ma' I'm trying to find Daron it's urgent…Yeah could you please…." I waited a couple of seconds for Aunty Vicki to call Daron.

"What up doe bro?"

"Nun you know I ain't rape that bitch…I need that lawyer's number you set up here…I think his name was Simmons or something like that…So you don't know who I'm talking about…Man I need a visit asap for real bro'…My visits on Monday, you know I don't fuck with this phone…Just call up here and see what time and shit…Oh you can come up here at eight o'clock, my mans just told me…Yeah I'm good just mad as hell about this bullshit…Alright then, love you bro'. Tell mom dukes I love her too. One."

CHAPTER 11

Kevin was stressed out. All he thought about was his baby brother. Kevin was confused; he didn't know if he wanted to kill his brother or be there for him like a big brother should. Kevin saw the news and saw Ms. Brooks. He couldn't believe what this bitch told the police. Kevin specifically told her to tell the police that he whooped her ass. This bitch told them he raped her. She had Kevin looking real bad. She had it coming and that was it. She was on Kevin's time now.

Kevin picked her up in a rental because he didn't want nobody noticing his car. The rental wasn't in his name nor could anyone trace it back to him at all. The rental was in a loyal customer's name he served on the regular. Kevin blew the horn to let Ranae know he was outside. Kevin couldn't lie, she was a bad bitch. She came out looking good as hell with her platinum Cartier glasses and her Cartier earrings. She got in smelling so damn good.

"This one of your new cars you haven't told me about?" She asked.

"Naw baby doll, I done had this Mustang for a while," Kevin lied. He loved to stunt. He didn't even have to, but sense he never really had it while growing up he stayed doing it. He loved to see the expressions on people's faces when he pulled up.

"Damn baby you look good as hell," Kevin said to Ranae.

"Thank you, you don't look to bad yourself," she responded back. Ranae knew she was dead wrong for what she did to his brother, but who would turn down forty-five stacks? She laughed in her mind thinking how Dre had dicked her down. She did have feelings because she didn't want to see his ass in prison for the rest of his life. She lied about being friends with Amber. She couldn't stand Amber, but Jevon was her sweetheart and Kevin was her fuck

80

buddy. That's how she always looked at him. She was a female version of Kevin: a money hungry hoe. She had promised herself to eliminate all the grimy people out of her life and start fresh. She was going back to school to get her Masters. She was tired of all the scheming ass niggas, her nothing ass home girls, and the bullshit ass job. She had a thing for guys in the joint so she had to remove herself immediately. She was thinking about getting married and having some kids of her own. These were all things that ran through her mind, but she never thought that this night was going to be her last.

"So where we headed baby?" She asked.

"It's a surprise," Kevin told her. Ranae was geeked up. She was going to get some dick and some dough. Kevin looked like a sugar daddy with a cowboy hat, and a long leather trench coat. He had his fake ID and his fraud ass credit card. He also knew the manager at the Hamptons. He stayed away from all the cameras at all times. Soon as they got to the room, Ranae gasped soon as she stepped through the door. Everything was set up like a scene that was supposed to be on a movie.

"All this for me?" She asked.

"Yeah, you know money ain't shit," Kevin said.

"*Trick ass nigga, but fuck it. If he wanted it, let him spend it.*" Ranae thought to herself. "*I'm about to put this pussy on this nigga and be out.*" Ranae hopped in the shower while Kevin waited patiently on the bed with one of his hands in his pants and one behind his head massaging the .22 under the pillow he was lying on.

The bathroom door busted open and Ranae stood naked in the doorway. She didn't need no Le Perla or no Victoria Secret shit He wasn't going to fuck her with it on. The shit was going to be ripped off if she liked it or not. She made sure she saved every dime when it came to somebody else. Kevin sat up on his elbows with his mouth wide open.

"Damn baby," Kevin managed to say. He couldn't remember the last time he saw her naked let alone fucked her. She walked slowly to the bed teasing him with every move. She started climbing on the bed like a cat. Kevin was staring down at her while she started to unbuckle his belt. After she tugged at his pants for a second she had ended up pulling them down. Kevin had a lump in his boxer briefs from watching her.

"Is that for me?" Ranae asked Kevin.

"What chu' think?" He asked sarcastically. She pulled down his boxer briefs and threw them. Kevin's dick stood straight up. Rane grabbed the base of his dick and started to squeeze it until it looked like it was ready to explode. Kevin let out a painful groan.

"You ain't smart now are you?" She asked. Kevin shook his head like a small child.

"Now that's more like it," Ranae said. She started to stroke his manhood with her small hands. Her titties were bouncing up and down. She started to bag away from his dick. She was on all fours with her ass in the air sucking his dick with no hands. She knew how to suck dick like a professional. She wasn't swallowing enough so Kevin put one of his hands on her head to push her down more. She liked it though. A lot of females would have been mad but she enjoyed it. She now had the whole dick in her mouth gargling and slurping every inch. She was biting his head every time she came up. She loved to see niggas faces when they were about to come. Kevin took his hand off her head and started to thrust his hips up so she could taste every drop. He never came in her mouth before. Maybe today would be different.

"Damn baby, I'm bout' to come," Kevin said between the slurps. She stop sucking and she started jacking him off with both hands. She played in the come like she just mesmerized how it looked. Kevin just watched hrr. Kevin's dick was limp now, but Ranae got it back hard

stroking it with her hands and licking his dickhead. After she got his dick back to life, she mounted him. She lifted up to guild his dick inside of her, but instead she rubbed his dickhead back and forth up her slit. She got turned on by teasing niggas. She finally slid his dick inside her pussy. Ranae let out a low grunt. She was riding him slow but her pace started to speed up.

"You ready baby? Is this the best coochie you ever had? This might be the last time you hit this so enjoy it baby," she said rolling her hips and coming up and down on his dick.

"Yessss, bang my walls down nigga," she said while staring at the ceiling riding his dick. Her eyes were now in the back of her head. Kevin grabbed her ass cheeks while she bounced and pounced on his dick. Ranae felt Kevin playing with her ass hole.

"Ohhh shit Kevin, take it out," she said between heavy breaths. Kevin continued to finger her ass hole. She started to bang her ass against his index finger. After her ass hole was loose, he stuck two fingers in. He was moving his two fingers faster back and forth.

"Damn baby, you got my ass hurting," she said while standing up.

"Girl quit playin' and come over here so you can bend that fat ass over," Kevin told her.

"Like this daddy?" She said while getting on the bed and bending over letting her ass and pussy face him. Kevin loved doing doggy style.

"You goin' saddle up or you just goin lie there and stare?" She said grinning. He got behind her parting her legs so he could get a good position to pound her down. When he rammed his dick in her pussy she tried to escape from Kevin's grip, but he had her hips locked with his huge hands.

"I feel it daddy," Ranae cried out. But that just made Kevin pump even harder. She was moaning to every

stroke. He felt her shaking and then ther nut started to leak every time he entered her.

"I'm cummin', right there. Ohh, ohhhh, ohhh. Here it comes." It was like a waterfall. Kevin still didn't get his nut. He continued to pump in and out of her.

He now had her ass cheeks spread apart. He knew he couldn't nut in her because DNA was something serious nowadays. He grabbed a Magnum out the dresser.

"What are you doing bay?" Ranae asked looking back.

"Arch yo' back baby," Kevin said slipping the condom on. She did as he said. He slid two fingers in her ass again to get her ready. She didn't know what he was doing, all she knew was that it felt good.

"You ready?" Kevin said speeding up his pace.

"Yesss, yes I'm ready," Ranae moaned out. Kevin shoved his dick in her ass and she let out loud grunts and fell out. Only thing that was holding her up was Kevin gripping her hips slamming his dick in and out of her ass. Her face was now in the pillow and she was now pounding her fist on the mattress. Kevin pulled her up by the hair to lift her head up and when he did he saw tears in her eyes when she looked back at him. That turned him on. She was trying to throw it back, but Kevin was like a wild beast. He knew he was about to come so he gave her hard long strokes. Three more pumps and he was now filling up the condom. They both fell out sweating and breathing hard. Kevin was still on top of her with his dick still in her ass. He finally got the strength to roll off of her. He stood up minutes later to take the condom off to flush it down the toilet. Ranae was sleep, well at least that's what he thought. Kevin packed all his shit. He made sure he didn't touch nothing and shit he did touch he wiped it down. After all his shit was packed it was time to off this bitch. Kevin grabbed the semi auto .22 caliber with the silencer and pointed at her.

"Sorry baby, but you gotta go," Kevin whispered.

"What the hell you talking about Kevin?" She said in a tired voice. Before she could open her eyes he emptied the clip. He didn't want to take no chances so he reloaded and put two more in her head to make sure she was dead. He changed his whole outfit and left out the room.

CHAPTER 12

"Damn, I been in here for almost three weeks," I said to Wes'. It was Monday morning so I knew I was getting a visit. I got up early, brushed my teeth, and showered. It seemed like it had been forever since I last saw Zaria. I needed to see her. Bout time I got out the shower I used Wes's brush to get my waves back in place.

"Damn Pilla, you just know you getting a visit huh?" Wes' asked while still lying down reading.

"Yep," I said while brushing my hair. I finally had got my commissary. I had ordered Wes' some hygiene and some cakes for looking out for me. He acted like he didn't want it, but I left it on his side of the desk. Soon as I jumped on my bed I put my deodorant on and lotion and waited for my visit to arrive. Me and Wes' kicked it until they called me for my first visit. I jumped down and grabbed my greens from under my mattress and ran out the cell like it was a fire drill. Soon as I sat down in the visiting booth Daron was looking me in the eyes. He was up here bright and early.

"What up bro/?" Daron said.

"Lay it on me bro'," I said.

"Well that bitch that said you raped her is dead. They found her body yesterday morning in a hotel. The good news is that the charges are gonna be dropped because she is dead. She never identified you. They're waiting on the DNA test from her right now," Daron said. A little smirk appeared on my face because karma was a bad bitch.

"Now about those murders, did you hear from Mr. Fitzgerald?' Daron asked me.

"Naw I ain't heard shit from em'," I said.

"I'm goin' get on his head, 'cause I just gave em' a stack to come see you and twenty stacks to represent you," Daron said looking upset.

"Good looking bro'. Man what the hell would I do without you?" I asked Daron.

"If it wasn't for Zaria it would've been more, but she's friends with his wife plus she put most of the money up," Daron said.

"Tell her to come up here like around eight o'clock or eight-thirty tonight," I said.

"Yo' sister should be up here too. I don't know what time though," Daron said.

"Man I'm so tired of this shit," I told him.

"I know Dre, don't stress yourself. You can call moms' house anytime you want," he said.

"Aight bro'. Oh, I got one more thing. You seen Kevin?" I asked. Daron looked like he froze up. After Kevin put a Mag in Daron's mouth years back, Daron didn't want no smoke.

"Naw, I ain't seen em'. Well I'm 'bout to go check the shit out this lawyer. Make sure you call me later on," Daron said.

"One," I said. I got back to the rock and everybody was still sleep except ol'school. I went back to the cell to holla at Wes'. I kicked it with Wes' until chow came. After we ate we played a couple of games of Casino until Wes' was tried of getting his ass whipped. I was about to go in the cell, but ol' school was calling me. Soon as I said what up he pointed at the TV.

"They had the young girl on there that said you raped her," ol' school said. Soon as the news came back on they showed Ms. Brooks' picture.

"Turn it up," I said.

"Black female was fatally shot in The Hamptons hotel in Southfield. The victim was identified as 26-year-old Ranae Brooks. The victim's body was discovered Sunday morning. More to come soon," the news reporter said. I was fucked up 'cause now I felt sorry for her. Everybody on the rock was looking at me different now

except Wes'. It seemed like they showed a sign of fear, but little did they know I had nothing to do with that chick getting killed. We ate lunch and watched Elimindate and Blind Date. After that went off it was almost time for the deps' to pass out the mail. I had wrote Zaria so I knew I had some coming, but I didn't know about the rest of these niggas. I went back to the cell to listen to the radio to pass some time.

"Aye fam', I wanted to know if you could give me three-way?" Wes' asked me.

"Yeah I'll see about it tomorrow 'cause I gotta get back right with my girl first 'cause mom dukes not goin' do it at all," I told him.

"Good looking pilla, I appreciate it," Wes' said.

"It ain't shit. If I got it you got it as long as you don't cross me," I said. I ended up dozing off for like thirty minutes until they called for mail. Wes' came in the cell loud as hell talking about his bitch wrote him. I was mad as hell 'cause this nigga woke me up. I heard them call Clark so I loosened up a little. The first letter I saw was Zaria's. She wrote three times. The next letter didn't have a name on it. It just had put Calvin Johnson on your visiting list visits wrote on the back of the envelope. I didn't know what to do so I ended up writing the name down on a paper for my bunky in case the social worker and I was in court. I told him to add that name to my list.

"Clark visit!" I heard the dep say through the thick glass window. I was jealousy in all these niggas eyes, but I wasn't tripping 'cause I dealt with that shit all my life. Soon as I got there I saw Carla.

"What up sis?" I asked.

"Nothing, well not nothing 'cause you probably don't know."

"Know what?" I asked.

"Well word going around is that Kev' had Ranae killed and I heard he put those bodies on you," she said

with her head down. I knew the last part ws true, but I had no idea why he killed Ms. Brooks.

"That's fucked up Carla," I said.

"So what do you be doing in here? Is it like prison?" Carla asked.

"Naw it's worst. Can't go outside, can't eat right. This shit all fucked up."

"What time your court date?" She asked.

"I think it's at ten o'clock in the morning," I said.

"Alright little brother, I gotta head back to work. Anything you need me to do?" She asked.

"Naw Carla, I'm good, just tell everybody I love em'."

"Alright, see you tomorrow. Love you so much," she said.

"Love you to sis," I said.

"Clark! You finished in here!"

"Yeah!" I said.

"Well switch booths 'cause you got another visit," the deputy said. Soon as I walked in the booth I saw a tall, skinny white guy sitting down.

"What's up playa'? Have a seat," the white guy told me. I couldn't believe what I was seeing and hearing. Man this dude had on Sean John and was talking like he was from my way. I was shocked.

"What up?" I asked. We shook hands and he told me he wasn't going to prosecute me. He was trying to be funny, but I wasn't in a playing mood. I sat down to see what he was talking about.

"Alright, first off how are you holding up in here?" He asked.

"I'm good. It could be worst," I said.

"I'm starting to like you more and more. That's a good thing. Well your brother Daron contacted me, but I was still looking over your case. I know all of this is some

89

bullshit. These crackers ain't got shit on you. Have any detectives came and talked to you?" He asked.

"Not at all," I said.

"They'll be up here trust me. You know better so I don't have to tell you to keep your mouth shut." I nodded my head and he continued to talk.

"I have your discovery packet right here. They can't place you at the scene. All they have is some heroin addict saying they saw you a couple times on that block. I'm going to be at your court date tomorrow to get you a bond, but it's gonna be high as shit. Youu don't have one body, you got three bodies. Anything or any questions?" Fitzgerald asked. He basically answered all my questions and more.

"So what's going to happen with this charge in Oakland County?" I asked.

"Well you should be going back for a dismissal real soon. I can't give you an exact date, but when I find out I'll be sure to inform you," he said.

"Umm, I don't know who this guy was, but he came and saw me. I only had his last name though. I think his name is Simmons," I said looking confused.

"Yeah I know who he is. He's the worst court appointed lawyer you can have to represent you. Horrible. Was he a heavyset brother with dreadlocks?" He asked.

"Yeah that's him," I said.

"You didn't tell him nothing did you because he's working with the prosecutor at all times. Big cases, small cases, it doesn't matter."

"Naw I ain't tell him nothing," I said.

"That's another good thing you didn't tell that slime ball nothing," he said.

"Anything else before I get out of here?" He asked.

"That's it sir," I told him.

"Well it was nice meeting you and I look forward to working with you," he said while shaking my hand. I went

back to the room and stretched out on my bunk. I guess things were looking good so far. Hoping like hell I get this bond tomorrow. Every time I closed my eyes, Zaria was standing right there.

"What up fam', I know you ain't sleep," Wes' said while coming in the room.

"Shit, my lawyer just came up here and my sister," I said.

"What they talkin' bout?" Wes' asked. I usually didn't fuck with niggas far as talking about my legal work, especially these county lawyers because these niggas a turn state on you with no hesitation. I thought different about Wes'. He was a cool little nigga. I kind of felt sorry for him because he rarely got mail let alone visits.

"Man it's looking good as of right now. The bitch that lied on me got killed a couple of days ago so it ain't goin' be no trial. She never identified me. It's sad that, that happened to her though," I said.

"You should be good then. What about them bodies?" Wes' asked.

"I don't know, but my lawyer trying to get me a bond tomorrow," I told him.

"Man that's where it's at," Wes' said. It got kind of quiet in the cell for a second. I was curious about Wes'. I wasn't really to interested in niggas cases, but I needed to know what type of niggas I was dealing with in case I started to fuck with a nigga heavy.

"Aye Wes'," I said.

"What up Pilla?"

"Not that it's my business, but what the fuck you do for you not to get no mail or visits?" I asked. When a nigga didn't get no mail and visits, he either fucked his people over or was in here on some foul shit.

"Armed robbery. Got a nigga for some Cartiers," he mumbled. I knew he was lying, but I listened until I was tired of hearing how he pistol whipped the nigga.

"Keep it funky Wes', you know that's some bullshit. I don't care what you in here for. I just need to know what type of nigga you is. A crime don't describe a nigga but by you lying to me explains a lot," I said. It was silent for a minute.

"Man, CSC and armed robbery," Wes' said. I wasn't surprised at all. It's niggas in the joint that you would never think would do some of the shit they were in there for.

"It ain't what you think Pilla," Wes' said.

"Man I don't care about that shit," I said.

"I'm still telling you. I was fucking with this chick and I fucked her. I stop fucking with her and started fucking with her friend. Big mistake. Man this bitch ended up going to the police. She set me up and said I robbed and raped her. Her friend wasn't going to help me so it was a wrap," Wes' said. I really felt bad for Wes' now. Man this nigga was little as hell. He was like 5'1'. Who in the hell could he rape?

"That's crazy. How much your bond?" I asked.

"Twenty-thousand ten percent, so it's two thousand," he said. Man that shit was extra cheap. I could've had that in two days.

"That's why I needed you to call my peoples," Wes' said. Me and Wes' kicked it all the way until dinner time. I couldn't wait to smash these hamburgers. The whole rock ended up getting extra trays, but that still didn't fill me up. The rock was laid back and the deps was cool as hell. On other rocks niggas was stealing out of niggas' cells and shit. Me. Wes', and ol' school played some spades until they called me for my next visit. I just knew it was Zaria. When I got in there my Uncle Devin and my younger cousin Will was in there. Me and Will were kind of close, but he lived on the other side of town. We made sure we kicked it hard for half an hour. I wasn't mad, but I was kind of because neither one of them wrote me or came to see

me. One thing my moms taught me was it was never too late to change. They threw some bread in my account and dipped off.

"Back to the crack house." We were finished playing cards because I wasn't 'bout to be watching that nasty shit. I took a quick nap. It was crazy how I kept being put in these fucked up situations.

"Damn," I said under my breath. I had court tomorrow too. I hated waking up that damn early. I couldn't wait until this shit was over. I had to get up because I couldn't sleep. Niggas was loud as hell. They knew I was trying to sleep. When I stepped out the room everybody turned their heads in my direction, but then got right back in their conversation. I couldn't believe these niggas were arguing over shit that happened on the outs.

"Aye dep, you got the time?" I asked.

"8:57!" The dep yelled from the booth. Man Zaria should've been up here. I was headed towards the phone to call Aunty Vicki. Soon as I pressed 1 the dep called me for my visit. I left out with the phone hanging off the hook. I had brushed my hair a couple of times before I got in the booth. Soon as I walked in, Zaria looked pissed.

"What's goin' on bay?" I asked.

"Did you use a condom?" She asked. Her eyes started to water, but the tears weren't ready to come down. Zaria knew I didn't use condoms. She's known me all my life.

"No," I said calmly.

"Why Dre?" She cried out. I felt like shit 'cause Zaria knew I fucked her and she knew I didn't rape her.

"Dre I didn't care about you fuckin' her. You didn't know what that nasty bitch had. Now look at cho' stupid ass. You make me sick. Sometimes I ask myself why am I still with you. I told you the truth. Yeah I was fuckin', but you best believe these niggas strapped up and ain't no nigga ever put their dick in my mouth. Did you eat her

pussy Dre? You know what I'm outta here. I'll see you tomorrow. Bye," she said in a dry tone. I just sat there looking stupid. After she left out I got up and headed back to the rock. I went to the cell and just listened to the radio. Wes' came in after me asking me was I alright. I ignored him. He didn't ask nothing else, he just left out the cell. I dozed off before they called lockdown so me and Wes' didn't get a chance to kick it.

I kept hearing a bunch of noise in my sleep. I was mad as hell. When I got up I heard it even louder.

"I know you aint sleep?" I asked Wes'.

"Yeah nigga I'm up. I probably been up longer then you," Wes' said sounded pissed off.

"Them niggas over there scrapping?" I asked Wes'. Before Wes' could answer my question I heard them arguing.

"Man I wasn't jacking off, I swear to God."

"Bitch ass nigga you was. You been doing this shit for the last two days," I heard a bang after that. All I heard next was somebody screaming for the dep banging on their door. Everybody was yelling 'whoop his ass'. Even the other rock was yelling. The deps finally came in and took both of them to the hole. I'm pretty sure one of them was going to medical 'cause he was looking bad. Everything was over and everybody was quiet. Soon as I closed my eyes they cut the light on in my cell for court.

"Bitch," I said out loud. I got up and got myself together. I had hustled up on a few cereals so I wouldn't have to eat my store food up. Before I left out Wes' said he'll pray for me. I didn't see anybody I knew when I was waiting to get on the elevator. After a hour past they finally called all seven of us on the elevator. When we got off we grabbed our one cereal and went to our bullpens. The corporal told me cell three. On my way to the bullpen niggas was staring at me griming me and shit, but I ain't care as long as they kept their dick beaters to themselves.

Soon as I came in niggas was in there rapping. It was way to early for that shit. The shit wasn't that bad though I just wasn't trying to hear that shit. Everything went sour when a nigga started asking niggas what were they in here for. Man it was to good to be true. It was always somebody asking about another nigga's case. Then I had to hear from these 'jailhouse lawyers. They called our bullpen out for fingerprints so I saw all them bitch ass niggas that was looking at me all crazy. All I heard was, 'that's the nigga that had that parole officer bitch killed.' I just flashed a small smirk and kept it moving. Niggas was crazy. We went back to the bullpen and waited until they called me for court. I had to hear these niggas for three hours complaining. They ended up calling me and five other niggas. I was so glad to leave, but when they said the last name it was the little nigga asking everybody about their case. The fucked up thing about it was he was only in here for a probation violation. We were escorted on the van and headed to the 36th District Court. When we got in there I started doing my crossword puzzles. They didn't let me change out because my judge was on the third floor. Niggas was jumping out of windows and escaping so we had to wear our greens at all times. Once they called me, they called the young nigga and three more niggas 'cause we all had the same judge. They called me first so I made sure I didn't have any eye matter in the crack of eyes. Soon as I walked in I saw all my folks, but I was searching for one person and that was Zaria. Damn where was she at. Soon as I looked to the left I saw her. My eyes were glued to hers until the judge told me to have a seat. They told me my charges, but it wasn't nothing but a bond hearing. They still denied my bond. The prosecutor was on my head. If I wasn't a ex-felon I probably would have got one. I heard Zaria crying behind me. I wanted to tell her it was all right, but the bailiff wasn't having that. I knew she still loved me, she was just upset. After they denied me I went back to

court holding pen with the other guys. One of them was gone when I got in there. It was two judges on the floor. The guy with the probation violation was last. When the other guy got back the young nigga left out. Thirty minutes later the young nigga came back crying like a bitch saying they gave him 90 days in the county without time served. Soon as I heard that I snapped.

"Man shut the fuck up. You in here crying about some bullshit. You a grown ass man. That petty ass time. At least you know you going home. I ain't tryna hear that shit," All them niggas was quiet as hell. I was the youngest in there, but none of them niggas attempted to say anything to me. The room was quiet until we got back to the other holding cell. The good thing was the van was here to pick most of us up. When we got back to the county everybody was asking what they do for you young dog'. I just ignored them. It took almost three hours to get back on the rock. I was starving. Them hoe ass cakes and beef and cheeses didn't do a nigga no justice. I made it back in time for dinners. I smashed that fake ass chicken drum and went to sleep. It was a long ass day. No mail, no bond. I mean what else could possibly happen to me?

"Aye man did you turn that visiting form in for me?" I asked.

"Yeah nigga, I took care of it."

CHAPTER 13 - ZARIA

Zaria was so depressed, she didn't know whether to forgive Dre or to leave him. How could he put his self back in a situation like this?

"Damn I love that boy 'cause that's exactly what he is, a damn boy," she said to herself. Her phone started ringing.

"Hello…Oh' what's up cuz?...Yeah maybe he'll get his bond on his next court date…When is it? Alright, love you too." She was glad to hear from Daron because she didnn't know that Dre's court date was two weeks from today. Zaria felt lonely 'cause her baby was gone and he could be gone for life. She gave her all in their relationship, but Dre found a way to fuck things up.

I had to go out and do some things for myself. I got dressed and hopped in the shower. I thought about taking my Monte because the Corvette was kind of hot.

"Nahhh," I said. I dropped the top and headed to the spa. O my way there I saw some guys trying to holla at me when I came off the freeway at the red light.

"Aye baby girl, you riding good, only thing you missing is me," a nigga in a 5 type Jaguar said. When the light turned green I just cracked a smile and drove off. When I got to the spa in Bloomfield, I walked in the spa with all my cosmetics in my bag.

"Appointment for Ms. Hicks," I said to the Asian woman.

"Yes please follow me." She led me to the end of the hall. The young Asian woman opened the door up for me. After the Asian woman left I took off all my clothes and looked at myself in the full body length mirror on the back of the door. I knew I was pregnant, but it didn't show. I was so mad at Dre. I didn't know what to do. I wasn't

97

about to get no abortion, it was a wrap for that shit. My mom was against that so that was out of the question.

"Damn I got to tell my mom what's going on with Dre," I said to myself. I started to have memories about Dre being over my house every day. My momma never tripped about him coming over. Sometimes she'll even let him inside. I wondered if Dre would have been around if my dad was still alive. I was nine years old when my dad died. He got shot right in front of me. Soon as he got killed I met Dre and they were close every since. I heard a knock on the door.

"Ms. Hicks are you ready?/" The voice behind the door asked.

"Hold on for a sec'," I said while putting my towel around my lower body so I could lie down on my stomach.

"Alright, I'm ready now," I said. The cocky woman walked in looking like the world's strongest man.

"How are you today?" He asked.

"I guess I'm cool. I just need a real good massage," I said.

"That's cool. That's what I'm here for," he said. I thought his hands were going to feel like sandpaper but they didn't. I felt so relaxed. After the massage I made sure I tipped the masseur a nice tip and dipped out.

Zaria was wondering if she went to hard on Dre.

"Nahhhh, he needed to feel like shit for a minute," I said while getting in the Corvette. I was mad at him 'cause he still hasn't called, but I didn't let that stress me out. I called Sunny to tell him I wasn't going to be able to make it in. I knew he would understand and plus he watches the news everyday so I knew he would understand. I called Suga to see if she wanted to go out tonight. Of course Suga said yeah. Even though me and Carla didn't get along, I still called her and asked her did she want to go to the River Rock.

"All come on girl. I know you tired of Aunty Vicki…Girl I'll be over there like around eight o'clock," Zaria said to Carla. Carla finally said alright.

Zaria wasn't feeling like wearing no heels so she put on her white Prada gym shoes and her skintight blue Guess Jeans with her white Guess shirt that hugged her breasts. Zaria heard Suga blowing her horn outside. She took like ten more minutes to come outside. Zaria came out and hopped in the car.

"Girl you looking good," Zaria said to Suga.

"Thank you, but you looking like a million dollars," Suga said. Suga always went hard anywhere she went 'cause Daron spoiled the hell out of her. She had on a tight Christian Dior skirt with her matching stilettos. When they got in front of Aunty Vicki's house, Zaria called on her cell phone to tell Zaria to come outside. Carla came out looking like new money. Her Gucci printed jeans were so tight on her, thong showing and all. She had her Gucci print gym shoes on with her matching halter top and to top it off she had on her Techno Marine watch to match her outfit.

Soon as we got there the music was so loud we could hear it over our music in the car. When we got out, we knew we were the baddest bitches there.

"Damn it's some sexy ass niggas in here," Carla yelled over the loud music. Me and Carla drank Apple Martinis most of the night. Carla danced with this young guy almost the whole night. The guy had to have money with that big faced Movado watch with all them diamonds in it. I had to admit he was a cutey. I danced with a few guys but that was it. Suga didn't even attempt to get up and dance 'cause Daron was known almost everywhere and niggas would hate and gossip like bitches, so she sat at the table and drunk all the drinks that were sent to the table by all types of balling ass niggas.

"Girl I think I'm going home with this nigga," Carla yelled to me in my ear.

"Girl you don't even know this nigga," I yelled back.

"Who said I had to know em' to fuck em'? Carla asked.

"Girl you trifling," Suga said putting her two cents in. They went back to the table so they could try to talk Carla out of leaving with a stranger.

"For real girl you don't even know that nigga," Suga said.

"Girl I'm good, 'Von gave me a .25 semi-automatic a couple years back. It's in your car right now," Carla said.

"Bitch you had a gun in my car that whole time and ain't say nothing?" Suga asked.

"If I would have said something you would of tripped on me and soon as I leave I'm going to go get it," Carla said while laughing. To still think of it I still had that .380 that Dre gave me. Since that incident with Man-Man I didn't get rid of it. Suga wasn't mad either because she kept hers at all times too.

"So you have your gun permit?" Suga asked.

"Girl you know damn well I got mines," Carla said.

"What about you girl?" Suga asked me.

"Naw, I ain't got mines, but I'm on the verge of getting one," I said. The club was about to be over because they started playing the slow music. Carla rushed out to the car to grab her purse.

"Carla leaving for real," Suga said. We shook our heads. We left out of the club a little bit after Carla. When we got outside we saw Carla getting into a red XJR Jaguar.

"He must be getting a lil' money by looking at his car," I said.

"Yeah, I just hope she'll be alright," Suga said getting in to her car.

"We gotta make sure we tell Aunty Vicki Carla not coming in tonight," I said.

"I'm pretty sure she goin' call Aunty Vicki and let her know. She got her little .22," Suga said while making her index finger look like she was pulling a trigger. We both started laughing.

"Damn I wish I could get some dick 'cause lord knows I need it," I said.

"Girl shut the hell up, Dre a be at home in no time," Suga said.

"I hope so 'cause I'm tired of this shit," I said. We were quiet the rest of the way back. Suga dropped me off and waited until I made it in. Soon as I got in I took off all my clothes and went right to sleep.

"Damn baby you look good as hell," Zetroc told Carla.

"You like it when I do this?" She asked while she danced slow to Mary J. Blidge and R,Kelly 'It's On'. Zetroc was getting dough. He owned a detailing shop. He had his youngins' steal cars, and he'll buy them and fix them up and sell them. He was the coldest on re-tagging. He never got down on his crew at all that's why they showed mad respect for him. He could have had any chick in the club tonight but he chose Carla. He was feeling her hard. He was 28 and he was looking to settle down 'cause he was tired of all the gold diggers.

"You goin' let me just dance all by myself?" Carla asked. Carla hasn't been intimate with anyone in a long time so she knew her juice box was full.

"Shit we been dancing all night baby girl," Zetroc said getting up and joining her.

She woke up in his arms the next morning. Zetroc got up and went to the bathroom. Carla was dick dizzy from all the fucking they did last night. Carla was feeling him hard. She was surprised that he didn't get up and leave her at the Marriot.

"Carla!" Zetroc yelled over the running shower. She was still in a daze when he was calling her.

"Yeah babe?" Carla smiled back.

"You goin' join me or you goin' sit there and listen to the shower run?" Metroc hollered back. She giggled thinking to herself about what she asked him last night. He was trying to be funny. She got up and went straight to the shower to join him.

"Damn baby girl you look good as hell," Zetroc told her. She loved the way he complimented her all the time, but she knew this wasn't going to last 'cause it was a one night stand. They made love in the shower and washed each other in the steamy shower.

"Aye Carla," Zetroc called out to her. She turned around with a surprised look on her face.

"Yeah?" She said.

"I'm feeling you, anytime you wanna go out or anything that you like to do give me a call okay?" Zetroc said looking in her eyes. She smiled and he gave her his number and drove off.

CHAPTER 14

"Chow!.....Chow!.....Chow on the rock!" The trustee yelled through the mechanic doors. I got up and grabbed Wes's breakfast, laid back down, and waited for my visits. I thought about giving Wes' that 3-way 'cause I didn't want him to think that I was spinning him. I knew Wes' was up because he was down on his bed tossing and turning.

"Aye Wes', you still alive down there?" I asked.

"Yeah nigga I'm alive," Wes' mumbled back.

"You still need that 3-way call?" I asked.

"Yeah fam', I really do need it," Wes' said. I stared at the ceiling for at least two hours listening to the oldies. I knew Daron was on his way so I finally decided to get up and eat my breakfast. I brushed my teeth and hopped in the shower. After I was finished they called me for my first visit for today. I threw my greens on and dipped out. Soon as I got in the booth, my brother Daron was in there.

"What up bitch?" I asked playing around.

"Man slow motion. It could be better if you was out here with me."

"You heard from your cousin?" I asked.

"Nigga she said call her. You need to get her back on the team 'cause you slippin' bro'," Daron told me.

"What the hell you talking about?" I asked getting a little upset.

"She constantly going out with Suga and Carla. Suga telling me that she tired of your shit, tighten up bro'," Daron said.

"You feel the same way about Suga going out?" I shot back.

"Hell naw. Shit her man right here. She ain't going home with another nigga, not saying that Zaria is but you know what I'm saying," Daron said.

"Naw bro', I don't know what your saying," I said.

103

"Bro' I didn't come to visit you to argue. Don't take it like that. Everybody just mad 'cause you gone," Daron said.

"I'm mad that I'm gone to bro' but what can I do about it? I can't control Zaria's actions. Ain't no tellin' what she out there doin'. You feel me?" I asked.

"Yeah I feel dat. You know Chris's birthday comin' up. It's next Saturday," Daron said.

"I know bro' and I promised him I was going to be there too," I said.

"Your court date coming up so we could probably try to get a bond for you," Daron said.

"Man I hope so dog 'cause I'm sick as hell," I said.

"I gotta go to the shop bro' so I'm goin' try to make it up here next Monday. Love is love, loyalty is law," Daron said leaving.

"You know what it is," I said leaving out. I got back to the rock and everybody was still sleep except this skinny, tall white dude walking around the rock. I went back to the rock and took a nap. Soon as I laid down they called me for another visit. I thought it was going to be that Calvin Johnson dude. I got out there and it was my big sister Carla.

"Hey big head," she said.

"What up doe sis'?" I asked.

"Nothing. Me, Suga, and Zaria been going out You know me I love clubbin'. I already know what you goin' to say, did I take some pictures? No, I forgot but don't be mad at me okay?" She said.

"I ain't mad, but I am 'cause you ain't wrote to let me know how you or my nephew were doing out there," I said.

"Boy I'm good ain't nothing going on, but the same ole stuff; people getting killed, robbed, and locked up. Your nephew doing good. He keep asking about you. How about

you, you doing alright? You ain't have to whoop nobody have you?" She asked giggling.

"Naw ain't none of that happened yet. Hopefully, I don't but you never know while being in here. I'm good just wishing these crackers drop this bullshit feel me?" I asked.

"I felt that, 'cause this place is dirty as hell," Carla said looking around the booth.

"Girl shut up, everything dirty to you. You just like momma. Remember when momma saw that roach in the house, she woke everybody up at two o'clock in the morning to clean the whole house up? What about when our cousins came over and momma told them to put their bags outside, bu Leslie brought her bag in anyway. Man momma whopped the hell out her for bringing that bag in the house," I said reminiscing.

"Yeah those were the days Dre. I miss all of them Dre so much," Zaria said.

"Me to Carla, it'll be alright," I said. We kicked it for about ten more minutes about the old days then the visit was over.

"Alright brother, I love you," Carla said.

"I love you too," I said. I felt good kicking it with my sister. Visits were over and chow was almost on the rock.

"Who came up here?" Wes' asked.

"My nigga, well my brother and my sister," I said. Me and Wes' played a few games of Casino until lunch time. The tuna mac was alright. Most people didn't eat it, but I did. I didn't care as long as it wasn't no pork. I went back to the room to go to sleep.

Soon as I woke up I asked Wes' did they pass out mail.

"They didn't call neither one of us for mail," Wes' said.

"What time is it?" I asked.

"Shit, it should be going on three o'clock," Wes' said.

"Soon as my girl get off work, I'm goin' call her so I can get you that 3-way," I told Wes'.

"Good lookin' Pilla," Wes' said. The whole rock was calling me Pilla. Me and Wes' played a couple of games of Chess until Maury came on.

"Aye Wes' at four-thirty I'm goin' call so be around and pay attention to the time 'cause I be getting caught up in this Maury," I said.

"I hear you," Wes' said. Watching Maury had me rolling. Maury was out his shit. The revelaed episode was on.

It was four-thirty on the nose when Wes' called me over to the phone. This was going to be the first time I called her since I been in here.

"Alright fam' here I come," I said. I dialed the numbers and I heard the operator say please say your name after the beep.

"Dre," I said. I waited for a few seconds to get through. Zaria finally accepted my call.

"Hey baby, I miss you so much….I'm sorry for not callin' you sooner. I thought you didn't wanna be bothered with me after all that bullshit," I said. We kicked it the whole fifteen minutes. I had a minute left.

"Aye baby, when I call back I need a favor…I need you to give my homeboy a 3-way so he could bond out…Alright baby I appreciate it…I love you too…Aye bay…Do you know a Calvin Johnson?" I asked but before she could answer the question the phone was disconnected.

"Man you better get the hell out the shower 'cause I'm 'bout to call back. My girl said it ain't goin' be no long ass call either," I told Wes'.

"Alright, I'm on my way out!" Wes' yelled from the shower. Wes' came out the shower trying to grab the phone.

"Damn fam', go put some clothes on I ain't even called yet," I said.

"My bad, I thought you were on the phone," Wes' said while holding his towel around his body. Wes' went to the room to dry off and put his clothes on. When he came out he handed me the number on a sheet of paper. When Zaria picked up she asked me who was Calvin Johnson?

"I'm goin' holla at you about that later," I told her.

"What's the name?" I asked.

"Monic," Wes' said loud enough for Zaria to hear him.

"Yeah, here you go, she on there," I said giving the phone to Wes'.

"Hello, yeah this Wes'. Why you ain't wrote?...I told Moe-Moe to tell you I was locked up...My bond...twenty-thousand ten percent, so it's two-thousand dollars...Alright, I love you too. I got something for you when I get home. Okay bookey see you soon," Wes' said. He gave me the phone back and told me good looking.

"Yeah bay, I don't know who this Calvin Johnson is but I'm goin find out tonight probably...What time you coming up here?....Aight baby I love you," I told her. I felt good. I didn't even have to ask her about going out because she came right out and told me. I had something special in my life. I had to get the fuck out of here. Soon as I got to the cell Wes' was packing his shit.

"I'm out this bitch tonight fam'," Wes' said.

"Straight up?" I asked.

"If not today then sometime this week. She getting the bread right now," Wes' said.

"That's good shit bro'," I said.

"Yeah that was my shorty. She been ridin' with a nigga for the longest. She talking about she was worried about a nigga and shit. Pilla, soon as I touch down you don't gotta worry about shit. I got you 100%. Only thing is

I ain't writing at all and I ain't coming up to this shitty ass county jail," Wes' said brushing his hair.

"Nigga don't tell me that shit, I seen to many niggas go home and ain't nan one of them niggas shoot no words, a money order, or even give me a number to call. All I can say is, if you 'bout that be bout that. Loyalty is law Wes'. No disrespect Wes' but I'm tired of hearing that shit. I just got done doing five years in the joint, so I heard that shit every other day. Niggas callin' me bro' and shit. I'm feedin' these niggas, looking out for em' and niggas still ain't shoot shit," I told Wes'. Wes' was looking confused. I guess he was fucked up off my reaction. I was mad as hell. I surrounded myself around disloyal niggas for five years.

"I feel you fam', but my twenty-five years of living it has never been a crooked bone in my body. Believe that," Wes said. It sounded like he was sincere, but I still kept my guard up. I laid down for a while after Wes' left the room. Moments later Wes' came in and told me I had a visit.

"Man quit bullshitin'," I told Wes' because I din't hear the dep call my name. "Nigga ain't nobody bullshitin',

Myself around disloyal niggas for five years. " I feel you fam', but my twenty-five years of living it has never been a crooked bone in my body. Believe that." Wes' said. It sounded like he was sincere but I still kept my guard up. I laid down for a while after Wes' left the room. Moments later Wes' came in and told me I had a visit. "Man quit bullshitin !." I told Wes' because I didn't hear the dep call my name. "Nigga ain't nobody bullshitin'. Get yo stankin' breath ass up and brush yo' grill ." I got up and brushed my teeth, washed my face and got the hell on. I waited in the bullpin for a second until the first bullpin open. Soon as I got inside the room my mouth dropped. I didn't know whether to throw a chair at the bullet proof window or just leave. He had an grin on his face. "Happy to see me? Have a seat little brother." Kevin told him. I didn't sit down. I stood up and the hatred I had for him could have broke through the glass. "Alright then fuck it, be hard headed. That's how you got locked up the first time fool." Kevin said. I was froze because this was the first time me and Kevin had been this close in a long time. "Well since you don't wanna talk to me I'll give you the good news. Your bond will be posted next Wednesday, so don't get out of line. Don't worry about none of this shit. Everything will be taken care of." Kevin said. I snapped. "You bitch ass nigga. You killed my brother and sister. You fucked my life up. I don't need shit from you, you disloyal bitch." I yelled. "Damn let me know you want me to be in here with you. You goin' let the whole world know what I did? Kevin asked. I just stood there breathing hard as hell. "Well you don't have nothing to say? So be it. I didn't give a damn about Von' or that friend bitch. I do what I wanna do. Who goin' stop me? Huh? You? Daron? You must be fuckin' kiddin' me. I run this shit. If you wanna keep talking to me like that I'll have that bitch Zaria filled with

holes quicker than I can snap my fingers." Kevin said. My eyes started to water but the tears didn't role down yet. I knew he would do it so I played it cool. "Now you wanna talk like men"? "Yeah man." I said putting my head down and wiping my eyes with my thumb and index finger. "What's the problem? I asked. The problem is you. You gotta get the fuck outta the state. I'll give you some dough and you and yo' bitch can leave. Kevin said. "Nigga I ain't going nowhere, you got life fucked up. You think you can buy me?" I asked. Kevin just laughed. He knew it wasn't going to be easy getting rid of his brother but something had to shake. "Keep talking slick if you want to and see what I do. "LEAVE TOWN ASAP." Kevin said slowly. Kevin got up before I could even respond. It had to be eight something. I was praying that Zaria didn't run into him while coming in. I still was confused on how he managed to get an attorney booth. Soon as I got back to the rock I went straight to the cell. "Damn Pilla, that was a long ass visit." Wes' said while coming in the cell. "Yeah it was." I said in a dry tone. "You look like you got a lot on your chest. You wanna talk about it? Wes' asked. I'll holla at you about it later fam'." I said. Wes' was about to leave the cell until I called him back. "A fam'. I said. You see what time it is?" I said. "Yeah hold on…It's eight-seventeen." Wes said. "That's it?" Wes' asked. "Yeah fam'." I said. Soon as Wes' left out I started talking to myself. "Damn Zaria, where the hell you at?" I asked myself. I sat on the bed waiting patiently. I knew my brother was crazy and I just put Zaria in a fucked up situation. "Clark visit." Deputy House Called over the speaker. House was one of those hood niggas with a good paying job. He was cool but he still had handcuffs. I almost fell sliding in my shower shoes trying to rush off the rock. All I heard was ol' school say 'damn boy, you goin' kill yo' self before you see yo'

visit.' Everybody started laughing. When I seen Zaria she looked normal but when she seen my face, her face instantly got screw up. "What's wrong baby?" Zaria asked. "Baby I love you so much. I don't know what I'll do without you. You my heart, baby I'm so sorry I fucked up. I never really had the chance to say I was sorry. I wish I could hold you right now." Zaria broke out in tears. "Where is all this coming from Dre'? She asked. "It's coming from my heart. Just know I'll be home sooner than you know." I said. We talked and laughed about all the funny shit we used to do when we were younger. "Visit up Clark." Deputy Johnson said. "Five more minutes Johnson?" I asked. "Make it quick Clark." Johnson said. I put my hand up to the glass so Zaria could put hers up too. "I love you baby, do you love me?" Zaria asked me. "Of course." I said. "That's it Clark." Johnson said. Zaria blew me a kiss and caught it and put it in my shirt pocket. I left out the visiting booth and set in the bullpen for a second because Johnson was busy. When he opened the gate, Johnson asked me was that my girlfriend. I told him yeah. "You better keep her." Johnson said. When I got back to rock I had a big grin on my face like I just got some pussy. That smile turned upside down when I seen Wes' eye. It was purple. It was also scratches on his face. I knew he was fighting because his fist were still balled up. Even though Wes' was older than me I was still like the big brother to him because he was so small. "What the fuck happened Wes'?" I asked. "Me and Corn had a few words and when I walked away he swung on me. He knew I was going home so he started telling everybody on the rock that I was fucking with babies." Wes' said. "School why ain't you break that shit up?" I asked school. He just shrugged his shoulders. I guess it wasn't his place to interfere with it. "A Corn you know what time it is?" I asked. Corn acted as if I

didn't say nothing to him. He just kept watching TV. "Did you fight back?" I asked. "Yeah I fought back. He just kept grabbin' me." Wes said. That's all I needed to know because if a nigga wasn't going fight for his self I wasn't either. I walked over to the table where Corn was sitting at. I already didn't like because he would steal niggas breakfasts if they didn't get up. Corn was little taller than me. He was at least six three. But I was still going to mangle him. "Awwww you mad 'cause I whooped your bunky. Nigga you betta get the fuck outta my face." Corn said trying to show off. When I looked in the deputy booth I didn't see no deps' in there so soon as I looked at Corn he asked me again what chu' goin' do?" I blew his shit out. Wes was right he wanted to grab. I hit him with two uppercuts and he let men go. After he started to leak he told me he was through but I kept going and started to ball up. Ol' school had to get me off of him. It was blood all over my county greens. I looked at him like what's up, telling him to run up on me. Only thing he did was call for the deputy. House wasn't here today we both would have went to the hole but instead they just moved Corn to another rock and locked us both down in our cells. "Wes you bet not ever let a nigga brag about beatin yo ass." I told him. "Pilla I fought to the end but he kept grabbin' me. Wes said. "Just know I got you straight up. Loyalty is Law." They didn't have the radio so it was nothing to do but go to sleep.

CHAPTER 16

Kevin chilled with his Latino chick. He rolled a blunt and she lit it. "When we goin to start going out papi?" Selina asked. "I don't know, I be tired girl." I said. "You know why you be tired, 'cause you be rippin and runnin the streets all day. Every time it comes to me and my needs you don't have any time. That's messed up papi." She said. "Girl why you tripping on that bullshit?" I said while inhaling the blunt. "You get on my nerves." She said. Selina was a good girl. She was a tall Latino chick with nice perky breast, she didn't have much of a ass but her face and model figure made up for that. Brown silky hair that came to her shoulders. She was smart and had a lot going for herself to be twenty-four years old. "Lets go get something to eat papi?" She told me. "What you wanna eat?" I asked. Lets go somewhere quiet like the Blue Nile in Greek Town." She said. "Since you wanna go somewhere quiet, then let's do the complete opposite and go somewhere fun and loud like Fudruckers." I said. "So what are you saying, the Blue Nile is boring?" She asked. "Well yeah." I said. They both laughed. After the blunt was gone I was zoned out. "All-right get dressed but before you jump in the shower let me get some of that punani." I said. "Boy you are a freak." Selina said whle getting on top of me. She lifted up so she could get her hands in my boxers. She rode me until I was drained.

I jumped in the shower while Selina soaked in the bathtub. Selina was the only female that knew where I lived. I trusted her. She slept over from time to time but that was it. "Baby you ready?" I yelled up the stairs. "Here I come baby." Selina said. When she came down, she

looked so good in skin tight white jeans and her Calvin Klein wife beater. I had to let her leave some clothes at my house because it wasn't no telling when we were gonna fuck or when she was going to spin the night. I had on my khaki pants with my white Ralph Lauren Polo shirt and my white Rockport Prowalkers. "What are we driving in papi?" She asked. I pointed to the Lexus. "The gold machine baby." I said. We were to Detroit fudruckers. I couldn't keep my eyes off that fat ass pussy print in her jeans. "I see you checkin out this punani. You better keep your eyes on the road before you get to exited and spoil our date." Selina said while laughing. "Girl ain't nobody studdin you." I said.

We got in pretty quick, even though the line was long as hell, but my pull game was crazy, plus money talked and bullshit walked. We took our seats and ordered our food. Everything was going fine until I seen Mindy come in. She was standing in the carry out line until she saw me and Selina. Before I could turn my head Mindy was headed my way. "You can't answer my calls?" Who the fuck is this bitch? Oh so you don't know who the fuck I am? When you had your dick buried in my ass you knew me didn't you?" Mindy yelled. Everybody was looking in our direction. The employees were trying to talk to Mindy. "Naw don't touch me. Are you gonna give me some answers?" Mindy asked with her hand posted on her hip. "Listen Mindy, I don't know how you took it that night, but it was nothing serious." I said in the calmest tone I could even though I wanted to rip this bitch head off. Selina just sat there listening to every word that was exchanged. "Bitch what the fuck are you looking at?" Mindy asked Selina. Selina wasn't a fighter even though she had all brothers, but the one thing they taught her was to never let

no one disrespect her. "Don't involve me in none of this mess. I would appreciate it if you left so we could finish our meal." Selina said. Everybody was still watching us like some kind of soap opera. Mindy slapped the shit out of Selina. She fell out of the chair. Mindy quickly grabbed Selina by the hair. Mindy drug Selina all through the restaurant until the police arrived and arrested them both. I bonded Selina out and left Mindy there at the precinct. "Baby I'm so sorry." I said. "Why didn't you stop her when she was dragging me around the restaurant?" Selina asked. He was laughing at her even though he felt kind of bad for Selina. "Girl I thought you could fight, you from Southwest right?" I asked making it into a joke. "Boy shut up." She said while holding the ice pack to her face, They put a couple of bandages on her and she was good to go. We ended up back at my crib. I had to make it up to her so I gave her a massage. I made sure I oiled her whole body. We both fell asleep. I was feeling her hard but I wasn't ready to settle down though. It was hard because I was getting old and wanted to have a son.

"Wake up baby." I said. "what Kevin, I'm tired." She said waking up. "I want you to have my child." I told her. "Boy stop playing." Selina said turning around facing me. "I'm serious Selina." I said. "Look Kevin, I don't have time to play these childish games with you. You out here fucking these bitches then they come to me tryna fight me for doing nothing." Selina said. "Baby it won't happen again." I said looking into her eyes. "Promise me." She said. "I promise baby." I said. She was scared but she believe him. "I believe you baby." She said. I climbed on top of her to enter her. After I started a good pace I put her legs over my shoulders and started hitting it harder. Selina always made Kevin use a condom but not this time. I felt

myself ready to explode. After I released my fluid inside of her I rolled off of her. She got on top of to stroke my dick to bring him back alive. It didn't take long for me to come back alive. After I was hard again Selina slowly eased down on my dick. She let out low moans as she continued to ride me to ecstasy. We both fell asleep on the couch.

In the middle of the night I woke up from a nightmare. I was sweating hard. I never thought I would see myself getting killed in my dream in all of my life. The scary thing about it was that I never knew who shot me. I ended up dozing back off to sleep.

CHAPTER 17

"Damn man I can't wait to get out this bitch Pilla. I should be gone today. She ain't come yesterday 'cause she worked all day on Thursday." Wes said. "What the hell you goin do when you touch down?" I asked. "Don't know Pilla, but I know I ain't coming back here." Wes said. "Jones! Pack your shit, you bonded out." The dep yelled though the intercom. "Fuck yeah, I'm out this bitch Pilla." Wes said while getting all his shit from under his mattress. "A Wes, stay out of trouble fam'." I said. "You all-ready know Pilla. Write your hook up down." Wes said. "You wanna stay or you wanna leave Jones?" the deputy asked. I gave Wes my hook up and me and Wes shook hands hugged each other. "Keep it real Wes and don't let these crackers jam you up." I told him. "I hear that." Wes said leaving. That was the last words I heard from Wes'.

I knew I was about to get a bunky so I hurried up and switched mattresses because Wes' mattress was fatter than mines. I stayed on the top bunk so I wouldn't be by the toilet. When dinner came it was a wrap. I wasn't really hanging out no more. I laid down and listened to the radio until it was lock down. I kind of missed that little nigga and them crazy ass stories he used to tell me. I hope all that shit they said about Wes wasn't true. It was cool though, Because I done ran into the good, the bad and the ugly.

It was Monday all-ready and I still didn't have a bunky. When I got up to get my breakfast it seemed kind of weird not grabbing two. I seen Ol' school watching the news. I only fucked with him on the strength of Wes. I knew that he had did some time in the joint and actually stayed to himself. I sat down and we kicked it but not on no

serious shit. "You think Wes is going to write you?" Ol' school asked. "I don't know, but I done been through this phase so many times so it really didn't matter if I heard from him or not." I told Ol' school I was going to catch up with him after lunch time because I was tired. I knew Daron wasn't coming up here because he was out of town. It was only one person I was waiting for and that was Zaria.

A couple of hours later I woke up and waited for lunch, After we ate Ol' school asked if I wanted to play some chess. "Yeah fuck it, I'll play a few games." I said. Man Ol' school beat the shit out of me. I thought I was cold until I ran into him. Beating on Wes' made me feel like a king but playing Ol' school made me feel like a servant. "Think about why you made that move. Always think two moves ahead. Don't just worry you catching me slipping, you also gotta worry about what I'm trying to do to you. Focus." Ol' school said. "This is going to help you in the future. Trust me." Ol' school told me. Ol' school was wise. All this time I could have been building with school soaking up all that knowledge. I just thought he was he was a bug. A bug is a person that's missing a few screws that has been to the joint or still in the joint. My moms always taught me never to judge a book by the cover. After a few games I was hanging with him but still was losing. Somebody ended up asking the Deputy what time it was. I heard him say 4:58. The rock was cool after Leon shot that move. "I gotta make this call, but we can get back popin' soon as I get off." I said. School just nodded his head. I sat down by the phone an dialed Zaria number. I listened to the operator say repeat your name after the beep. "Dre." I waited for Zaria to accept the call. "Hey baby….Thinking about you….Yeah he bonded out last week. He was cool, he haven't wrote yet but I ain't tripping bay…Naw bay I

would have asked you to pay his bond…..How's my nephew doing?....I should be out soon, but listen to me carefully, Be safe out there. We gotta lot of stuff to talk about when I come home. Do you still got that." I asked her. Hoping that she knew I was talking about the gun. "What time you coming up here?....Well I'm about to take a nap so I'll see you at 8:30…I love you too." I couldn't tell her over the phone what was happing with Kevin because she probably would have flipped. I hung up the phone and sat there for a hot second until I had enough strength to get up off the floor. "A School, right after they bring chow we goin get it in on the chess board." I said. School said all-right and finished watching the 5 o'clock news.

Chow came a little late so it was almost like six o'clock. I didn't really want the veal pattie but I was hungry as hell. After I brushed that nasty ass taste out my mouth I was ready for School. He had the board already set up. I sat down and asked him was he ready. "The question is, are you ready?" School asked me. "Of course." I said. We played so many games, I was tired of looking at red and black squares. Time flew past so quick it was like eight o'clock, so I had to bounce and get ready for my visit. "All-right School this is my last game so play your hardest." I said. "Well I'm going to take my queen off the board." Ol' school said. I had to take full advantage of this. After fifteen minutes had gone past School had got a stalemate. "All-right School enough of all this I'll probably play after I come back from this visit. I said. "That's cool with me youngin'." School said while putting the pieces up. I went and brushed my hair because Zaria told me I bet not have her waiting out there no more. I brushed 100 times in the front, 100 times in the back, and 100 times on each side. I put my doo-rag on and laid down. All there was to think

about was Zaria and Kevin. I couldn't tell Zaria but I had to because I was putting her life in jeopardy. I wasn't no bitch, but getting out of the hood didn't sound bad, but fuck that ain't no nigga just goin' run me up out the hood. I had to get a new parole officer so that was going to be hard. I was starting to worry after I asked the dep' the time. "He told me it was four minutes til'." I was pacing up and down the rock. When I walked past School he told me she was coming, sit down you making me tired. Soon as I sat down they called me for a visit. "Thank God" I said taking my doo-rag off. When I got out there I asked Zaria where the hell was she at? "Boy quit it out." Zaria said. "For real, you had a nigga walking up and down the rock." I said. "Boy I had to get my hair and nails done so I could look good for my baby. You can look good and I can't?" She asked. "I was just worried, that's all baby, but you are looking good as hell." I said complimenting her. "Thank you baby. You looking good too, even though you got those greens on." Zaria said laughing.

We talked about Kevin but not to much on that subject because we didn't have enough time to. The deputy let me and Zaria stay a little longer because she was one of the last visitors.

After the visit was over I went back to the rock. I still didn't have a bunky. It was ten minutes until lock don. I went to the cell to see what was on the radio. The quiet storm wasn't on yet but it was about to come on at ten o'clock. I said a silent prayer to myself and dozed off.

I woke up to the Deputy calling my name. "Clark you got court." Man what the hell was this? It was a lot of guys going on dry runs because of screw ups from the deputies. I wasn't in the mood for this shit. "Man you sure

it's Clark?" I asked opening my cell door. "Dre Clark right?" The deputy asked. "Yeah." I said. "Well yeah you got court." The deputy said getting irritated. I brushed my teeth and got ready. I grabbed a couple of beef n cheese and some corn chips. I stayed in the bullpin for almost seven hours waiting on court. They finally called me. I was the only one they called. Soon as they cuffed me, asked one of the corporals what was I going to court for. "Bond hearing." The corporals said. Only thing that ran through my mind was Kevin. My brother was plugged in with somebody. When I got in front of the judge she asked me was I here for a bond hearing. "Yes, your honor." I said. "If I gave you a bond and were able to pay it, will you return back to court?" the judge asked. "Yes your honor." I said. "Do you understand that you are an ex-felon?" She asked. "Yes your honor." "I'm setting your bond. One million percent." She said. "Thank you, your honor." I said. "Your welcome Mr. Clark just don't make me regret this. This court is dismissed." She said. Man, I hope Kevin bitch ass come through. He's the one that put me in this fucked up situation. He probably wants me to pull a capias. When I got back to the bullpin niggas was asking what they do for me. But I still didn't answer them because ain't shit changed.

I finally made it back to rock and the dep save me a tray. "Good looking Johnson." I said. He nodded his head and continued to talk on the phone. The pizza was cold but it as better than them corn chips and beef n cheeses. Next thing you know I was knocked out. I jumped up when somebody opened the cell door. It was my new bunky. He was a older Latino dude with a bunch of tattoos. I notice the big initials S L on his neck. "What's up homie?" He asked. "What up doe." I said. "They call me Esco." He

said. "They call me HP." I told him. "They got me on bs so I should be out tonight." Esco said with confidence. I could tell he was cool but I wasn'y in the mood to make new friends so I put my cover back over my head.

"Clark you got mail." One of the deputies said. Soon as I read the name I was surprised the little nigga wrote. The letter read:

WHAT UP PILLA,

SHIT WITH ME, AIN'T NOTHING OUT HERE. I HOPE YOU GET THE FUCK UP OUTTA THERE. I HOPE THAT YOU'RE NOT GONE YET SO YOU GET THIS LETTER. I KNOW THAT SOUNDS KIND OF FUCKED UP. DON'T TAKE IT LIKE 'CAUSE I KNOW YOU READY TO GET OUTTA THAT SHIT HOLE. GUESS WHAT MY NIGGA? THEY ENDED UP DROPPING ALL THE CHARGES BECAUSE THEY LIED AND THE EVIDENCE WASN'T ENOUGH TO CONVICT ME. WELL IM GONE, TELL OL' SCHOOL I SAID WHAT UP? HERES $20 NIGGA.

CALL ME, 248-273-5191

LOVE IS LOVE

LOYALTY IS LAW

Damn that little nigga wrote for real. Real recognize real. I got to make sure I shoot him some words back. I told Ol' school what Wes' had said. Ol' school really didn't care about nothing, he had county time to do. He probably was going to be leaving real soon to be a trustee. When I got back to the cell Esco was just staring at the wall. "You aight' in here?" I asked. "Yeah I'm good, just thinking about my kids." "How many do you have?" I asked.

122

"Three, I got two sons and a baby girl." "You kind of young to have three kids. You about twenty-four?" Esco laughed. "Naw homey, good looking on the compliment though. I'm thirty-two." "Damn." I said looking surprised. "That comes from doing time homey." He said. We kicked it for a while until chow came. I didn't eat nothing so Ol' school had a field day with that nasty ass pork chop. Time was slowing up because I knew I was about to get up out of here. I paced up and down the rock for a while. Ol' school was mad at me because I wouldn't play chess with him. He just wanted me to stop pacing. Ol' school stepped in front of me. "A man you gotta stop that shit. You acting like that crazy ass white dude down the hall that be cutting on his self. You pressing my bit and yours." Ol' school said. He was serious too and he also was right. I had to tighten up. I sat down and wrote Wes back. I had so much on my mind. Let me see what's up with this nigga.

WHAT'S GOOD FAM'? I GOT YOUR LETTER TODAY. I KNEW YOU WHERE GOING TO WRITE BUT NOT THIS SOON. GOOD LOOKING ON THAT MONEY TOO, YOU KNOW I REALLY DIDN'T NEED THOUGH. I'M GOING HOLLA AT YOU BUT IT'S GOING TO BE PHYSICAL, NONE OF THIS PEN AND PAPER SHIT, SO LOOK OUT FOR ME. I GOT YOUR NUMBER SO I'LL FIND YOU. STAY OUTTA TROUBLE FAM.

LOVE IS LOVE

LOYALTY IS LAW

HPILLA DRE

CRIME BOY

After I sent the letter out it was kind of late. I kicked it with Ol' school for a hot minute because I needed some of that wisdom that Ol' school had bottled up. "Lock down." The deputy yelled. "Take it in gentlemen." He said. Esco was all-ready sleep so it didn't take long for me to follow suit.

CHAPTER 18

Damn I might be up out this bitch today. I gave my breakfast to Esco because I didn't have a appetite at all. I didn't know an exact time when I was going to bond but I was going to be right back locked up for murder because Kevin had to go. I couldn't leave the states with this case pending. He had to be up to something. I couldn't trust him at all. I thought about all the possible ways how Kevin could set me up. I got headache so I had to get a drink of water. Esco asked if I was al-right. I told him I was cool. I didn't feel like being bothered. I got in the shower to cool myself off. I made sure I got in every morning and at the end of the day. I wasn't about to miss no shower and the shit was free, even if it wasn't for free I still was in this bitch. These niggas took showers every three or four days. They were horrible. After I got out I laid down to take a nap. "Clark pack your shit." I heard one of the deps say. I ain't pack shit. I left everything with Esco and Ol' school. The only thing I took was my letters. I grabbed Esco hook up from him and dipped out. I stayed in the bullpin for a minute because it was a long process. They finally called everybody that bonded out. We changed out and sat back in the bullin. It was eight of us in there. I seen a couple of guys that was in the joint with me so I chucked the deuce and kept it moving. We waited a couple more hours until they processed us out. When I walked out it was a Latino chick pointing in my direction letting the deputy know it was me she was bonding out. When I came out she was standing there with her blue and grey pin stripe suit with her jacket to match. "I'm not here to converse with you, I'm just here to do my job. I have all your court papers in the car that's waiting for you." She pointed to the green

2000 Mustang. "That's your rental, return it to this address a week from today." She handed me the address, not knowing that I was going to return it today. "This is also for you." She gave me a envelope that said Calvin Johnson on the front. "Here are the keys, good-bye Mr. Clark." The Latino chick said. She wasn't that bad looking, she also looked familiar. When I got outside I read the note which read: Wait until they throw the case out then you can leave the states, but if you choose to run you won't be putting a dent in my pocket. You'll only be hurting yourself. After I read the note I looked up and seen the Latino chick hopping in a red Lincoln Ls. When I thought about getting into the car all I thought about was the Casino when they put that bomb under Robert DeNiro car. I looked in the back seat to see if anyone was back there. There wasn't. I open the door and got in and before I shut the door I looked under the car to make sure. People were looking at me like I was crazy. I felt like a damn fool. I shut the door and laughed to myself. I started the car up and drove off. When I got far enough I popped the trunk to see if anything was in it. The car was cool so I kept it moving. It took me 30 minutes to get to Oak Park thanks to the Mustang. When I pulled up in front of the house the Monte Carlo wasn't in the driveway so I checked of the garage and the Corvette and the bike was back there. The Taurus was parked on the grass in the backyard. I parked the Mustang five houses down. When I got out I felt good only thing I had to do was get in the shower and get this county smell off of me. When I walked in it smelt so good. Zaria had plenty of candles and oils so I didn't have to worry about buying any of that stuff. I went to the nearest wall which was Northland Mall to go pick up a few things that would set the mood when my baby got home. I bought some white roses and some chocolate strawberries. I had a little cash at the crib plus I had the

check from the county from money that was in my account. When I got back I hoped in the shower to get that county jail soap off of me and put some clean boxers on. I heard Zaria pulling up in the driveway so I cut the Bel Biv Devoe on. When can I see you smile again was playing in the background. Soon as Zaria walked in I stood there with the plate of chocolate strawberries with my boxers on. I couldn't even explain the look she had on her face. I walked up to her and fed her one of the chocolate strawberries. I took off her coat and led her to the tub where she seen the white rose peddles in the water. I helped her take off all her clothes. I washed her body like she was a toddler. She let out a low moan when I washed between her legs. When I was down bathroom where her lingerie and a small note were lying on the bed. When I was leaving out the bedroom I heard Zaria giggling.

She did what the note said and slipped in her lingerie. She walked in the bedroom with the chocolate strawberries looking like a model. She climbed on top of me and started to feed me. After she was finished, I turned her over on her back. I planted soft kisses on her stomach and neck. She moaned my name out telling me how she didn't want me to stop. She tried to reach for my dick but I move her hand. "I wanna please you tonight." I whispered in her ear. I continue to kiss and suck on her. I got off of her and told her to turn over. She did as I asked. Zaria was laying on her stomach and her ass looked like two basketballs. I undid her bra so I could massage her. I caressed her like I was a Masseuse. I kissed my way down her back. Her ass was so fat, it sat up perfectly. I kissed each cheek. I could see Zaria gripping the sheets after each kiss. I made my way down her thighs to the back of her legs to her sexy feet. "Dre please I can't take this

anymore." She moaned out. That's all I needed to hear. When I rolled her over I could see sweat beads dripping off of her. I pulled her panties down leaving her with both legs in the air. She was taking off her bra while I just stared at her. I was ready to taste her asap. I licked the outside of her pussy with long slow strokes. "You make me feel so good Dre." Zaira cried out. I teased her clitoris until I felt her juices run down my chin hairs. She grabbed the back of my head and mashed my face into her tender spot. I kissed my way back up to her face with her juices still on my lips. "I want you to ride me baby." I said. I laid on my back and Zaira proceeded to mound me but she didn't know I was talking about my face. "No baby my face." I said. Zaira moved up to my face. She buried me within seconds. She had both hands on the headboard rocking back and fourth. "Oh yes, don't stop. Mmmmmm." She moaned out. Those were her last words before I tasted her sweet juices. Zaria stood up over me barely because her legs were shaking. She played with her pussy slowly inserting her index finger in and out. "I want you so bad, I want you inside of me." I pulled my boxers down and kicked them off. I haven't had no pussy since my encounter with Ms. Brooks. She slid down on my dick slowly. Her pussy muscles was working because I could feel them contracting around my dick. "You like that don't you?" She asked as if she knew what she was doing. I couldn't even answer because I was on the verge of coming. I exploded inside of her. She managed to stand up again looking at the cum leak out of her and the rest leak out of my dick. She started giggling. "Baby what's so funny?" I asked. "Nothing baby" she said and giggled again. "Don't worry baby, I'll get it back up." She said. She played with my dick stroking it gently, then with faster pumps. I started to rise but not to the full length. That's when she wrapped her lips around my dick. She didn't get

128

all of it in , but it was enough. She started sucking my dick making all type of popping and slurping noises. "Baby I'm bout to cum." She looked into my eyes and kept going. I tilted my head back and put one of my hands on the top of her head. Her eyes widened a little when my nut came out. But she kept going until I had nothing left. "You taste good baby." She said while licking her lips. "Bend that fat ass over." I said getting on my knees. She bent over looking back at me. Her pussy looked so good tooted up. "You want it like this?" She asked with her hands on the bed on all fours. "Or like this?" she asked with her back arched and her face on the pillow. I instantly got hard. I moved my dick head up and down her slit. "Put it in Dre." She said. I did as I was told and put my dick in her throbbing pussy. My flesh smacked up against her while I pounded away in her pussy. Her walls were so tight. Zaria started to buck back. I could feel her shaking but kept going. She looked back biting her top lip. She reached her right hand to stretch her ass check so I could see all of her. I couldn't take it no more. My third nut was in her pussy. I kept thrusting until every drop was out. I fell on top of her breathing heavy as hell. I rode off of her and she turned over to looked me in the eyes. "I love you baby." She said. "I love you more baby." I told her. We slept good the rest of the night.

Zaira woke me up for breakfast but I was drained. I couldn't move, so she brought it to me in bed. She made me some Belgian waffles two sunny side down eggs and a couple slices of turkey bacon. She had also made me some of her homemade orange juice. "You didn't have to do this for me baby." I said. "Anything for my man." Zaria said pouring me a glass of orange juice. After we ate breakfast, I washed the dishes while she showered. I had to call Daron. He should've been back from Kentucky. Nobody picked up

so I was going to try later. When Zaria got out I got in. "Damn baby I like how you ran out all the hot water." I yelled from the shower but didn't get a response back. When I got out I looked for Wes phone number through my county bag. I sat on the couch with my towel still wrapped around my wet body. I dialed Wes number and he picked up. I put him on speaker phone so I could put my deodorant on.

"What up bitch?"

"Who dis?"

"Nigga this Pilla."

"What it is?"

"Shit ready to kick it."

"How you doing in there?"

"Nigga I'm out."

"Straight up? Where you at so I can come scoop you up?"

"Ummm, meet me on 7 mile and the lodge freeway at the Pizza Hut in twenty minutes."

"All-right fam, one."

"Aight Wes."

I got dressed and told Zaria what I was about to do. I kissed her and told her I love her. I threw on some gear and hopped in the Corvette. The engine sounded good still. I got to Pizza Hut quick as hell because I was right around the corner. I order a cheese pizza while waiting on Wes. I made sure I sat by the window so I could see him pull up. I seen Wes pull up in a black on black "87" Monte on triple

gold 20' Daytons. His shit was beaten too. Soon as he came in a big ass grin appeared on his face when he seen me. I gave him some dape and we sat down. "What's good Pilla?" "Shit man I bonded out yesterday." Straight up?" Wes asked. "Yeah, I spent the hole day with my woman though." I said. "Aww that ain't shit, I spent almost a week with mines." Me and Wes both busted out laughing. The pizza came and Wes asked me why had I only ordered a cheese pizza. "Nigga you know I don't fuck with all that bullshit. Plus it's my money." I said. We both started laughing. Since Daron didn't answer his phone I needed Wes to take me to Metro Airport so I can return that Mustang. "I need you to come with me to drop this car off. I gotta return it to the airport." I said. I couldn't explain everything to Wes because it wasn't his business. "Aight." Wes said. We finished our pizza and Wes left a $10 tip. I hopped in the Corvette and dropped the top. "Damn Pilla, Why you ain't tell me you had a Corvette?" Wes asked. Same reason why you didn't tell me you had a Monte sitting on them thangs." I laughed and said. "You evea rode in one?" "Hell naw, I ain't even sat in one." "Wes said. "Well we even 'cause I ain't never rode in a ol' school sitting on nothing." "So who car we taking my mines or yours?" Wes asked. "First follow me to my folks house." I said. Wes hopped in his Monte and followed me to Highland Park. I didn't want to let Wes know where I live so I went to Auntie Vicki house instead. Couldn't take him to Daron spot because he didn't fuck with a lot of niggas plus he lived too damn far. When I was driving I could have sworn I seen Kevin riding past me but I kept going. I had to see my nephew. I wanted to take him out with me. His birthday was in two days. When we get on her block I didn't see her car so I parked the Corvette in her driveway and hopped in Wes whip. One thing I did like about Wes

131

was that he didn't ask no questions. The inside of his ride was out cold. It was peanut butter all over. "This bitch clean as hell." I told him. "Yeah this my baby." We drove back to Oak Park to pick up the Mustang. I glanced at the house to make sure everything looked normal. Zaria Monte was gone so I knew she was off to work. Here go the car right here. We stopped right next to the Mustang. I hopped out before closing the I told Wes to follow me. We drove to Romulus where the airport was located. It took us almost an hour to get there but we made it. Before I got out I looked around to see if everything was intact. I followed the directions and left the keys in the visor and dropped out. "We goin go back to get the Vette matter of fact leave it there, let's just ride out. I told Wes. "You wanna hit this blunt?" Wes asked. "I'm good fam, plus I'm on papers. I said. "Alright Mr. Angel." Wes said putting the blunt back. we drove to All Stars on 8 mile and Hubbell. It wasn't too many people in there because it was still daylight plus I didn't like being around a lot of people anyway. Wes had all the females on him. I didn't even want no lap dances, I was good. Wes didn't even tip none of the strippers because they all knew him. It was a little after four and I knew Zaria was on her way home. "A Wes let me use your cell real quick." Wes unclipped the Nex-tel off his hip and handed it to me. I called Auntie Vicki to tell her that I dropped my car off earlier. I also told her to tell Zaria to go to her house after she got off work. I told her I loved her and I hung up. "Yeah Wes it's getting kinda of late, I gotta get back to the crib." I told him. "Damn you ain't get no dances or you ain't had shit to drink." Wes said. "Oh I forgot to tell you, I don't drink either. I said. "Awww man what type of nigga is you?" Wes asked. A lot of guys were happy me and Wes were leaving because all the little bad chicks were surrounding us. We got outside and it was bright as hell.

We hopped in the Monte and Wes had that Lil John and the Eastside Boyz playing. That shit was loud as hell. "Bia Bia why you actin like a hoe, like hoe? Bia Bia why you actin like a hoe, like a hoe?" "Just drop me off where you dropped the Vette off at." I said. "You talking about in HP right." Wes asked. "Yeah." I said. Wes hopped on the freeway and we were there in no time. This bitch rode smooth as hell. I didn't want to get out but I had to check on Zaria. When we pulled up in front of Aunty Vicki's house she was sitting on the porch and Chris was running around the front yard. "Naw, I know what you're thinking, but that's not my son he's my nephew." I said reading Wes mind Wes just cracked a smile. I dug in my pocket and grabbed a hundred dollar bill and gave it to Wes for gas money. "Man I don't need that." Wes said trying to give it back but I was already outside the car. "All-right fam, I'm goin be calling you soon so we could kick it." I told him. "All-right fam." He said than scurted off. I walked in the front yard through the gates and Chris came running up to me. I picked him up and took him up the steps to Auntie Vicki. "Hey Ma. How are you doing?" I asked. "I'm doing fine and why don't you come in when you drop that car off in my driveway?" She asked. "I didn't think you were here." "Boy you know that key been under my flower pot for years." She said giving me a hug. "All right now me and Chris about to go in because it's getting late. Love you. She said. "Love you too Ma. Did you call Zaria for me Ma?" "Yeah boy I called, she's working overtime." She said before shutting the door. Damn I forgot she was working overtime on Thursdays now. It had to be around 6:00 o'clock. I walked around the hood looking at how everything has changed. Everybody still was doing the same shit though; hooping, fighting, selling dope, and fucking with the hood rats around the hood. They been

doing this shit their whole lives. Just wasted talent. No high school diploma, no G.E.D, half the niggas didn't make it out of middle school. I wasn't going to be like that. I knew it was going to be hard because I was a ex- felon. But I was going to succeed. When I got back to Aunty Vicki house I went inside and made a peanut butter and Jelly sandwich. I couldn't get enough of them. Jeopardy was on but I wasn't feeling that today. I flicked to the news same ol' shit somebody shot, robbed, or killed. I wonder where Carla was. I haven't called to let her know I was out. She should have been here. I wanted to drive past my old house to see what was going on with it. After that bullshit with Kevin, ain't no telling what he did with it. He made me sick to my stomach. Sitting here flicking these channels made time fly by. I seen some headlights out the side windows. It had to be Zaria. I looked out the window and it was her. When she got out she looked tired. I was standing at the door waiting for her. "Hey baby" She said hugging me. "Missed you." "I missed you too" She said. "Where's aunty at, is she sleep?" She asked. "She should be upstairs with Chris. I told her. "Okay let me go tell her I'm here." "All-right I'm gonna be sitting on the porch." "All-right baby." She said going up the steps quietly. She came back down tip toeing. "Aunty said if we're staying tonight make sure we lock all the doors." "Good, because this is where I wanna be tonight." I said. We went outside and sat on the porch looking at the stars twinkle. Zaria head was leaning on my shoulder while my arms were wrapped around her body. "Baby what's wrong, Why did you wanna sleep here tonight?" "First off I wanna tell you that I'm sorry not for telling you that I was coming home. I just wanted to surprise you. I feel like I been neglecting my family and loved ones. I don't want to be shit like Kevin. Me and my nephew should be closer." I said. "Baby I know, everything is gonna be fine. We just

gotta work harder. It just takes time." She said. I didn't wanna tell her that Kevin bonded me out but I had to. "I have something else to tell you Zaria. "What Bay?" She asked. "Daron didn't bond me out." I said with my head down. "Who did?" Zaria asked. She lifted her head up and looked into my eyes, it took me a minute to answer her question. The words finally came out. "Kevin bonded me out." I said. Zaria look like she seen a ghost. She was confused. "Why didn't you tell me this?" She asked looking clueless. "He wants me to leave Michigan after I beat this case but I don't wanna leave. He told me if I didn't he was gonna hurt you. She put her hand over her mouth and tears were starting to build up in her eyes. "He said he was going to give me some money to leave and everything but I don't wanna leave you here." "Baby I would go anywhere you wanna go." "Where do you wanna go Zaria?" I asked wiping here tears away. "I wanna go far from here. Some where hot. We don't need his money either. "Zaria said. I knew Daron would help us plus I would give it back every time, even though he might not want it back. "Baby I gotta beat this case then we outta here." I kissed her on the forehead and we went inside and I made sure all the doors were locked like aunty Vicki asked. We went upstairs to Daron's old room and went to sleep.

When I woke I was in the bed by myself. Earth Wind and Fire was playing all though the house. A song along because this is my moms favorite song. "Do you remember, the 21st night of September." That's all I knew but I liked it and it was a good song to start your day off with. I went downstairs and saw Zaria in some hoop shorts cooking and she was even singing. I snuck into the bathroom to wash my face. Aunty Vicki always kept a couple of toothbrushes in her bathroom just in case

company had to sleep over. I opened up a new one and went to work. I love brushing my teeth. I had to brush after every meal because food I was left a nasty taste in my mouth. I wash my face and open the door as quietly as I could. I seen Zaria still singing looking into the refrigerator. I walked up behind her and hugged her. "You think I didn't see you go into the bathroom boy." She asked laughing turning around and kissing me. "I was thinking about something baby." I said "And what's that?" She said putting her hands on her hip. "I wanna take Chris with us." I said. "Baby I don't mind. Anything to put a smile on your face." She smiled then kissed me on the cheek. "All-right we got children in the house. Aunty Vicki said bringing Chris into the kitchen. "Good morning ma." I said hugging her and kissing her on the cheek. "Good morning to you too. Did you put some Lawry salt on those potatoes?" She asked Zaria. "Yes aunty, I got the water boiling for the grits and the grease is heating up for the potatoes and sausage links are still in the pack." Zaria said. "What's up lil man?" I asked Chris. "Say hey uncle Dre." Aunty Vicki told him. "Hey uncle Dre." Chris repeated after Aunty Vicki. I put Chris in his hi chair so he could get ready to eat breakfast. While we were eating I asked Aunty Vicki could I take Chris out with me today. "Son go ahead, just bring him back at a reasonable time." Aunty Vicki said. After breakfast I went upstairs to watch the morning News. Nothing was popping so I turned the TV off. I thought about Daron and why he hasn't returned none of my calls. I thought about Esco too. "Let me write this nigaa." I said to myself. I wrote a little note and put my number down. I put the letter in the blue jeans that I had just put on. I got Chris dressed so we could go out and spend some time. "Don't forget to grab his car seat out of my truck." She yelled downstairs. Zaria was already in her car. I grabbed the car

seat out of auntie Vicki's Escalade and put it in the Monte Carlo and we were headed home. As soon as we get home Zaria got in the shower first while meeting Chris watched Sesame Street. After she was finished I hopped in right after her. It was a quick shower because we had a long day ahead of us. I put on some black hoop shorts and a crispy white T-shirt and my white Air Force ones. When I got into the living room Zaria was dressed and ready to leave. "I bought you something too, it's on the kitchen counter. I'm taking the Vette right?" She asked. "Yeah, drive safely baby. I love you." I said. "Love you too. Give me a hug Chris. Zaria said while extending her arms towards Chris. Chris ran right to her. I went into the kitchen and saw a cell phone on the counter. It was a Sprint. I flipped it open and I seen a name pop up and it said Wifey calling. "Hello." I said. Zaria was standing inside of the doorway in the kitchen. "All you have to do is give $50 a month and don't go over your minutes. Oh, and me, Aunty Vicki, your sister and Suga better be the only females in that damn cell-phone. Make sure you get Chris in that car seat good. I love you bye bay." She said leaving and shutting the front door. I called her back and told her the only names and her phone better be me, Sonny, Daron and Uncle Phil. I looked at the time and it was time to head out. "Chris you ready?" I asked him. He shook his head up and down. We were about to leave until I remembered I forgot about Esco's letter. I hurried up and grabbed it out of my jeans. I went to the den to grab a envelope and a stamp out of the drawer. Only problem was I had to find his hook up. It was on top of my dresser. Mario Lopez. I hurried up and jotted it down on the blank envelope with my new cell phone number inside of it. We left out the house and I dropped the letter in the first mailbox I seen. Soon as we got inside Northland mall Chris wanted to go into every store. I had a little money from the

county. It was almost six or seven hundred dollars thanks to Daron. It was females everywhere all in my grill. "Is that your son?" One of the females asked me. "Naw, this is my nephew." I said. My hormones were jumping up and down but I had to control myself. I ended up buying me and Chris some Timberland boots I also bought Zaria some boots to match ours. We got some McDonald's because all of the walking we did. We ate our food and continue to shop. When we left out Chris was sleep with his arms wrapped around my neck. We got home like around 4. I laid Chris down on the couch and sat in the lazy-boy. I was tired as hell too. I will sleep within minutes. I jumped when I heard the door open. It was Zaria. "Hey sleepy head, how was your day with your nephew?" She asked. "Tiring" I said stretching my arms. "That boy wanted everything in the mall" I said. "I see. y'all didn't even have time to put the bags up. You should be ashamed of yourself. Did you call auntie Vicki and tell her that Chris was staying over? She asked. "Naw bay, I was too tired. Could you call for me?" I asked. She picked up the phone and dialed auntie Vicki number and told her Chris was staying over. Soon as she hung up she picked Chris up and took him to the backroom with her. I follow right behind her. The three of us went right to sleep.

CHAPTER 19

Today I had court for dismissal. Mr. Fitzgerald had called me yesterday and told me that the prosecutor wasn't going to waste her time on a weak case. I didn't know what type of shit Kevin was on but I was going to find out. I was super tired because we partied for Chris birthday over the weekend. Me, Carla, Auntie Vicki, Suga, Daron, Zaria, Uncle Devon, Will, and Uncle Phi went to Major Magics. We had a good time too. I put some khakis and a white button-up on with my white Nikes. Zaria had to work, so I drove myself. It was like three people inside the courtroom with me I seen the same Latino chick that gave me the Mustang and bonded me out. "Due to the lack of evidence, this case is being dismissed without prejudice." The Judge said. I will still fucked up because they could bring the shit back up. When the bailiff gave me the papers I was out. "Mr. Clark" somebody called my name I turned around and saw the Latino chick. "Damn what now?" I said under my breath. She walked towards me holding a burgundy leather suitcase. "This was from Mr. Johnson, he's giving you two weeks to leave. Have a nice day." She said handing me the suitcase. She hopped in a Benz Jeep and drove off. I hopped in the Corvette and drove off slowly. At every red light I couldn't stop looking at the suitcase. I stopped at a nearby Coney Island to get something to munch on. I grabbed the expensive looking suitcase and went in. "Hello, may I help you?" The white blonde haired waitress asked me. "Yeah, let me get two orders of cheese sticks and a fish dog with cheese. I said. "Is that it sir?" "Umm, let me get a large water to go with that." I said. "Okay your total is $6.89." I handed her a $20 bill and gave her a $2 tip for being polite. "Thank you Sir" She said smiling I went and sat down at the table by myself. I waited for a minute to

open the suitcase because it wasn't no telling what was in there. I ain't really have nothing to lose so I opened it. It was full of hundred dollar bills. When the waitress came with my food I hurried up and closed the suitcase. "Everything okay sir?" She asked. "Yeah, everything good." I said smiling. She gave me a smile but not a regular smile was more on the flirting tip. She was good looking but I wasn't studding her right now. She walked away swaying her hips trying to move the little butt she had. I opened the suitcase again and couldn't believe it. It was a small note on the inside of the suitcase. I read out loud. "Leave, don't make me hurt you" I ate my food and left out winking at the waitress. I knew her pussy got wet instantly. I had call Daron and told him I had to leave the states. I told him I would explain later. I called Wes and told him the same. Zaria had dropped Chris off at auntie Vicki and let her know I was taking Chris with me out of town. I had to call him Mr. Fitzgerald and asked him about the other pending cases in Oakland County. He told me don't worry about it and everything has been taken care of. He also said that whatever state I would move to, my new parole officer would contact me. I called Zaria to tell her that it was time to leave and Chris was coming with us. Before I left Michigan I had to visit my brother, my moms, and my three sisters grave sites. It was fucked up looking at their stones. I couldn't believe they were gone. It was just me and Carla. It was so much shit going on. I didn't have a clue to where we were going to move to. It was a little after five o'clock, I had to go see Daron. It was kind of windy so I kept the top on the Vette while I drove down Seven mile. I pulled up in front of the store and it was packed. Lil Lou was outside with the four clearance racks. I hopped out still wearing my court clothes. "What up doe Dre?" Lil Lou asked. "Shit, chilling like a villain. Where Daron at?" I asked. "He in

there somewhere." Lil Lou said letting out a low giggle. I ain't know what he was laughing at, he probably was laughing at this ridiculous outfit I had on. Soon as I walked in I seen big Bo behind the cash register. He looked up as I came in. "What's up Dre?" He asked. "Same ol' shit." I said. "Daron somewhere in the back." Big Bo said still playing with his cell phone. I walked in the back and opened the back door where the couch was and I seen Suga sucking Daron's dick. Suga never saw me but Daron did and he smirked at me when he saw me. Suga had both of her hands wrapped around Daron's waist while Daron had one hand on top of her head. I had to leave because it was kind of weird looking at my bro and his chick. It was all good we were younger but not now we were grown. I quietly walked out. Now I knew why Lil Lou was laughing. I came out rubbing my temples with my thumb and my middle finger. A few minutes later Daron came out. Suga went in the bathroom. "She's a freak." Me and Daron said at the same time. We always said it when we were younger every time I see him coming out the mop closet with a broad or when he see me coming out the school auditorium with a chick. "What's good bro?" I asked. "Man tired of wondering why we gotta leave. I didn't wanna ask too many questions over the phone." I told him and he was pissed. "Man, is that nigga crazy? He got to go. Straight up he gotta go." He said. I just stood there with my head down. "I'm serious bro" Daron said getting angrier. "Hold on man lets go to the back." I said that looking at all the customers that was watching us like a TV. "Listen man, he said he was going to kill Zarya, so I think it's best for me to leave." I said. "I can understand that but you better let me know where you going and what's going on." He said. "All-right bro. Love is love. Loyalty is law." I said. I left out and nodded to big Bo. "Alright Suga." She gave me a hug and a

kiss on the cheek. Why is the hell did she have to kiss me? "All-right Dre be safe." She said. I ain't leaving right now but it will be soon. I left out and chucked the deuces to Lil Lou and hopped in the Vette. I smell the Michigan weather because I knew it was going to be a long time before I smelled it again. I called Wes on my cell phone and told him to meet me on Fenkell and Livernois. I waited at Kentucky fried chicken for about twenty minutes before Wes showed up. I wasn't in a rush so it was cool. He pulled up in a green Escalade. This nigga had a different whip for every week. he got out the big truck looking like a teenager. "What's good fam?' I asked while leaning on the Vette. "Shit, what's good with you?" Wes said. "Waiting on you. I see you in that big boy." I said. "Naw, that's my girl shit. She wanted to drive the Monte. Naw but what's up?" "I'm bout to leave state for a minute but I'm goin keep in contact though." I said. I didn't tell nobody about half the money not even Daron and Zaria. "You straight?" Wes asked rubbing his index finger, middle finger, and thumb together. He was talking about on the money tip. "Yeah, I'm good." I said. "You know where you going?" "Naw, not right at the this moment, but trust me I'm goin to let you know what's up." I said. "Know when you leaving?" He asked. "I don't know yet. Maybe two or three weeks." "What chu bout to do right now?" I gotta go kick it with my girl and see where she wanna go." "You got my cell number so call me when you settle down fam, for real Pilla. I owe you one." "You don't owe me nothing but your loyalty. Dre didn't know it but he was like the brother Wes never had. I got chu fam." "all-right my nigga, keep your head up and stay out that funky ass county." Wes said. "All-right fam. A Wes, that number I called you from is my cell phone number." I yelled out the window. "All-right I got it save." Wes yelled back. Me and Wes went our

separate ways. I had to get to the crib so I could get some sleep cause I had been up all day. I kept thinking about what Daron said at the shop. "We can kill him right now." Daron couldn't stand Kav. It had to be a reason though. He didn't like him before this shit happened. I had to get my mind off Kevin because all that did was made me stress so I thought about Zaria and Chris.

When I get home Zaria was cooking dinner. After we ate Chris went to sleep while me and Zaria talked. "Why you ain't tell me Chris was here?" I asked. "Because I wanted to surprise you boo." Zaria said with her feet in my lap. I told her about the money, but she wanted nothing to do with it. "Did you find out where you wanted to go?" I asked. "I don't know baby. I been trying to contact my mother but she's a busy woman. We ended up falling asleep on with the TV on. When I woke up Zaria was gone. It's been almost a week since I seen the Latino chick. I didn't have to much time left, and still had to holla at Carla. It was going to be a boring day. Me and Chris was stuck in the house. We had to do something. I think the State Fair was open, matter of fact it was the last day. When I walked in the living room I seen some mail on the table. Zaria must have gotten it out of the mailbox for me before she left. I knew exactly who it was, from the name on the envelope...... Esco, so I opened it.

WHAT UP HOMIE?

I BEEN DOING GOOD HOMIE. BY THE TIME YOU GET THIS LETTER I'LL BE OUT SO COME SEE ME. MY NUMBER IS 313-995-8423. CALL ME AFTER SIX O'CLOCK CAUSE I'M A BUSY MAN.

SOUTHWEST ESCO

143

That had to be a good room to move in 'cause everybody that was in there went home. I had a cold idea. I kill two birds with one stone. I called Zaria and told her I was taking Chris to the Fair. I called Wes and Carla to see if they wanted to go. I didn't even attempt to call Daron because I knew he was busy. Carla said she didn't care and of course Wes said he didn't mind because all of the females. We got there early. We rode in Carla's Lincoln Ls. Me and Carla finally had a chance to kick it. It felt real good to. Wes was too busy getting numbers from females. After we rode most of the rides, I won Chris some prizes shooting hoops. I seen Wes checking out my sister out the corner of his eyes, but I couldn't do nothing about it because she was grown. After the concert we left. I let Carla take Chris with her to her new apartment and me and Wes hopped in his Monte. He had met us down there. We drove down Woodward banging 'Chedda Boys'. I had already stored Esco number in my cell. "Bro you gotta step yo game up and get chu a Nextel. Sprint aight, but Nextel poppin." I ain't care what kind of phone I had as long as I had one. I called up Esco to see if he didn't mind if me and my homeboy slide though. He said he didn't care. I hung up my phone and Wes looked at me. "You wanna shoot this move with me to Southwest. I asked. "Shit I don't care." Wes said. On our way there we stopped at Wes men's house. "Yeah I gotta put this heater away. Niggas be on some shiesty shit at the Fair." Wes said while getting out. He got back in and we drove off. Soon as we got to Esco spot it was like a hundred Mexicans in the front of the address he gave me. They were all looking in the car and shit, so I called Esco to tell him I was outside. When I got out all the Latino chicks were checking me out. Wes stayed in the car with it still running. I stood by the passenger side door and waited for Esco. I finally seen him. He came out

144

with his red bandana hanging on out his khaki shorts and his flip flops. This nigga had so many tattoos on his chest and stomach it didn't make no sense. "What's up homey?" He asked shaking my hand. "Shit, same ol' thang" I said. "'Who's that in the car?" He asked. "That's my man's Wes, He was my bunky before you was." I said. "Oh, that's the one that wrote while I was your bunky?" "Yeah, he solid doe" "Alright I just wanted to know because I don't fuck with too many motherfuckas homey." He said. "Same here" I said. "Tell him to get out, it's disrespectful not to introduce yourself." Esco said. I walked over to the car tell Wes to hit the engine and get out. Wes hit the engine got out. "What's up homie, Dre tells me your good people. They call me Esco." Esco said while extending his hand out. "They called me Wes" Wes said shaking his hand. "You from Detroit homie?" "Yeah I'm from the mile." "5, 6, 7, 8?" Esco asked. Wes laughed a little. "Naw, it's only one mile and that's seven mile." Wes said. "Why don't you and your friend come in and have some drinks?" Esco said. "I ain't really got nothing to do. What about you Pilla?" Wes asked me. "I don't drink but I'll go in and holla at chu for a lil minute." I said. Soon as we went in it was so many Latinos in this nigga crib. "Damn what's this a party?" I asked. "Naw homey, we do this all the time." Esco said while pouring the drinks. "You got mad females here." Wes said. "Yeah it's normal, they come around often. Help yourself, the homies ain't gonna trip." "Shit I don't got nothing to lose." Wes said asking the Latino chick to dance. "What about you homey?" "Naaa, I'm straight." We kicked it while everybody partied. "A homey, I gotta talk to you." Esco said. We went to the back. When I walked inside the back room it was two Latino chicks snorting white lines. "Get from back here puntos. I told yaw about that shit." Esco yelled. They both ran out leaving behind left over

lines on the glass table. "I don't know where to start but I gotta start somewhere." Esco said. "What chu talking bout?" I asked. "I know about you and Kevin" Esco said. The words shocked the shit out of me. "You said what?" "Listening, you don't have to play crazy. I know everything and more homey." I was confused now. "Your brother came to me a minute ago. He had a hit on you but I told him to give me a little time. I didn't even know that it was you in the county. I'm sitting up here sleeping with the guy I'm supposed to kill. That's crazy homey." I was now kind of scared because this guy had me in his house and I was trapped, me and Wes. I had to play it off though. "Yeah, I'm fucked up behind that. "I just wanted to holler at you. You looked out for me. You didn't know me from a can of paint and you were loyal. That $25 helped me get out the county. Nobody would give me a three way until I offered to pay somebody. I'll never forget that. I owe you." He put his hand up and stopped me. "You don't owe me nothing Esco. I owe you." Any situation you and your brother get into, you can call me and get what ever you want." "Naw I'm good Esco. This is my problem because you have did enough. I don't wanna involve nobody else in this shit." "I can respect that homey, but know this Dre, anytime you need me I'm here. I own this shit, anything that happened in southwest I'm the one. I take care of my peoples." Esco said. "So what are you going to do about the hit?" I asked. I was just curious. "You know I couldn't take that hit. "I'm glad that we talked though because I was seriously thinking about it. But to be honest with you I never really fucked with the guy at all. He's a snake. I know what's going on and that wasn't a reason to kill you. He wanted to put a bomb under your car. So for future references do not take nothing else from him." Esco said. "You said if I need anything or your help I can ask right?" "Yeah homie those

146

are my words." "Well I'll be hitting you up." I'm only one call away." Esco said. "I'm going to get back with you then." I said. We both left the room and headed back to the front. "Come on Wes it's time to bounce." "Damn man Wes said leaving the thick Latino chick. It was three in the morning when Wes dropped me off at my house. "All-right fam, keep ya head up." "Same thing Wes said peeling off. Zaria was knocked out when I get in. I took my clothes off and got in the bed with her.

CHAPTER 20

A couple of weeks later Kavin found him self laying with his woman. "Wake up Selina." "What baby? I'm tired." She said. "Alright I'm about to go pick up a few things from the market. "Do you need anything?" Kevin asked. "Yeah, just get me a strawberry milk. Make it two." "That's it?" "Yeah baby" "I see you gaining all that weight too." Kevin said while washing his face. "I know bay, but shoot I be hungry." Selina said laughing. "Are we gone have time to talk?" Kevin asked. Selina nodded her head and put the covers over her head. Kevin brushed his teeth and dipped out. Kevin rode all around Detroit to check on his businesses. He was thinking about if Dre had left yet. He didn't let that get him off track so he focused on getting to his car wash. He finally made it to his car wash on Puritan. He had to collect his money. "Solo, What's good?" Kevin asked. "Shit, gettin these little niggas in check. It's been kind of slow doe." Solo said. Kevin could understand where he was coming from because the seasons were changing. Solo was a quiet nigga but when beef was on the floor so was he, but since his daughter was born he calmed down a little. Kevin paid him real good. It was basically his car wash. "Well I'm goin get at chu' later." Kevin said rolling his window up. Solo through the peace sign up and went back into the building. Kevin stopped at a nearby gas station to get Selina's strawberry milk. Selina lived on eight mile and Cherrylawn. When he pulled in her driveway he noticed a bunch of young niggas in red griming him but he wasn't worried at all. He laughed because he could of had those little niggas popped but it just would of been unnecessary beef, plus Selina lived right down the street. "Baby I'm home" Kevin said. Selina was laying on the couch watching re-runs of Seinfeld. "You had to talk to me

right?" Selena asked. Kevin handed her, Her milk and said you first. She looked Kevin in the eyes while he stood up in front of the TV. "I'm pregnant Kevin." Selina said while taking the milk out of Kevin hands. "What Kevin asked looking shocked and scared. Kevin wasn't ready for any kids. "Yes Kevin, I'm three months pregnant. Well aren't you going to say something?" She asked. "Are you gonna have it?" Kevin asked. "What the fuck you mean am I going to have it?" "Of course I'm gonna have it." Selina said getting irritated. "Okay it is what it is" Kevin said. "What the hell is that supposed to mean? Sometimes I don't know what the hell be going through your head. Are you gonna leave the streets Kevin?" Selina asked. The question hit Kevin hard. He was froze. "Selina now you know I can't make no promises like that." "I'm not trying to bury you baby, I love you and I don't want you to be in nobodies casket." "Don't ever say that, don't ever say that shit again." Kevin said. "I'm just scared baby." Selina said breaking down in tears. "Baby I'm sorry. Come here. Kevin said pulling her up in his arms. "Everything gonna be okay. I promise. They both sat down on the couch. Kevin massage her feet then the rest of her body. They fell asleep right on the couch. Kevin woke up because his phone was vibrating in his pants pocket. He didn't notice the number but picked it up anyway. "Who dis" Kevin asked. They didn't say nothing. All Kevin could hear was somebody breathing real hard, then he heard the line click. There wasn't to many people that had his number. He went back to sleep after he got tired of trying to figure out who it was.

Kevin woke up smelling sausages and eggs. He got up and brushed his teeth and walked into the kitchen. "Damn baby what the hell you cooking?" "I'm making you some bacon, sausages, scrambled cheesy eggs, grits and

butter toast." "Damn you must love your man." "Yes I do love you papi." "You looking good as hell." Kevin said looking at her tight boy shorts and the tiny T-shirt. He hugged her from the back and kissed her neck. She could feel Kevin hardness while he hugged her. "That friend of yours don't know when to stop playing." Sclina said. "I guess not." They both ate and watched The Real World. "Baby I gotta go shoot this move real quick. I'm gone be back later on. I gotta go check on my crib." "Didn't you have something to ask me yesterday?" She asked. Kevin thought about it for a minute then he finally remembered. "I want you to move to Benton Harbor with me?" He asked. "I told you already Kevin, I've been living here since I was younger. My mom practically raised me here. She stayed here all of her life." Kevin just shook his head and walked out. "What time are you coming back?" Selina yelled while he was closing the door. Kevin didn't even respond. He was heated. As soon as he opened the door he seen the same young niggas he seen yesterday. They were shooting dice in front of this abandoned house. It was probably a spot. He hopped in his DTS and rode past the young niggas. He tried to get a good look at most of their faces. He could of sworn he had seen one of the niggas somewhere.

He finally made it to his crib. He noticed his driveway was done over. "Damn I forget I called the contractor to do my driveway over." Kevin said. He parked on the street and walked to his crib. Before he could walk away from closing his door and locking it back he heard a knock on the door. Kevin hung his jacket up and went to see who it was. When he looked out to see who it was, it was the next door neighbor two houses down. He was trying to get some pussy but she had been playing around.

The bitch was bad. She looked like Carman Electra twin sister. Kevin opened the door and. "And what may I do for you miss?" Kevin said. "Ummm my husband is at work and my stove is really acting up. I wanted to know if you could check it out for me." "This bitch was desperate. She knew damn well I didn't know how to fix the damn thing. Kevin thought to his self. "Yeah, I can look at it. Give me a sec." "When Kevin came back downstairs he seen her checking out his spot. "You like what you see?" Kevin asked. "Do I? I've been in love with this house for the longest. My husband never looked into it though." She said. "Well that's a loss for your husband. Are you ready?" Kevin asked. "Yeah I'm ready." She said. "Where are your tools?" "Oh I got all the tools I need." Kevin said while laughing to himself. Soon as they walked in her house she led him to the kitchen. "I didn't catch your name miss." Kevin said. "Because I didn't throw it at you." The Carman Electra look alike said. "Alright then" Kevin said. "I'm joking. My name is Stephanie and yours?" "Kevin but you can call me Kev." "Which one do you prefer?" She asked. "It doesn't matter." Kevin said. "Well here's the problem." She said pointing to the stove. She bent over to try to turn on the oven but it wouldn't come on. Her spandex were so tight. All Kevin could see was her fat ass pussy print between her legs. It looked like her pusy lips was putting the middle finger up. That's how fat her shit was. He could tell she was damp down there because he seen the wetness between her legs. Kevin could see both of the problems. A young white horny bitch with a old husband that didn't get any dick and a loose gas line. "I think I know what the problem is Stephanie." Kevin reached over her and grabbed the gas line to show her it wasn't plugged up all the way. After Kevin was finished he seen her looking over his shoulder. "That's it?" "Yep, that's it." "How much do I

151

owe you?" She asked Kevin looking down at the huge bulge in his pants. "You don't owe me nothing, I'm good." Before Kevin got his last words out she grabbed his dick and her eyes lit up like Christmas lights. She fell to her knees and unzipped his pants and wrapped her lips around the tip. "Mmmm this chocolate stick is good." Stephanie moaned out. "Damn girl." Kevin said grinning his teeth. Stephine started to go faster. Kevin was now bagging up because it felt so good but she kept a lock on his dick. Kevin was now leaning on the kitchen sink with his head tilted back. Kevin looked down to see if it was real and it was. She had his whole dick in her mouth and the tip of her tongue was licking his balls. Kevin almost fainted but he grabbed the cabinet to hold on. Stephine pulled his dick out and started licking it like a blow pop. "I can't wait til you cum. You like sticking your dick in little girls mouths don't you?" kevin couldn't really make out what she was saying because the head was so good. She kept sucking until she tasted the semen. "There it is. Mmmm, that was so good." She said while stroking his dick. "What do you mean little girls?" Kevin asked barely getting his words out. "Oh you didn't know?" She asked still stroking his man hood. "What the hell are you talking about?" "I'm only six-teen that's what I mean. My mom passed away after I was born." She said while massaging his balls. He couldn't believe what he was hearing. "So are you going to come get this tender pussy?" Stephine asked. All I could do was moan because she took him in her mouth again. Kevin snatched her up and pulled her t-shirt over her head exposing her d-cups. Her titties were so fat with the pinkest nipples Kevin had ever seen. Her stomach was flat as a ironing board. "Yes yes, don't stop big daddy. She said watching him while he sucked her breast. Kevin licked down to her navel. He started pulling down her purple

spandex shorts and she didn't have on any panties. Her pussy was so fat and pink. She didn't have a lick of pubic hair down there. Kevin was tempted to eat her pussy but he couldn't. Stephine rubbed the top of his head. "Taste it baby, I promise it's sweet." She pushed Kevin's head towards her pussy. Kevin started licking her clean shaved pussy. "Oh yes, don't stop. Ohhhh." Stephine moaned out over and over again. Kevin had one of her legs over his shoulder. He lifted her up on the sink and now she had both her legs over his shoulders. Kevin licked furiously. "Yes baby, yes baby. I think I'm bout to cum for you. Uggg, oohhh shit." She exploded all over Kevin face. Kevin had to admit she did taste good but now it was his turn to get his dick wet. "I been ready to feel this dick for the longest." She said getting down from the sink. She led him to the den. Kevin was now on his back. When she took off his pants his dick was sticking straight up. She got on top of him and started to ride him. Her pussy was tight. She had to only had one or two partners but she was riding the dick like she had to have many partners. Her titties moved in a circular motion while she bounced on his dick. "You so big, I want you to hurt my little pussy. Knock everything down." She said while looking at the ceiling. She scratched him all over his chest while rolling her hips. Kevin rolled her over on her back and quickly drove into her. She let out a loud grant. Kevin loved to see a female in pain from him fucking them. He now had both of her legs over his shoulders, driving in and out of her with powerful thrust. Kevin knew she was in ecstasy. Her boyfriend probably never put it down like this. Kevin thought to himself. "Yes daddy. I'm finna cum all over your dick." She yelled out. Kevin felt her liquid flowing but wasn't finished yet. He turned her over quickly. She was so small and fragile he could do anything he wanted to do. "Ohh I love it up the

ass." Stephine said thinking Kevin was going to have anal sex with her. Kevin didn't want to fuck her in the as though. He stuck his dick in her pussy from the back. Stephine almost collapsed. She bit down on the pillow and started growling. Kevin entered in and out of her repeatedly. Her ass cheeks was soaking wet from all the sweat. He opened her ass cheeks exposing her even more. Her asshole was the same color as her nipples. He pulled his dick out and slowly put it in her asshole. "Ohh my God, oh shit. Go all the way, all the way." Her ass was super tight. "My father never puts it in my ass." Stephine yelled out. This bitch was all the way fucked up. Kevin couldn't believe what she was saying. This was some perverted shit but it turned him on even more. Kevin felt his self about to explode. He pumped her slow and hard filling her asshole with a fat nut. She laid on her back and played with her pussy. Kevin stood up with his dick in his hand wit cum still dripping out. This little bitch was out her shit. Kevin was now getting back hard. His shit was hurting from getting back hard but he couldn't control it. Stephine smiled at the sight and got up and sucked his dick until he was empty. Kevin left her dazed out on the couch.

After Kevin washed all the sex off he was thinking about how he fucked a teenager. "That lil bitch talked me into eating her pussy." Kevin mumbled to his self. When he was drying off he looked in the mirror. He thought about Selina and his unborn. He was mad at his self for not being loyal to Selina. He slipped on a jogging outfit and some Timberlands. Soon as he stepped out of his crib, he hopped in his DTS. He saw Stephine in some tight ass blue jeans. She was hugging her dad in the front lawn. Her dads back was facing Kevin. She stuck her tongue out and licked the

154

top of her nose. Kevin dick started to rise but he couldn't do nothing about it so he drove off.

CHAPTER 21

Even though I had $300,000 it didn't mean shit because I wasn't going to enjoy it with my family. The only thing I could be thankful for was Zaria and Chris. We were now living in Arkansas. Zarya mom owned a couple of houses here so she let us stay until we get settled. It wasn't far from the dirty glove but it felt like it. The environment was totally different. It was a lot of white folks down here and they were nosey as hell. Zaria family stayed in Atlanta so we were right around the corner. We stayed in a small city called Searcy. We were like thirty minutes from Little Rock. The air was fresh because it wasn't a lot of factories down here. It was mainly farms and shit. Sunny had plugged Zaria in with one of his family members that owned some clothing stores, but they weren't like our clothing stores, they were behind. Fashion was real slow down here, but soon Zaria would have her own clothing store. I never told anybody how much money I had received from Kevin. I didn't need any new friends. Me and Wes stayed in contact strong. I kicked the Esco every now and then. Me and Daron stayed on the phone talking shit. He expanded his business. He was doing his thang. My sister Carla was doing good, she was doing her at a nice Salon in Southfield, where she stayed with her new boyfriend Ferric. I was getting Chris ready for kindergarten next year. He was already smart so I didn't have to do much. As for myself I had to step my game up and be a good role model for Chris. I bought Zaria a small building so she could have her own clothing store. I didn't want to enroll in school until I was finished with my parole. I had eighteen more months and I would be off papers. I've almost been out for six months. Christmas was right around the corner and Daron was suppose to come down here but I

didn't believe him because that was one busy nigga. I'll probably call him tomorrow. I had to stay home with Chris, it wasn't shit though because it wasn't shit out there to do anyway. The malls and shit were like forty minutes away so it was a wrap with all that driving shit. I had to get my drivers license together so it wasn't going to be no driving. I'm suppose to take the test tomorrow. I knew I was going to pass it with flying colors. I looked outside and thought about how this was going to be the first Christmas without snow. It was a little warm out compared to the weather in Detroit around this time. I stayed reading hood books, especially my girl Trei Woods. I was filling her. She came hard in every book. When Zaria walked in from work, I noticed she looked sleepy. "You look tired baby, you actually been looking like that for the last few days." "Naaaa, I'm alright baby." She said bending down and kissing me on the cheek. She was going to surprise Dre. All this work could kill a bitch. She thought to herself. She was so tired of carrying his baby. She was ready to get it out the way. "Why don't you go in there and lay down and me and Chris a jazz you up something." I said. Zaria took my advice and went to her room and took her clothes off and came back out with some basketball shorts and a T-shirt on. She laid on the couch and watched 106 & park. I cut up the potatoes and flattened out the hamburgers. I salted everything up. Chris watched me in his highchair. After we got finished eating I rubbed her feet until she dozed off. I had to call Daron. He said that he was going to come down here so I had to make sure. Might as well call the nigga and see what was up. I went to the back room I could put him on speaker phone while I ironed my clothes. He picked up on the second ring. "Hello. What up nigga?"

"Shit, man just waiting for this day." Daron said sounding geeked. "What Christmas?" I asked. "Nigga fuck Christmas, I'm bout to propose to Suga tomorrow."

"Man that's where it's at bro."
"You the only person I told. I ain't having no big ass wedding." I congratulated Daron because that was a big step in a relationship. "So when you going to ask my lil cousin?" Daron asked. "Man I don't know right now." "Don't fuck up something good bro, you got a rida, nigga you better cuff her." "I know she a ride bro, but I ain't ready yet, especially with all this shit going on." We kicked it a little longer before Daron had to go.

Christmas Eve was here and it was a little snow on the ground. "Uncle Dre is Santa Clause coming?" Chris asked me. "Yeah, he'll be here tonight but you can't wait up for him or he'll be mad and won't show." I ain't never believe in Santa Clause but I wasn't going to spoil Chris day. "You gotta leave him some milk and cookies." I said. "Aunty are you going to help me make some cookies?" Chris asked. "Sure baby." We watched the Christmas story all day because it was on for 24 hours. It was my moms favorite movie. Next thing you know we were sleep on the couch.

" Santa Claus came, Santa Claus came. He ate all the cookies too Auntie." Chris yelled waking up. Me and Zaria had to put a few gifts out when he was sleep. I had a little change so I bought me a '99' Range Rover when I get down here. I had sold the Corvette and the motorcycle. Zaria still had her Monte Carlo. She also sold her Taurus. She was going to be ready to get rid of the Monte too. "You ready Chris?" Zaria asked?" Chris jumped out my lap with

the quickness. "Is this, is this mine?" Chris asked. "Yep" Zaria told him. She sat there smiling the whole time. Chris ran through so many gifts that didn't make no sense. When he was finished he was laid out on the floor with gift wrapping all around him sleep. Zaria picked up a small box and gave it to me. "You going to stare at it or open it?" When I opened it was a red box that said Cartier. I opened the box and it was a platinum chain and a cross full of diamonds. "Damn baby, Thank you." She gave me another small box and I opened it it was a grey rubber band watch with diamonds around the face. I didn't really like it at first. "What, you don't like it baby? It's a Techno Marine." "Yeah it's cool, it just look a little childish." I said. Soon as I put it on I fell in love with it. "Huh, here's one more thing." She handed me a small rectangular box soon as I ripped the wrapper off it had Cartier in gold letters on the red box. When I popped the box open, there were a pair of glasses like Daron's but mine was platinum wood grain. I looked up as Zaria and gave her a kiss on the lips. "Well put it all on and grab the green gift sitting in the corner." "You doing a lil to much Zaria." I said. "So, I love you nigga." I grabbed the box and unwrapped it. It was a pair of shoes. "Prada?" I asked. "Yeah open the box." She said. They were some grey on grey Prada gym shoes. "Now put all of it on." She said. Soon as I put everything on I was acting like I was one of The Chedda Boys. I was rapping 'I'm a Chedda Boy' Zaria was rolling. Zaria really loved the shit out of me and it was the same here. Now it was my turn. "Grab that big pink one right there." I said. She grabbed it and sat down next to me. "This seems empty." She said. "Girl just open it." I said. Soon as she opened it, there was a bunch of cotton inside of it. "What's this about Dre?" "Girl quit playing and dig inside." 'No you didn't, what the hell you done got me?" She asked finding a key.

159

"Go look out the window." I said. Zaria jumped up and looked out the window behind the couch and almost fell off when she seen the all white Lexus convertible with a pink bow tied around it. All the neighbors were smiling and giving me the thumbs up. She didn't even find the other key to her building. "Zaria it's something else in there." She turned around with tears of joy coming from her eyes. "Baby what are you crying for?" I asked. "I don't know." Zaria said grabbing the box and searching for the other gift. She finally found the other key and she looked at me with a confused expression on her face. "What's this for? I held up a picture of her new building. "This is your building for your clothing store." Zaria hug me so tight crying over my shoulders telling me how much she loved me. "I have one more gift for you baby." She said. "Girl you better stop trying to be so competitive." I said. "Boy whatever." Zaria laughed. "Dre, I'm pregnant." I was froze for a minute. I didn't know how to react to what she just said, so I just stood there with water building up in my eyes. I didn't want to let Zaria see any tears come down so I rubbed my eyes. I got down on my knees and hug her by the waist line. "I love you baby" I told her.

Zaria whipped up breakfast, because we didn't cook no big dinner. We just had a big breakfast. Wasn't nothing opened around here so I hooked the PS2 up and me and Chris played almost the whole day while Zaria slept. I went in the room and watched her while she was sleeping. She was so damn beautiful. I prayed that she would have a girl. I didn't want a boy, we had Chris.

The next few days we were busy with the New Years planning. She had got us a room at the Hamptons. I threw on my jewelry and my Cartiers. "Yall ready?" I said. "Yeah baby here we come." Zaria yelled from the other

room. Zaria come out with her Donna Karrine outfit with her three quarter Gucci Loafers. Chris had on a Polo outfit and some Jordans. We hopped in the Rang Rover and we were on our way to the Hamptons. When we got there I told Zaria I had to make a run. "Where you going Dre?" "Baby I'll be right back." I said. They got out and walked towards the entrance. I made sure they got in and I drove off. I had to check on Zaria's building to see what was done to it. It took me a minute to get there but I finally made it. "A lot of progress." I said to myself. I drove around the city a little more to see if there was any competition, but it wasn't. Only stores that were potential threats were Hudsons and a Footlocker. My phone started vibrating. I put the Nextel on speaker. "What up?"

"Nigga where you at?"

"All-right baby hurry up."

"Love you"

"I love you too Zaria."

When I hung up I noticed a police car in my rear view mirror, but I was good. I had all my shit in order. They tailed me for a minute before they flicked their lights. Soon as I pulled over, two big red necks got out. "Damn what next?" I whispered. "Cut your car off Sir." The officer on the driver door side said. "License and registration." I gave him my license and registration and he took it. "Any reason to why you pulled me over sir?" I asked. "Well I'm going to be honest with you sir. We don't get a lot African Americans driving expensive cars like this. Usually if they do, their drug dealers or they carjacked the vehicle. This is my city and I never seen you around here. When you were snooping around I felt uncomfortable. I also can tell your from the city." The officer said. "Yeah I'm from the city but nor am I a drug dealer or do I steal cars for a living." I

said. "Well I'm going to run this Id to see if you have any warrants." They both went to their car. Seconds later both officers came back. "I see you're on parole Mr. Clark." The driver side officer said. "Yes, I have one more year and I'm off." I said. My phone started to vibrate on the dash broad. I knew who it was but I didn't answer it. "Aren't you going to answer that?" the passenger side officer asked. Soon as I answered it Zaria was cursing me out. "Zaria I just got pulled over, you need to relax….No baby I'm not going to jail baby calm down….I'll call you when I'm on my way….Love you too." "Your wife?" The passenger side officer asked. "Soon to be." I told him. "I had to ask you these questions because it's part of my job." "Do you have anything illegal in your vehicle?" "No Sir." "Do you mind if we search your vehicle." I knew my rights and if they didn't have a reason then they had to ask, but I didn't care because it was nothing in here. "Sure." I said. "Could you step out please?" I stepped out and the passenger side offer came around and led me to the back of the truck. He searched me and had me sit down on the curb. After he was finished searching my car he told me I was good. I got in my truck and he handed me my license and registration back. "Don't take it personal Mr. Clark, you're an ex-felon so I have to follow protocol." The driver side officer said. "I understand." "Have a nice day." He said. "You too." I said before driving off. "Fucking cracker." I said. Black or white officers it didn't matter, they never want to see you doing better than them. I had did five years in prison so I knew how to talk to them. Shit, I guess being in prison actually helped a nigga. I finally pulled up in the Hamptons parking lot. Soon as I walked into the room. "SURPRISE!" Wes, Daron, Suga, Big Bo, Lil Lou, Freaky Rell, K-dog, Carla, her boyfriend Zetroc, Aunty Vicki, Sunny, Uncle Phil, Will, Uncle Devin, Esco even

162

showed up. Zaria eyes were bloodshot red. I knew she was worried about me. she came and hugged me and told me she was scared. "You gotta stop worrying baby. That's not good for the baby. I'm serious Zaria." "Okay baby." She said. We all danced and kicked it all night. We were all in the ballroom downstairs. We had rented it for a few hours. After we get tired we all went to our own separate rooms. The guys went to theirs and the females went to theirs. Our rooms were connected together. We played Madden most of the night while the women gossiped. Chris didn't have anyone to play with so I took him to the kitchen area. "What up nephew?" I asked Chris. He just smiled. "What up doe nigga?" Wes said walking up. "Nothing really. Shit going straight I guess. I said. "What up lil man?" Wes asked Chris. "Wat's sup?" Chris said. Wes started laughing. "Yeah the streets miss you dawg. That's really as hell how you left and shit. but fuck it you had to do you. Didn't really have a choice." Wes said. I did have a choice, I just chose the best one for me and my family. I said to myself. "Yeah it's fucked up I had to leave." I said. "Everybody still wearing them shirts. Daron still having parties too. He still holding you down for real." Wes said. I was thinking about all the shit Daron had done for me and all I could think about was why. After me and Wes kicked it, me and Esco exchanged a few words. He had brought two of his homies with him. It was almost 1twelve o'clock so the females came back to the room. "Excuse me everybody." Daron shouted. "Can I get everyones attention?" Everybody was now looking at Daron. "Michelle Reese." He got down on one knee. "Would you be my wife?" Daron asked Suga. She broke out in tears. "Yes baby, yes baby. I will be your wife." She said hugging him. Daron put a dumb ass ring on her finger. Zaria was so happy for Suga, shit who wasn't. They'd been together forever. "Yaw

163

ready to bring the New Year in?" Uncle Phil yelled over the music. Everybody started to count down. "10, 9, 8, 7, 6, 5, 4, 3, 2, 1, HAPPY NEW YEARS." Everybody yelled. We all clowned a little longer, then everybody started leaving. They hugged me, Zaria and Chris, some even gave us money. Everybody went to their separate rooms while Carla stayed a little longer. Her boyfriend asked her did she want anything before he went to the room. "Naw, I'm straight baby, thanks though." Carla said. "Carla I miss you and I'm really concerned about." I told her. "Dre you know I'm good. I gotta job, my own money, my own car, and my own hair." I busted out laughing. "Girl you crazy as hell. So what's up with this Zetroc dude?" I asked. "He cool, he keep me looking good, and he take care of my needs financially and sexually." She said smiling. "Come on Carla, I ain't trying to hear that shit about cha sex life, save that shit for Zaria and Suga." "Boy shut up. I know you ain't talking. Zaria be tryna tell me about you and her. I be telling her the same thing you just told me." "Yaw both some freaks." "And what does that make you?" She asked me. "Man shut the hell up girl." But on the serious tip Carla. Have you seen Kevin?" "Dre I don't even wanna talk about that evil nigga." "I just don't want nothing to happen to you out there." "Boy I told you I'm all-right. I don't even be studding that negro. All I do is work all day anyway, so he's the last thing on my mind." My sister was strong, but it wasn't that much strong in the world to know that your brother killed your brother and sister and even threaten to kill your baby brother and nephew. "Alright if you say so Carla, well that's it. I love you and I'll see you before you leave tomorrow." "All-right lil bro, I love you too. "Gone somewhere girl I ain't little no more." I said while trying to stop Carla from kissing me and grabbing my cheeks. "Alright yaw take care." Carla said before leaving.

"A Zaria." "What's up babe?" "How the hell you get all those people here?" I asked. "I looked in your phone. I told you I was going to be checking." She said smiling. She came and laid on top of me and we fell asleep.

CHAPTER 22

After everybody left and went back to Detroit we stayed for a few more days. We got up and shower we were on our way home. "Dre hurry up and get Chris ready." Zaria said. We left the room before noon. Zaria had been looking out for me since I came home now it was my turn to lookout for her. Her store should be open in a month or two. She wanted to decorate it herself. Zaria had got a plug from Sunny so she was good on clothes. Daron even gave her a few numbers to get hooked up.

Zaria's new clothing store was opened by Valentine's Day. 'Get wit it or get lost'. Her store was doing good. It was all type of doe boys flooding inside. Especially cause of the holiday. I was so proud of her. She had got her license in everything so everything was legitimate. I stayed helping her because we didn't hire anybody yet. We thought it was best if we kept it in the family until someone we could trust came along and that was going to be hard with me. Chris stayed in the back until we were done. I kept him busy with toys and made sure I checked on him all the time. "We did good our first day baby." I told Zaria. "Did you check on Chris?" Zaria asked. "Yeah I went back there like three minutes ago he's back there playing with his Hot Wheels cars. "Just make sure he's alright." She said. When I went back there he was still playing with his cars. "What's up big fella?" "Nothing." "You hungry?" I asked. "Mmm um." He said shaking his head. "What do you want?" I asked. "A Big Mac." Chris blurted out. "you think you can eat a Big Mac huh?" at I asked while tickling him. Zaria closed up the shop while me and Chris played the game in the back. "Are y'all ready?" Zaria hollered. We cut the Nintendo 64 off and left out the back. We headed to McDonald's to eat and went home. When we get home Chris was knocked out.

"Baby, I love you so much." Zaria said. "I love you too. I can't wait to be a father." I said. "You're already a father baby." Zaria said.

Time was flying, it was April and Zaria was due in a couple of months. She was getting big her cheeks, hands, and feet were huge. Zaria had hired two females she met while getting her nails did at a small beauty salon. They were in high school. That bought a lot of customers to the shop. Chandra and Mya were their names. They were both smart. They kind of reminded me of Leslie and Lisa but they weren't twins though. I looked out for them when they needed anything. Mya was the youngest, she was 16 and Chandra was 17 going on 18 next month. She was about to graduate from high school. Me and Zaria ended up meeting their mom. Kim was a single mother trying to do the best she could for her three girls. Zaria had to do a background check. She didn't just want to hire anybody so she trained them like Sunny trained her. Since then they both knew the tricks of the trade. We got real cool with Kim. We started paying her to babysit Chris to put some extra money in her pocket. I guess southern hospitality was true.

Zaria birthday was in two weeks and I didn't know what to get her. She had everything. I always had something up my sleeve though. I had to ask Kim if should baby sit Chris on Zaria's birthday. I made sure I called her ahead of time so I wouldn't intervene with anything she had planned. "Hello may I speak to Kim please?....This is Dre....That's what I was calling about. I wanted to know if you could watch Chris while I took Zaria out for her birthday?......All-right Kim, thank you so much....I'll be sure to tell her....you too." I said hanging up. Kim was cool ass hell. She a daughter around the same age as Chris so now Chris has somebody to play with Zaria's birthday tomorrow so I laid

it down.

I woke up at 5:30 in the morning. Got in the shower and made sure I was fresh. I woke Chris up and got him dressed to go over Kim's house. "You ready little man?" I asked. "Yes." He said while putting his coat on. After I made him something to eat I dropped him off at Kim's it was 6:50am. I had cooked Zaria breakfast. "Wake up baby. Happy birthday." She didn't even move. "Come on girl and eat your breakfast." "I'm tired bay." Zaria said pulling the covers over her head. I opened the blinds to shine the sun in the room. Zaria finally lifted her head up and saw pancakes, bacon, sausage, and scrambled eggs. "Ohhh thank you baby. You didn't have to do this. Where's Chris?" She asked. "I dropped him off at Kim's." "Dre what are you up to? You know I'm pregnant, so if you think you getting some of this coochie you must be crazy. You can taste it though." Zaria cracked a smirk and pointed between her legs. "Man, whatever, ain't nobody tryna put no lips on you." "You act like it's nasty or something to put your lips on my coochie. You wasn't saying that four months ago." "Girl eat your food and get in the shower. We got a lot to do today. I'll be in the front room waiting." I gave her a kiss and left. "Dress comfortable too." I said before leaving the room. "Boy shut up." Zaria said playing. I had everything planned out. "Come on girl." An hour later Zaria came in the front room looking like a pregnant model in street clothes. "You like?" She said pointing at her belly. "Damn, baby you look like a million dollars. I told you to just put something on, you went in there and put on the flyest thing on." I said. "First off, I look like a zillion dollars and F.Y. I this is simple." She had on a BeBe outfit. Black shirt with BeBe across her breasts, Black stretch capris on with her black stilettos with the straps that came below her calves. "Girl you ready?" I asked in a smart but

funny way. "Yeah." She said trying to sound like me. We hopped in the Lexus and drove off. "So where we headed bay?" Zaria asked me. I just looked at her. She was so beautiful. I was froze for a minute. "Boy are you going to answer my question?" She asked. "What are you talking about?" I asked. "Why you gotta answer my question with a question?" "Ain't that how you do me?" "Boy I can't stand you." She said cracking a smile. "Bay just sit back and enjoy the ride. Zaria folded her arms like a little kid. It took us 30 minutes to get to the skating rink. After dropping Chris off I stopped at Walmart to get some skates because I couldn't be caught in none of them broke down skates. It wasn't no one there yet so we went to the movies first. After the movies we ate lunch at this little restaurant that served outside and inside. We talked about a lot of stuff. It was crazy how we bonded. I took her shopping, bought her a couple outfits and shoes. It was Sunday so the shop was closed. It was still early so I waited a little longer so we wouldn't be the first to get there. Zaria love to skate. She didn't even see me passed by it. "Damn bay you 23 years old." "Yep, I'm getting old huh?" "Naw, just more beautiful." "You think you got game don't you?" "Nope, but I got chu." When we got to the mall we went in almost every store Zaria wanted to go in. I couldn't stand shopping with a female. They made it their job to go into every store, even stores that they never even heard of. After our arms were hurting from carrying all the bags, we left the mall. It was almost five o'clock. When we got in the car Zaria told me she was hungry. "Oh hell nah you ain't bout to keep eating." I said trying to be funny. "You make me sick boy." When we got to the skating rink it was almost six o'clock. I got out first and grabbed the skates out the trunk. "Come on girl." "No you didn't, I know we ain't bout to go skating." "Yeah you're right, so come on pretty lady." She got out

smiling hard as hell. We went in and it was packed. It was Ol' school Sunday, so it was a lot of older people there. We had a good time. They play everything that came out before I got locked up. I couldn't believe how Zaria was skating. She was moving like she wasn't even pregnant. We were now skating backwards together to the slow jams. "Zaria Hicks please go to the middle of the rink." The DJ said over the microphone. Zaria was looking confused. "Well aren't you going to go?" I asked. "What is all this about?" She asked standing in the middle of the rink. "Dre has something to ask you." The DJ said. She turned around and looked at me. "Do you love me?" "Yes Dre I love you." "Well I love you too and I'm asking you to marry me?" I said getting on one knee. Zaria was in tears. "Yes Dre, I'll be your wife." she said. I put a nice diamond ring on her finger she couldn't stop looking at all the baguettes surrounding the fat rock in the middle. I stood up and she hugged and kissed me. Everybody was clapping all you heard was female saying "You go girl." We parted until the Shaking rink was over. "Did you call Kim to tell her you were on your way?" "Naw bay, I'm going to drop you off first so you can get some sleep." I said. After I dropped Zaria off I hopped in the Range and headed towards Kim's. I called her and told her I was close by and to have Chris ready. When I pulled up I seen the porch light on. I knocked on the door and Kim answered it immediately. "Hey Dre. How was it?" Kim asked letting me in. "It was good, we had a good time." "Well did you ask her?" "Of course I asked." "What did she say?" "You already know what she said. Yes." "Congratulations. I wish the best for you two." "Thank you Kim." I picked Chris up off the couch, he was knocked out. "All-right Kim, I appreciate everything." "Anytime." She said leading me out. I put Chris in his car seat and headed home. When I pulled in the

driveway my phone went off. It was Suga. "Hello. What….slow down Suga everything goin be all-right….I'll be there ASAP….Love you too.

CHAPTER 23

Back in Michigan things were getting crazy. The summer time was on its way. Now that Daron had two more stores he was never around. He had one in Dearborn and one on the east side of Detroit. He had upgraded to a 600 Benz. He bought Suga a 5LK convertible Benz. Everything was looking good for him. Suga was pregnant and she was due in September. She rarely went out to the clubs anymore. "What up doe?" Daron asked freaky Rell. "Shit all is well." "All-righty." Daron said back. "Where k-dog at?" Daron asked. "That nigga somewhere riding around in his Caprice." "You know he threw some 23's on it." Freaky Rell said. "Straight up." "Yup, that nigga don't know how to act." "So what's up with that situation?" Daron asked. "With dog?" "Yeah." "Oh I been peepin 'em, you know his girl stay down the street from lil B." Freaky Rell said. "oh yeah?" "Hell yeah. I ain't seen 'em in a minute doe. You know his girl pregnant too?" "The Latino chick?" "Yeah the tall one. I think her name is Selina." "She bad?" Daron asked. "Hell yeah, the bitch cold." "We might have to holla at that." Daron said while laughing. "We goin' talk about that later, let's worry about Kevin right now." Daron said. "You heard from Dre?" Freaky Rell asked. "Man fuck that nigga. He act like he to good 'cause he done came up and got his hands on some money." Daron said while frowning up his face. "Straight up?" "Fuck yeah. I see why Kevin played 'em." "Well it's whatever." Freaky Rell said. Daron couldn't wait to catch up with Kevin. Kevin had pulled a pistol on him and slapped him. "I see you done put some 22's on the Monte." "Yeah you know it ain't shit compared to that 600 bitch you riding in." Freaky Rell said. Daron just laughed. "What's up with Suga?" "She good, she don't be coming out that much

because she pregnant." "You know what chu having?" Freaky Rell asked. "A boy nigga. I don't produce no girls." Daron said. They both laughed. "I'm gone catch up with you fam." "All-right. "All-mighty." "All is well." Daron said while pulling off. Daron was just as money hungry and grimmy as Kevin. His pull was just as long as Kevin now but he needed some niggas on his team. He had drove to a city called Dearborn to check on his clothing store. Dearborn was on the outside of Detroit. when he got there Big Bo was leaning on the counter. "Everything good?" Daron asked. "Yeah, it's been kind of slow doe." Big Bo said yawning. "Give it some time. Daron had Big Bo and Big Bo's little cousin Rah-rah running the show. "All-right Bo, I'm bout to go check on Lil Lou. "Where Rah-rah at?" Daron asked. "He went to Pizza Hut to get lunch." Big Bo said. "Tell him to call me when he gets a chance." "Alright." "Yup." Daron said. It took Daron a minute to get to Detroit east side because that was on the other side of town. Daron had called Suga to see how the shop was doing on 7 mile. She told him everything was good. Just what he wanted to hear. When he got to the shop on the east side it was packed. Lil Lou and Uncle Phil son L was running it. L has been fucking with Daron for the longest, he just wasn't around because he was living with his moms in New Jersey. It was so many hoes in the inside when Daron walked in. Daron had on his platinum and wood Buffaloes. He had at least three pair of Cartier glasses. He had paid twenty-hundred for the pair he had on. "What's good L?" "Shit tryna get on these lil hoes flocking around the shop." L said. "Don't get distracted. Get that money." Daron said. Daron was two years older than L so he treated him like his little brother. "Lil Lou, man please get him right. Don't let these hoes get to yo head." Daron said. "Man we good, you know these hoes come and go." L said.

"You ain't never lied." Lil Lou said cutting in. L was real childish and he played all day. Daron didn't do to much of the playing but he made a exception for L because it was Uncle Phil only son and Uncle Phil had treated his mom well and him too. "Yaw just keep doing what chall doing, don't let these hoes get just walk around, get these hoes to buy something. Daron said. "We got chu covered." L said. "I'm out." Daron said leaving looking at a young chick ass. He hopped in his Benz and drove off.

Kevin was just coming back from Miami. The first place he stopped was Selina's house. He made sure she wasn't in need for anything. "Damn baby I missed you." Kevin said hugging her. I missed you too papi. "You know I'm do in anytime?" she asked. "Yeah, I can't wait to see my son." Kevin said rubbing her swollen stomach. After he left, he called skeebo up. "Hello….Yeah….I need a favor…..I got this lick. I don't want nothing. Yaw keep it all…..I don't know what's in there….It's probably a few bucks in there…..I'll meet you at the spot….One." A couple hours later Skeebo, Osama, and Sambo was in the Cutty headed to the lick. "Yaw niggas ready?" Skeebo asked while loading up the Mac-11. "Man what kind of question is that bitch?" Osama asked playing. "All I'm ready to do is put a bullet in anything or anybody who gets in the way." Sambo said rubbing his hands together. Only thing they needed was a stoley to get away in. Skeebo pointed out a green Durangos with tinted windows. Sambo hopped out tiled it up. He peeled out and Osama follow him. Skeebo lived in the D for seven years so he knew where to go and how to get away. They parked the Cutty and hopped in the truck with the masks, gloves, bags and guns. "Yaw make sure nobody runs to the back." Skeebo said. They parked right in front of 'Money talks'. All three hop out with their guns in broad daylight. The store only had three customers in it.

"EVERYBODY GET THE FUCK DOWN!" Sambo
yelled. Skeebo ran to the cash register and put the .45 to the
bitch head that was behind the counter. "Get on the
ground." Skeebo shouted. "I can't I'm pregnant." She yelled
back. "I don't give a fuck." He yelled. She finally got on the
floor. "Yaw watch." Skeebo told Sambo and Osama. They
had put all the customers behind the counter with the
pregnant bitch. Sambo had locked the front door and put
the closed sign up… Skeebo was now in the back. He had
a duffel bag in his coat. He searched all the rooms but one.
When he went inside he did see nothing unusual until he
looked at the old mirror. He broke the mirror and he
realized it was a door. He opened it and went back there.
He grabbed all the money he could. He couldn't fit the guns
in there but he made sure it wasn't no more money or drugs
back there. He came out the room and had headed towards
the front with the duffel bag full. "Yaw ready?" Skeebo
asked. "Why yaw doing this?" One of the employees asked.
"Bitch I do what the fuck I wanna do." Sambo said. "Stand
up bitch, you got a attitude?" Sambo asked. "Please leave
her alone." The pregnant bitch asked. "Shut the fuck up."
Osama yelled. Skeebo was mad because it wasn't no need
for that. "Bitch stand up." Sambo yelled again. The blonde
headed chick finally stood up. When she did Sambo shot
her in the shoulder. She fell to the ground. "Anybody got
any questions?" Sambo asked. "Yaw got what yaw wanted
please, please leave." The pregnant bitch asked. Sambo
upped the pistol towards her. "Come on man we don't do
kids." Skeebo said grabbing his wrist. "Thank my mans
bitch 'cause he just saved your life." Sambo said. They left
out with the duffel bag. They hopped in the truck and sped
off down 7 miles Osama Cutty. They got to the Cutty and
left the Durango running. They hopped on the freeway and
headed back to Benton Harbor. Three hours later they were

counting their lick money. It was $73,000, 5 kilos and 16 pounds of weed. "How to fuck you manage to fit all that shit in there?" Osama asked laughing." Nigga I had shit all around my waist line and in my sleeve." Skeebo said laughing. They had called Kevin to tell him they hit the lick and good looking.

Back in Detroit, Diamond was bleeding bad. Suga got up and called 911. "Pleased Diamond your gone make it. She tried to call Daron but he didn't answer. Her next resort was Dre. "Dre somebody robbed us and they shot Diamond, Daron's not answering his phone. Please she's dying."

Daron had drove back to the shop and swooped the little young chick up to see what she was talking about. "You goin' get in or you goin' stay out there?" Daron asked. All her friends were pushing her towards the car. She finally came up to the car and bent over on the passenger side window. 'What's your name?" Daron asked. "Janeen." she said looking innocent. "You wanna get something to eat?" She turned around to see if it was alright with her girlfriends. She looked back in the car and said she didn't care. Get in." Daron said. She got in smiling hard as hell. "So Janeen how old are you?" He asked. "Seventeen I'll be eighteen in two months." She said making her point clear that she was close to being an adult. "How old are you?" She asked. "Twenty-four about to be twenty-five." She laughed at his answer. "So what type of things are you into?" Daron asked. "I don't know." She said being shy. "You know that that's my store right?" "Naw I didn't know that." "You probably was in there trying to buy your boyfriend something." "Nope, I dumped him not too long ago." "Why?" Daron asked looking at her at the red light. "'Cause he didn't get with the program." "And what's the

176

program?" "Satisfying my needs." "Ohhh okay. The needs thing huh? And what are your needs?" He couldn't satisfy me sexually and financially." "That's it?" "Yeah that's it pretty much." Daron knew the bitch was gullible so he made sure he was going to have his whole dick in her mouth and her back. He took her to L's complex on the east side. "Who's apartment is this?" She asked. "This my nigga shit." "He ain't here is he 'cause I ain't no busto or nothing?" "Naw, why would I try something like that?" "Because a lot of niggas do." "Well I ain't a lot of niggas." Daron said opening up the door. When he walked inside she had seen that the house was plushed out. L's shit was laid for real. He had everything. Janeen was a red bone with light brown eyes. After Daron shut the door Janeen was standing there looking clueless. Daron grabbed her and tongued her down. She kissed him back. Once Daron figured out she was into it he cuffed her ass. She let out a low moan. L kept all the condoms in a drawer next to the couch. Minutes later Janeen was sucking his dick. She couldn't suck dick but he didn't care. He could tell she didn't know what she was doing because she was trying to hard. She said her jaws was hurting. She had her panties and bra on, so Daron had her take everything off. Her body looked good too. He heard his phone go off but he didn't answer it. "You ever had it from the back?" Daron asked." No. What's that?" She asked looking confused." It's going to feel good." He said. "Alright, anything for you." She said bending over all fours on the couch. Daron got behind her. He slid the condom on. "Arch yo back a little more." She did as he asked. He had one hand on her hip and one on his dick. He stuck his dick in her small tight pussy. It felt so good. "Damn, baby you a virgin?" "No I had sex before." Daron didn't care. Once he was all the way in he started off slow. Janeen was screaming and moaning. But

they soon turned into pleasure moans after he opened her up. He kept fucking her harder and harder. He was pulling her hair so she could look up. It was a mirror facing her so he could her face. Little did Janeen know, the couch and the mirror was there for a reason. They had brought so many females to this couch and she wasn't going to be the last one. Daron was about to cum, but he was mad because the pussy was so good. He wanted to keep fucking her. He felt her muscles gripping him and that made him explode in her. He kept pumping in and out of her. "Ohh, I never felt like this." Janeen moaned out. She had came and kept cuming. Daron filled the condom up. She was looking at him though the mirror get his last pumps off. He wanted to fuck her again so bad but he knew his dick wouldn't get back hard because she couldn't suck dick worth shit. "Damn, I ain't never been fucked like that." Janeen said swiping the sweat off her forehead. "Straight up?" "Hell yeah." She said. She was putting on her clothes while Daron was looking at her. This bitch was bad. "You going to call me when you get a chance?" Daron asked. "I don't even have your number." She said walking out the front door. "I'm gone give it to you." They hoped in the Benz with the tinted windows and drove off. "This my friends house right here." Janeen said. "You going to give me a going away present before you leave?" Daron asked rubbing his dick through his pants. She unzipped his pants and pulled his dick out and started pulling at it. It hurted him but it felt good at the same time. She was now sucking his dick. He tilted his seat back and let her go to work until he came in her mouth. "Is that a good gift?" She asked wiping the corners of her mouth. "Yeah you did good." Daron said reaching in his pants pocket. He pulled out a donkey kong and pulled three crispy one-hundred dollar bills off and gave it to her. "This for me?" She asked.

"Yeah you said sexually and financially right?" Daron asked. "Thank you Daron." She said hugging him and kissed him on the cheek. She got out and walked up the porch. She turned around and waved. He waved back and drove off.

Kevin felt good. He didn't even want none of the money. It was trump change. The kilos didn't sound bad though. Kevin had traded his DTS in for Escalade. He kept it black and put some bang in there. He left the factory rims on there because he wasn't going to keep it for long. "A Solo roll that blunt up." Kevin total him. Him and Solo got cooler. Even though Solo wasn't in the game he still fucked with him. "So you ain't heard from Dre." Solo asked him. "Naw, all I heard was he was trying to go to school. But he aight. Kevin said. "What's up with that bitch ass nigga Daron." "That bitch ass nigga wanted out on the deal because he didn't have enough heart. He played it cool with lil bro. He was holding him down but when it was time for Dre to come home he wanted to step up and be 'Big Brother.' I don't understand. When I told Daron how much money he was going to get he was in but when shit started to hit the fan, he turned on me." "I knew he wasn't right. I just didn't say nothing." Solo said rolling up the blunt. After Kevin and Solo smoked the blunt he dropped Solo off at his crib on Linwood. Kevin was still trying his best to get Selina to move in with him, but she wasn't buying it. Before this year was out, Selina was going to be living with him, he didn't care what she said.

Daron had checked his phone he saw that he had three missed calls. Two from Suga and one from Dre. He tried to call Suga back but she didn't answer. Dre probably didn't want nothing so he didn't return the call. Daron was worried cause Suga usually didn't call twice in a row. He

179

hopped on the freeway and sped to the shop. She probably wasn't feeling to good. Now he started thinking about if she was in labor. When he got on 7 mile he noticed a bunch of red and blue flashing lights where his store was at. He started to panic when he pulled up he seen yellow tape around the glass door of his shop. "What the fuck going on?" Daron yelled hopping out his car. "Stop right there sir." One of the officers told him. "I own this place." He yelled. "There was a shooting here and a armed robbery." The officer said. "Yeah someone named Diamond Reese was shot and is in critical condition." The officer said. "Do you know what hospital they at?" "I'm pretty sure their at Grace." The officer said. Daron hopped in his Benz and sped off. Daron banged on the dashboard screaming no. He made it to the hospital in five minutes. He parked his car illegally and ran into the hospital. "Where is Michelle Reese?" He asked the lady behind the counter. "Are you family?" She asked. "I'm her fucking husband." He said lying. Security was now coming in his direction. "It's Okay." She told the security guard. "She's in emergency with a cousin." The lady behind the desk said. The security guards opened the emergency doors so he could go in. Daron walked down the long hallway until he saw Suga. "Oh my God. I thought I was never going to see you again." Suga said standing up and hugging Daron. "They shot Diamond baby." Sugar cried out. He looked over at Diamond she was breathing through tubes. "Is she going be alright?" He asked. "The doctor said she'll have to stay because they're not sure if she is capable of breathing on her own." Suga said looking at Diamond. "Baby are you all-right?" "Yes, I was so scared. They shut her Daron, right in front of me." She said hugging him again. "Don't worry about it, we're gonna find out who did this."

CHAPTER 24

The next day I was stepping off the plane. The air was still the same. My parole officer was cool. He let me come up here because I told him what had happened. I had called Wes to come pick me up. When Wes pulled up he was in the ol' school smoke grey Caprice with 20inch spokes. "Damn man you stay in something." I said getting in. "Nigga I you ain't talking you down there whippin that 4.6. "Shit, what up with you?" Wes asked. "Shit man, I know you heard what happened?" "Yeah that's fucked up and the crazy part is they don't even know who did it. Whoever did it hit a major lick. I think it was seven or eight keys, over fifty racks, and some pounds of regos." Wes said. "Straight up?" I asked "No lie." Wes said while hopping on the freeway. "Damn, that's crazy. Did ol' girl survivor?" I asked. "I don't know for sure." Wes said. "You gotta take me to go get a rental." I said. "My girl got a dog ass hook up on the rental tip. What kind of whip you looking for?" Wes asked. "Man something simple." Wes grabbed his cell phone so he could call his little chick. "I'm gonna call my girl right now." Wes said while dialing the number. "A bay, my homeboy need a whip hold on….Something fast, truck, what?" Wes asked me. "Man it don't matter." I told him. "Get 'em that new Yukon Denali…….All-right bay…I love you too." Wes hung up the cell phone. "She going have it later on. How long you gonna be here?" Wes asked. "Man I don't know 'cause I ain't no tellin what's going happen." I said. "Don't even worry about it. I got it." Wes said. "So what the hell you been up to?" I asked. "Same shit fam, I ain't been back to that hoe ass county doe." West said laughing. 'How yo girl doing?" "She straight, she didn't want me to come up here, but it was a wrap." I said. "My girl ain't gonna have that

truck until like five o'clock and it's only two right now So what chu tryna do?" Was asked. "Hold on let me call Esco to see what's up." I said. Esco told us to swing by. "You been kicking it with Esco?" I asked. "I'll slide by there every now and then but not on no everyday thing." "Straight up?" I said. "He cool doe, you know I don't fly with that gang banging shit." Wes said. "Shit I don't either." When we got to Detroit, it still looked the same. It was getting hot. Hoes was out and schemimg and niggas was out plotting. We pulled up in front of Esco house. Ain't shit changed. Niggas was still deep in front of his crib. I made sure I left my chain and glasses at the crib because niggas wasn't shit. I still had my watch though. "Esco in the crib homey." One of the Latino niggas said. Me and Wes went inside we didn't see Esco. It wasn't too many people inside but it was full of weed smoke. Esco came out the back with a blunt in his hand. He took a puff and left the smoke in his mouth. "You still on papers homie?" He asked while letting smoke out his nose. "Fuck yeah." I said. Esco past the blunt to one of the females on the couch. "Follow me to the back. You didn't wanna hit that did you honey?" Esco asked Wes. "Naw I'm straight, good looking though." Wes said. We followed Esco to the back and went out the back door. "What's up homie?" He said giving me some dep. "Shit, what up with it?" I asked. "Same shit homie? What up with you homie?" He asked Wes giving him some dep. "Man slow motion." Wes said. "I heard what happened to your home boy. You got any idea who might have did it?" Esco asked. "Naw fam. Ain't no telling who my bro beefin with. I haven't even talked to him yet." I said. "You need anything, pistols, vest, some of the homies to ride?" Esco asked. "Naw, I'm good fam. I really appreciate it though." "Anytime you need anything, you make sure I'm the first one you come to." Esco said

patting me on the back. We left and went to Wes crib. He had moved with his girl on Joy Rd. When he get out he looked at me stupid. "Nigga get out, you ain't no stranger." Wes said shutting the door. I just laughed and get out the car. "Nigga yo girl might be trippin." I said. "My girl ain't gon say shit." Wes said opening up side door. "Monica we got company so put some clothes on." Wes said opening up the door. We walk down the basement steps. "This my shit down here." Wes said. His shit was decked out. A pool table, a Pac-man arcade game, a big screen TV, with the X-box hooked up to it. Not to mention a small bar. "Why the hell you got all this down here?" 'Nigga 'cause I don't like being upstairs." "Wesley why you ain't come up here?" A female voice yelled from upstairs. "Girl why you yelling?" Wes yelled back. "Boy don't be tryna show off in front of your company." A dark skin bad chick said coming down the steps. When she got all the way down the steps she was even colder. She had short hair, real short hair. Wes was probably trying to show off but she wasn't having it. "Girl why you gotta come down here?" "Cause this is our house. OUR HOUSE." She repeated herself. Wes was turning red. It was funny as hell too. "Are you going to introduce me to your friend?" She asked. "Dre this my girl, Monica. Monica this is my home boy Dre." Wes said. "So your Dre huh?" I said yeah. "Wesley has been trying to go visit you but I ain't havin it cause he don't know how to act. He don't call or nothing. All he wanna do is go to the strip club and blow his money. He got a chick that will strip for him for free but he don't wanna see that. Do you go to the strip club?" She asked. Man she was blunt as hell. "Naw, not at all." Wes looked at me like I was stupid. "Well it was nice meeting you Dre." "You too." I said. "What are you gonna do with that truck?" She asked. "Where is it at?" Wes asked. "It's in the garage." Monica said. "All-right baby."

Wes said kissing her on the lips. "Umm, I'm bout to go pick up a few things, do you need anything?" Monica asked. "Naw, I'm good. Oh them Jordans coming out this Saturday, see if you could get 'em for me." Wes said. "That's it?" "Yes baby." Wes said. "The keys on the mantle." Monica said going up the stairs in her hoop shorts and her extra big T-shirt. After a few games of March Madness, I had to leave 'cause it was getting close to five. "I gotta get up outta here." I said getting up. Wes went upstairs and grabbed the keys to the truck. When he came back down, he threw me the keys. "You don't owe me nothing, just bring it back when you ready to go back to Arkansas." West said. "Man I'm gonna throw you something regardless, so don't even be on no bullshit." I said. "I'll throw all that shit in the air." Wes said laughing. We went outside and opened the garage door. When it opened it was a forest green Denali with 22inch Dubs. "Man I'm goin be not as hell driving this." I said looking at the truck. "Man quit trippin, you said something normal right?" Wes asked. "Nigga this ain't normal." I said looking at the big boy grill in the front. "So what chu want me to tell Monica you want something else?" Wes said. "Naw I'm good, good looking doe man. You goin have these young niggas out her tryna kill me." I said. "Man you good." Wes said handing me the keys. I hopped in the truck looking down at Wes. "Man anytime you get in trouble let me know." Wes said. "All-right fam." I said starting the truck up. I pulled out and headed to Daron's shop on 7 mile. Man it was so many heads turning when I was stopping at the red lights.

When I pulled up I seen that the shop was closed. I called Daron but he didn't answer. I ended up calling Suga. She answered and told me she was at the hospital with her

cousin. I told her I was on my way. It took me a couple of minutes to get there but it took even longer to find a parking space. I went inside and Suga was in the lobby waiting on me. Her stomach was poking out a little and her cheeks were fat. "Hey Dre." Suga said hugging me. "Hey Suga, you aight?" "Yeah I guess I'm alright." She said. We went upstairs where Diamond was being treated. "How is she?" I said. "The doctor said she'll be alright but she'll be here for a minute because she lost a lot of blood." She said. "Where Daron at?" I asked. "Probably tryna find out who did this." Suga said. "What happened?" I asked. She gave me a funny look. "It's all-right you can tell me." I said holding her hand. "It happened so quick. All I know is me and Diamond was talking about new movies that just came out and all I seen was three niggas walk in with guns. They told us to get on the ground. The customers that were in there, they made them get behind the counter with me and Diamond. One went to the back and the other two watched us. The nigga came back with a big duffle bag full of money, dope, and weed." Suga said. "What?" I asked. "It's a long story, the two dudes that was watching us was talking shit. He asked Diamond what she was looking at and she said something smart, so he told her to stand up and when she did he shot her and I ran to her side and he pointed the gun at me but the other two told him to stop because I was pregnant. They left out and I called the police. When I tried to call Daron he didn't answer so I tried again. Still no answer, so I called you. Dre I was so scared. They questioned me for the longest at the station." She said hugging me. "When I tried to call that nigga he ain't never pick up. Where's his new shop at?" I asked. "On the East side in the mini mall on 7 mile and Gratiot. He closed the shop in Dearborn because of the incident the happen at the shop. "Who's L?" I asked. "That's Uncle

185

Phil's son, he just moved to Michigan not to long ago." She said. "Do L got a cell phone?" I asked. "I don't even know it." "Have you talked to Carla?" "Naw, she been with her boyfriend. I think they living with each other." "How's Aunty Vicki?" "She all-right, she's worried about Daron, praying that he don't do nothing stupid." "Well I'm about to stop by there and see how she's doing." "Love you Dre." Suga said hugging me. "Love you too sugar." I said. Diamond was still sleep when I left. I was on my way to Highlight Park to see my moms. I didn't have no cd's so I had listen to WJLB FM 98. I missed the shit out of WJLB. Arkansas radio station was alright but it ain't have shit on WJLB. The windows were tinted and I was glad. I didn't want nobody recognizing me. When I got to HP, it felt good. I loved Highland Park but a lot of people were confused with loving yo hood. You can always love your hood but the hood will never love you. It wasn't to many people outside because it was kind of chilly outside. When I pulled in Aunty Vicki driveway, I seen her Escalade parked on the street. I got out and knocked on the door. "Who is it?" I heard Aunty Vicki yell. "It's me ma." I said. "Hold on baby, here I come right now." She said. She opened the door. "Heyyy baby." Aunty Vicki said hugging me. "Hey ma." I said. "How you been, you like it down South?" She asked. "Yeah, it's all-right, kind of hot but I'll get used to it." I said. I walked in and smelt chicken. "What chu in here cooking?" I asked. "Oh, I'm making some barbeque chicken." ,She said. "You be throwing down don't you?" I asked. "Boy quit it out. I been cooking like this since you were little." Auntie Vicki said playfully hitting me in the back. "Where Uncle Phil at?" I asked. "He at work. Speaking of work, do you have a job?" She asked. "Not at this time but I'm getting ready to go to real-estate school, I just wanna get off papers first." "That's good

baby. I'm glad you're doing something positive. How's my cupcake?" she asked. "Zaria all-right, she didn't really approve of me coming up here but I had to check on my family." "Yeah, how's Chris doing?" "Oh he doing real good. He's growing up. He'll be starting preschool this year." "That's good." "How's Daron doing?" I asked. "I can't say. He's driving me crazy Dre. He's doing stuff that's illegal. He's changed. Aunty Vicki said starting the Cry. Daron was her only child. She loved Daron to death. I hugged her. "It's going to be all-right. I'm going to talk to him." "Please, for me." She said sniffling. "Do you know where he would be?" "He's probably over Levon's house over there on Lafayette. You want the address?" She asked. "Yeah because he's not answering his phone." "Hold on for a minute." Aunty Vicki said going into the other room she came back and gave me the address. I gave her a hug and told her everything was going to be alright. She hugged me and I dipped out. I had to see what was up. I called Carla but I got her voice mail, so I left a message. Why the hell wasn't nobody answering their phones? I drove downtown to the address that I Aunty Vicki gave me. It took me about thirty minutes to get there and find the complex. I got out and knocked on the door. "Who is it?"

Zaria couldn't believe Dre had left to go back to Detroit. She was so upset. She couldn't get too depressed because she didn't want to have a miscarriage. It had got to a point where Chris was always over Kim's house. Even though Chandra was younger than Zaria, she still hung out with her when she turned 18. Zaria had bought her a Tiffany necklace for her birthday. Mya was too young to hang out but she'll still be around but Kim wasn't having that. Chandra was like a little sister to Zaria. Chandra didn't have too much. She wasn't used to having things but Zaria

changed all that. She helped her get her money right. She also helped Kim with Olivia and Mya. She even took Kim out with her a couple times. Kim wasn't the party type. She said she stopped going out when she had Mya. "Girl you gotta get out more." Zaria told her. "Girl Please, you ain't going be doing nothing when that baby pop out." Kim said laughing. "Girl I don't know what I'll do without you. God is good Zaria." "Yes he is. I'm just trying to get Dre to believe in him because he's completely lost." Zaria said. "Don't give up on him honey. You know I'm enrolling Olivia in this summer program. Do you want to sign Chris up?" Kim asked. "What kind of program is it?" "It's for a preschoolers and kids that's in kindergarten. Teachers teach them how to read and write. It's like a summer school. "Sure, how much is it?" "Hold on, let me get the brochure." Kim said. Looking on her messy coffee table. "Here it is. It's $275.00 for the whole summer." Kim said. "That's not bad." Zaria said while looking at the brochure. "When dose it start?" Zaria asked. "It should be in the back." Kim said. "June 19th to August 8 huh?" "Yup." Kim said. I guess I gotta check with Dre first. There's no telling what he has in store for Chris. But thanks for the information. I gotta go, I'll be back to pick Chris up at 8:00." "All-right drive safe." Kim said. "All-right Kim." Zaria said leaving out to go to her doctor's appointment. She was going to get a ultrasound. She was 18 weeks pregnant. She knew she was having a girl but she wanted to surprise Dre. After her doctor's appointment, she had went to the shop to check on it. Chandra and Mya was there. "How was your doctors appointment?" Mya asked. "It was good." Zaria said putting down her purse. "Did you tell Dre you were having a girl and did you give her a name yet?" Mya asked. "No I haven't told Dre. I'm going to surprise him and I'm thinking about naming her Sa-riyah." "That's a beautiful name."

Chandra said. "I see it's kind of slow today. Where all your friends at?" Zaria asked. We don't know, we just left school and came right to the shop right before you left to go drop Chris off at our house." Chandra said. "I'm saying it's Friday, don't they supposed to be out shopping?" Zaria said. "Well maybe there at the mall. You know everybody goes to the mall. That's where people go to get numbers. Ain't nobody bought to be in here trying to get no number." Chandra said. "Well I'm glad they went to the mall, 'cause ain't nobody bout to be in here walking around pulling numbers from each other." Zaria said. A couple of customers came in so Chandra took care of it while Zaria went to the back. She tried to call Dre but he didn't answer. She was starting to stress. She couldn't believe this nigga had her like this. Why I let that nigga leave?" Zaria kept asking herself over and over. "You alright in there?" Chandra asked knocking on the door. "Yeah, I'm alright just thinking about the baby." She lied 'cause she didn't feel like talking. "Alright let me know if there's anything I could do okay?" Chandra said. "Okay Chandra."

CHAPER 25

"Damn baby, you gonna let me hit or what?" Daron asked her. "It's two of y'all. I don't get down like that." The high school girl said. "That's my brother doe." She looked over at L. He is kind of cute." She said. Minutes later Daron was blowing her back out. Him and Levon had been fucking all the high school females after school. They were in the back room fucking while Levon waited outside the room because she said she didn't want two niggas in the room together. Daron didn't even nut yet and L was banging on the door. "Man come on. You always go first." L said. He was 25 years old but he acted like a teenager. Daron couldn't understand how he had all these hoes acting like that. L opened the door and just walk right in the room. The chick didn't even say nothing. L pulled his dick out and put it towards her face. Daron was still hitting it from the back. She grabbed his dick with one hand and put it in her mouth while she balanced herself with her other hand. Daron wasn't feeling it so he stopped 'cause it didn't feel right. It was cool when they were young, but they were grown now, so he left out while L and ol' girl stayed in the room. Daron wasn't mad because this was a everyday thing. He lit a blunt and watched fear factor. Twenty minutes later L was coming out the room buttoning up his pants. "Damn took you long enough." Daron said getting up and going back to the room. "You ain't gone leave the blunt?" L asked. "Hell naw, row yo own shit." "That's some bullshit." L said plugging up the PS2. He heard ol' girl in the room moaning loud as hell. L knew she was faking but fuck it he already had his fun. L heard a knock on the door so he paused the game and said hold on. It probably was another chick trying to get dicked down.

190

"Who is it?" L asked. "Dre is Daron here." L looked through the peep hole to make sure. It was Dre. He had only seen a picture of him but never met him. L opened the door and let him in. "What up doe? I'm L. "what up? Where that nigga at?" I asked. He in the back. I'll tell him you here." L said going to get Daron. L knocked on the door. "Aye, somebody here for you." L said. "Man get the fuck on." Daron said from the other side of the door. "Man Dre here. He in the front waiting for you right now." L said. L heard a bunch of moving around after he said Dre was here. Daron opened the door a little. "Who you say?" Daron whispered. "Nigga you heard me, Dre." "Where he at?" "He in the front." L said. "Hold on." Daron said shutting the door. When he opened it he had some hoop short on and a wife beater. Daron went to the front room while L walked in the room and seen ol' girl hands handcuffed to the headboard and of the bed bent over. Her ass up in the air facing L. "Is that you Daron?" She asked. "Mmm mm." L said rubbing his hands together shutting the door. "What up bro?" I asked Daron. "Shit, What up wit up?" Daron said hugging me. "Man what the fuck you was doing?" I asked. "Shit." He said. We both sat down on the couch. I heard loud moans coming from the back. "Who is that?" I asked. "Oh, that's L girl. You remember Uncle Phil son don't you?" "I think so." I said. The moans got even louder. "Man we gonna get up outta here." Daron said going to the back. Daron opened the door and saw L balls deep in ol' girl ass. He didn't say nothing he just grabbed his keys and jacket. He came back in the front room with some sandals on. "You ready?" Daron asked me. "Yeah." I said. We walked outside and Daron asked me when did I get there? "Today." I said. "Suga told you where I was at?" "Naw, mom's did." I said. "Where your car?" Daron asked. "Right there." I said pointing to the Denali. "You riding

191

real good." Daron said. "It ain't nothing but a rental."
"Nigga that ain't no damn rental and why you ain't tell me
you was coming up here? I could of had you a whip and
everything." "Man I wasn't concerned about none of that,
Suga called me so I came." I said. "So you heard huh?"
Daron asked. "Yeah bro, it fucked me up too." I said. "You
wanna take a ride?" Daron asked me. "Where you trying to
go?" I asked. "Nigga just come on." Daron said. He headed
towards his white 600 Benz. "This you." I asked. "Yeah I
had to step my game up." Daron said getting in. I got in on
the passenger side. "All leather huh?" "Yeah nigga, it's a
2001." Daron said pulling off. It felt good to be with my
brother. "So you got any idea who did this shit?" I asked.
"Nah I ain't got nothing or heard nothing." Daron said.
"Mom's told me you was out here on some BS. What's up
with that? I asked. "Man she went tripping lately. She
keeps saying if I was there they probably would of killed
me." "Man she right bro. You know she ain't lying. What's
up with the shit they took?" I asked. I didn't tell him that
sugar told me what they took. Wes had told me too. "They
just took a little over 100,000. It's cool doe." Daron said it
like it was nothing. I never thought Daron would lie to me.
Maybe he didn't want me to know he was selling drugs. But
it still wasn't like him to lie to me, but I didn't say nothing
about it. "What chu mean just a $100,000? That's a lot of
money bro." I said. "I'll get it back 'cause somebody name
gone pop up, believe that." Daron said while driving
gripping the wood grain steering wheel. I could see the
change in him, it was weird. I never seen him like this.
"Where Big Bo and Lil Lou at?" I asked. "Lil Lou, Big Bo
and their little cousin Rah-rah looking for them niggas."
Daron said while stopping at Burger King. Welcome to
Burger King, how may I help you?" The female said over
the speaker. "Let me get a King size #4. You want

something?" Daron asked me. "Yeah get me a 7, King size it too." I said. "And let me get a number 7 King size." "What type of drinks sir? She asked. "Let me get a Sprite and." Daron said looking at me. "Pink lemonade." I said "And a pink lemonade." Daron said your total is 9.89. please drive to the next window." She said. "Man I'm hungry as hell." Daron said pulling up to the next window. "That will be 9.89 sir." The pretty cashier said. Daron gave her a twenty-dollar bill. She handed him his change. "Keep it, put it in your tip box." Daron said. She blushed. "You too beautiful to be working here miss." Daron said. "You can call me Ashley." The cashier said. "I'm looking for a couple of females to work at my clothing store. Here's my card, call me if you're interested. She took it and put it in her top pocket. She shut the small doors. Our food was ready in minutes. She opened the small doors and handed Daron the food. "Thank you, Ashley." Daron said driving off. "Nigga what was all that about?" I asked. "What?" Daron said. "All that flirting, Suga a kill yo ass nigga." I said making it into a joke. "Man ain't nobody flirting nigga, we need some workers at the shop." "Yeah, right some workers." I said being funny. I grab my food out. "Nigga what chu doing?" Daron asked. "What?" I asked. "Nigga we not bout to be eating in here. The park right up the street." Daron said being serious. "All right Mr. clean." I said putting the chickn sandwich back. We parked and hopped out and sat on a nearby bench. "You got anything to tell me bro?" I asked. "Naw, I'm good." Something was wrong and I was gonna find out. "How long you goin up here?" "Not for long, I just had to check on my fam." I said. "How's my lil cousin doing?" "She all-right I said. "And Chris?" He asked. "He straight. He about to start school soon." I said. "You seen Carla lately?" I asked. "You know what, I ain't seen her since we came and visited

193

yaw." Daron said. "Straight up." "Yeah, she bent in her own lil' world." "You seen or heard from Kevin?" I asked. I seen a spark in his eyes. It was something I never seen Daron do. "Nope, ain't seen 'em or heard about 'em." Daron said while sipping his Sprite. "You sure you don't wanna get nothing off your chest?" I asked. Daron felt fucked up. He knew Dre loved him like a brother but he couldn't tell him. Dre would probably kill him, so he made a lie. "Bro I ain't ready to be a father." Daron said. "We both gotta step our game up. We don't got time to be bullshittin. We grown now it's time bro. You bout to get married, I'm bout to get married. We got women at home that love us to death. You feel me?" I said. "I feel you bro. It's just so much shit going on. Niggas plottin bro, niggas jealous. I ain't did nothing to nobody." Daron said. "Everything happens for a reason. It could of been something you did ten years ago, five years ago. Fuck that shit bro. Like you said it ain't nothing but some change. Don't let yo pride get you killed or in prison." I told him. "I feel you bro. It ain't nothing but trouble in Detroit. "Niggas is born haters." Daron said. "Michigan period." I said "You right too bro." Daron said. After we finished eating, we hopped back in the whip and peeled off. "How you and Suga doing?" I asked. "Worrying." Daron said. "You can't be putting her through that while she pregnant. Man she'll fuck around and have a miscarriage." I said. Daron didn't even respond, he just kept driving. When we get back to L's crib I seen a young chick coming out the house walking funny. "Ol' girl look young as hell." I said. "She eighteen, she go to King high school." Daron said getting out the car. She waved at Daron. "You need a ride home?" Daron asked her. "Yeah, I appreciate it." The young girl said. "So where you staying?" Daron asked me. "I don't know yet but it'll probably be a rinky dink hotel." "Why don't you stay

194

here?" "Naw, I'm good it's a little too much going on over here." I said. "Whenever you change your mind let me know." "All-right bro." I said. "Love you bro." "Love you too." I said hopping in the truck. "Is that your other brother?" The young female asked. "Yeah that's my other brother." "He looks just like you." She said lying. "Yeah right." Daron said being sarcastic. "Are you ready?" Daron asked her. "Yeah I'm ready." She said. She hopped in and he drove off.

I was on my way to see my sister. I had called her to see if she was home. She told me to come on over. It was like 8:00 o'clock when I got to Southfield. I seen Carla's Lincoln in the driveway. Her house was small but it looked good though. I got out of knocked on the screen door. "It's open." Carla yelled. I walked in and everything was white. It was bright as hell. "Have a seat, make yourself comfortable. It should be some chicken fingers in the microwave." Carla yelled from the other room. "I'm good." I said. "Fine with me." she said coming out in some jogging pants and T-shirt. "Hey brodder." She said hugging me. "You look different now that you cut your hair." I said hugging her. "I know, you like?" She asked. "Yeah I guess." I said "Hater." She said let me go. "So how's Zaria and my nephew doing?" She asked. "They good. And you?" I asked. "Oh I'm fine. I couldn't ask for much. It'll be even better if the rest of the family was here with us." Carla said putting her down. "Yeah, that would be nice." So what brings you back to The Dirty glove?" She asked. "You ain't heard what happened to Daron store?" I asked. "Yeah, that's bold as hell. Did he find out who did it?" "No, I told him to leave it alone but I don't think he is. His pride is in the way." I said. "Is Suga alright?" "Yeah she good but her younger cousin Diamond still in the hospital." "I gotta call

195

Suga 'cause I know she going through a lot right now."
Carla said. "You heard anything about Kevin?" "Nope, I
ain't seen that nigga in so long. I don't keep up with him
anyway. I can't stand that nigga." Carla said. "Where your
boyfriend at?" I asked. "He at worked." "Where he work
at?" "Damn what's all this about? You trying to be a
detective?" Carla said. "I'm serious Carla. It's only me and
you. You my sister and I can worry about you." "Fine then.
He works at a detail shop. His uncle owns it but he's trying
to buy it from him." Carla said. "He treating you good?"
"Of course. I don't have time for no young niggas. He takes
good care of me." Carla said. "I just wanted to know if you
were straight. Well I gotta get up outta here sis." I said.
"Where you going, you only been here for a minute." Carla
said. "I got stuff to do. I'll be in contact with you." I said.
"Love you big head." She said. "Love you more." I said
leaving out the front door. I needed somewhere to stay. I
remember Esco saying if I needed anything he would come
through. It was 9:00. I called Esco and told him I needed a
favor. He told me to ride through there.

Kevin was spending more time with Selina now.
Taking her out to eat, shopping and all. He needed to get
her trust back. "Girl you getting big." Kevin said. "Yeah,
'cause I'm carrying yo big head baby in here." She said
laughing. Kevin kissed her on the lips and told her he loved
her. "I love you too." Selina said. "I'll be back later on, I
gotta go check on the shop." Kevin said helping Selina out
the truck. When Kevin pulled out the driveway he didn't
notice black Intrepid just sitting on the corner. Kevin drove
up the block and stopped at the stop sign. Kevin didn't even
see it coming.

Freaky Rell was tired of following this nigga. "Man
make sure you don't let this nigga see us." K-dog said.

"Man shut the fuck up." Rell said. "Nigga I say we just chop this bitch up right now, fuck that hoe in the car. She know what type of nigga he is." Rah-rah said."Naw man, Daron said leave her outta of it." K-dog said. Kevin was pulling in the driveway. "Keep going, we goin wait at the corner." K-dog said. "Yeah I got it." Rell said. "Look she getting out." Rah-rah said. "Hand me the choppa." K-dog said. "Naw nigga I'm using this." Rah-rah said. "Nigga grab the Tech and quit playing." Rell said. Rah-rah gave the choppa to K-dog and grab the tech. "Here he come, here he come." Rah-rah said. "Yaw ready?" Rell said. "Yeah." K-dog said. The black Escalade stopped at the stop sign. They rolled up on the side of the truck with blue bandanas around their mouths. K-dog was out the sunroof letting the choppa off. Rah-rah was in the back letting the tech spit. The truck tried to pull off but the truck crashed into a school fence. Rell pulled off leaving the Escalade rattled with holes.

Kevin was always paranoid so he wasn't never caught slipping but today they had caught him. When he seen the Intrepid pull up on the side he hurried up and jumped all the way in the back while the truck was still in drive. Kevin managed to make it all the way in the back. Without being hit. The shots kept coming. After he felt the truck crash he didn't hear no more shots. He stayed down for a second but then thought about if the dudes was going to open the doors so he looked out the tinted windows and they were gone. He would of been dead if he still would of had that DTS. Kevin opened the door and ran up the alley to Selina's house.

197

CHAPTER 26

The next day they were all chilling at L's apartment. "Did you get the nigga?" L asked. "Man I don't know. I know he ain't see us though." Rell said. "That nigga K-dog was shooting all stupid." Rah-rah said. "Man shut the fuck up." k-dog said. "I knew I should've had Big Bo and Lil Lou do it." Daron said. "Yeah he would of made it to the 10:00 o'clock news tonight." Big Bo said. "Yeah whatever." Rah-rah I said. "So what's up with Dre?" K-dog asked. "Ain't shit up. He on some peace shit right now, talking about leave it alone. Fuck that, soon as I find out who did this shit it's closed curtains." Daron said. "At least the nigga showed up." K-dog said. "Yeah, he did, but he showed up playing the pussy role. It wasn't on no let's go get these niggas bro or where them niggas at? When it was time for me to ride I rode." Daron said. "The nigga still on papers?" Lil Lou said. "Yeah." Daron said. "Suga still at the hospital with Diamond?" L asked. "Yeah she still there. She said the doctors told her Diamond doing good and she's recovering." Daron said. "That's good." Rell said. "Light that blunt up." Lil Lou said.

I was tired as hell. Esco let me stay upstairs. He had a two family flat. These niggas partied every night. I wanted to lay low. I didn't want Kevin to know I was here. I called Zaria first thing in the morning. "Hey baby...I miss you....you know I'm staying out of trouble girl.... How's Chris doing?.....When he wakes up tell him I love him....Naw they didn't find out who did, but your cousin is trying his hardest to find out....Suga all-right, she's worried about Daron. I talked to Aunty Vicki too, she's depressed also because she thinks Daron is going to get in some trouble....Yeah make sure you call them because they need somebody to talk to....I don't know when I'll be back but

I'll be back soon 'cause fucking around with Daron a have me back locked up.....I'm telling the truth Daron has changed for real....Yeah, but I gotta see how the situation gone play out. Daron was there for me so I gotta be there for him.....I love you too, bye bye." I hung up my cell phone and hopped in the shower and threw some clean fresh clothes on. I didn't bring much up here. I had brought a couple of throw-back jersey that Zaria bought me. I threw my Larry Bird Celtics jersey on with some black Gibauds. I only had brought two pair of shoes. My Pradas and white low top Air Force ones. I put my forces on and went downstairs. "Damn homey, it's 8:00 in the morning, Where you headed?" Esco asked. He was woke and walking around the house. "I'm a early bird. You been to the joint before so you know how it is. I gotta take care of some business. You need anything?" I asked. "Nah homy, I'm good but good looking out." Esco said sitting on the couch. I had parked the truck all the way in the back so nobody would steal it. Esco had about five pit bulls in the backyard. They was out all night, he probably would lock them up in a day. They were loud as hell. Barking early in the morning. I knew Esco neighbors couldn't stand him. I let the truck warm up for a minute. I got out and went back in. Esco was still on the couch. I went back upstairs to chill for a minute. when I get up there I notice a bunch of pictures of a young Latino chick everywhere around the house. I probably didn't notice it because I was sleepy. She looked so familiar but I couldn't tell where I seen her at. I went back downstairs to ask Esco if that was his sister. "A Esco is that your sister?" I asked. "Yeah, that's my little sister homey. It's only two of us. She used to stay up there. I put pictures up there so I wouldn't forget her." Esco said. "She passed away?" I asked. "Naw homey, she just left and never came back. I talk to her every now and then but I can't convince her to come back. I miss her so much." Esco said. "Don't beat yourself up about it. Don't let me come

back and you hangin from the ceiling fan." I said making it into a joke. Esco laughed. "Man get the hell out of here." Esco said still laughing. I walked out the back door and hopped in the truck. I tried to call Wes but he didn't answer. I didn't even know what I was doing back in Michigan. I had to leave, I wonder where Kevin was. I couldn't wait to catch him. His days were numbered. When I tried to call Daron nobody answered. I called Suga she was still at the hospital. I had stopped by the hospital and bought some food for her. Diamond was doing much better. I left and tried to call Wes again. "Hello, what up doe?...shit, riding around bored as hell…. All-right I'm on my way." I hung up my cell phone and drove to Wes crib. When I got there Wes Caprice was parked in the front. His girl Escalade was in the driveway, so I parked in front of his neighbors house. I got out knocked on the door. Wes girl Monica had answered it. She was talking on the phone when she let me in. I walk right in and it was clothes everywhere. She had to be a booster. She looked out the door to see if anybody was behind me. She hung up her cell. "Hey Dre, Westley a be down in a minute. I like that jersey, how much did it cost?" she asked. "I'm not sure, my wife bought it for me. I'm guessing she paid like around $300.00." I said. "300.00? That's too much. I got 'em for $250.00. I gotta couple of throwback jersey dresses for your wife too." Monica said. Wes came downstairs. "What chu tryna do Monica hustle my mans?" Wes asked. "Naw I seen him with that throwback on and he spent $300.00." Monica said pleading her case.

"$300.00?" Wes' blurted out. "Yeah, that's to much or something?" I asked. "Fuck yeah!" Wes' said. "My wife down south selling the shit out em'." I said. "Well whenever you up here my girl got everything you want. She tryna get her hands on them Gucci forces but she been bull shittin'." Wes' said. "I ain't bull shittin' soon as I get em', you got am', so don't even trip." Monic said. "That jersey nice though, I got a couple of em', matter of fact I might as well throw mines on too." wes' said going upstairs, "Sit down, you don't have to stand up." Monic said. "Shit ain't no where to sit," I said looking around. Monic came over to where I was and moved the shoe boxes on the floor. "Now it's a spot." She said. Wes' came back downstairs with a Lakers jersey on. His shit was long as hell. I never thought about it cause I thought it would look tacky but he was rocking the shit out of it. He had some wheat Tims on with it. "Yeah this that Jerry West boy. This my first time wearing it." Wes said. "That bitch cold." I said. "Where you bout to go?" Monic asked. "I'm bout to go hang." Wes' said grabbing his keys. "Make you call me." Monica said. "All-right baby I'm goin' let Dre park the truck in the garage okay? Wes asked. "Yeah whatever, you just make sure you call me." Monic said. "All-right baby I love you." Wes said leaving. "Love you too." Wes'

pulled Monica Escalade out the driveway so I could put the Denali in the garage and I hopped out. "You ready?" Wes asked. "Yeah." I said. "Huh, here go the keys to the Caprice, you driving." Wes' said. "Straight up?" "Yeah nigga." I hopped in and started it up. The engine was quiet. I ain't put no 350 in there, I left the 305 in there." Wes said. "So where we going?" I don't know, it's Saturday. Where you wanna go?" Wes asked. "Shit lets go to to the Isle." I said. "Belle Isle?" Wes' asked "Yeah it's kind of windy but I bet it's slammin'." "All- right it's all you." Wes said giving me a cd. I put it in and Wes turned it up. The shit came in knocking. "What this?" I asked. "This that new Lil' Jon' and the East side boys." Wes said bobbing his head. "Put it on 4." Wes said. "Bia bia, bia bia...Bia bia bia bia well you scared, you scared, you scared, you scared, stop actin' like a bitch you scared, you scared." "This shit pounding fam'." "I'm surprised you ain't never heard it. You down south and shit." Wes' said. We was clowning.

When we got to the Belle Isle bridge we started seeing so many hoes. We wasn't even on the island yet. "I told you this bitch goin' be poppin'." I said. "Nigga this bitch always like this." Wes said. "Man I ain't been down here in so long. I remember I was scared as hell of the giant slide. My moms use to always be like go ahead, don't be

202

scared. Your brothers and sisters are gonna be right there. I always ended up between my sister legs sliding down the slide." I said "Man I don't even remember the last time I went down that slide. It had to be years fam'." Wes' said. We rode around the isle for a minute. Wes' was scopin' out hoes. I wasn't paying none of them no mind. "Bro', you gotta get chu a next-tel fuck that sprint. You won't even have to call you could charp me." Wes said. "I ain't with all that new technology shit. Give me a regular cell phone and I'm good." "Whatever nigga."

Chapter 27

Kevin was mad as hell. Selina wasn't there when he ran back to her house after they shot his truck up. He went in through the back door and called Skeebo and told em' to come and pick him up. He wanted to tell him what happened but he didn't because he didn't trust the phones. Kevin couldn't even sleep. Selina didn't come in last night. He was now worrying about her. It was nine in the morning. "Where the hell she at." He said to himself. He heard somebody pulling up in the driveway. He looked out and seen her blue Cherokee. He sat down on the couch in the dark and waited for her to come in. He heard her keys rattling in the door and she opened the door. When she shut it she turned around. "Where have you been?" Kevin asked. Selina pulled out a chrome hand gun and pointed it at Kevin. "Who the fuck are you and what the hell are you doing in my house?" Selina asked while pointing the pistol at him. "Put the gun girl, you act like you didn't recognize my voice." Kevin said. "Kev baby?" Selina said lowering the pistol. She cut the light on and seen his face scratched up and cuts on his arm. "Did you get into a fight or something?" She asked. "This not about me. Where were you last night?" Kevin asked. "Since you wanna know so bad I was taking care of my aunt. She's very sick so I

stayed with her last night cause I knew you weren't coming back." Selina said putting her things down. Kevin was just staring at her. "Well, what happened to you?" Selina asked. "Nothing." Kevin said. Where the hell yo' truck at?" Selina asked. "Somebody tried to kill me yesterday." "What?" Selina screamed. "Yeah on yo' block. They shot my truck up while I was in it, but I managed to get out and run back to your house." "Did you see who it was?" "Naw only thing I saw was blue bandanas around their faces." Kevin said. Selina walked over to Kevin and hugged him but he didn't hug her back. "What's wrong?" She asked. "We gotta leave this house. All this shit, just leave it. We don't need none of it. We can donate it all." Kevin said. "Kevin you sure they didn't have the wrong person?" She asked. "You know how stupid you sound." Kevin said. "Don't talk to me like that. You been out here doin' all this dirt and it caught up with you, don't be mad at me for your faults." Selina said leaving the front room and going to the bedroom. She slammed her door and turned on her music. "Damn why I do that." Kevin said to his self getting up and going into the bedroom with her. "Baby I'm sorry." Kevin said. "You don't have to many sorry's. left Kevin. You putting me through hell. You don't ask me if my aunt was all-right, you don't even ask if I'm all- right. You need to grow up

Kevin. You're not in your twenties no more." Selina said taking off her clothes. "You right baby?" "I know I'm right." Selina said cutting him off. You couldn't win with her no matter what you said or what you did. She always wanted the last word, that's why Kevin loved her cause no other woman would even think about talking to him like that, "All- right, I'm goin' have my home boy come pick me up." Kevin said. "So you not goin' stay with me? That's the shit I'm talking about. All you wanna do is rip and run the streets." Selina said cutting him off. "All you wanna do is argue. I don't wanna hear that all day. Somebody just tried to kill me and you talkin' bout spendin' some time with you? The shit not only happened, but it happened on your block." Kevin snapped back. Selina had tears in her eyes. "Baby I just don't wanna lose you. You put me through so much bullshit, it don't make no sense. You gotta son on the way you shouldn't even be doing what you are doing. If I didn't care about you I wouldn't be telling you this Kevin. You the one I love. I ain't out here fucking every nigga I see. I got my own shit Kevin. Money is not the issue. I wanna spend the rest of my life with you. I'm really having doubts about that." Selina said crying. Kevin hugged her. "I know baby, I know. I just don't wanna bring this shit to your house. What would I do if something

happened to you cause of me? Huh? I'll be fucked up Selina. I wouldn't be the same. I'm goin' stay for a little while then I gotta go. It's not safe here." Kevin said still hugging her. After Selina went to sleep Kevin called Skeebo again and told him to come and scoop him up. Skeebo told him he'll be there in three hours. That was way too long. He had to leave now. He picked up his cell phone and called Solo. "Hello...What up doe?...I need a favor...I need you to come swoop me up... I'm on Cherrylawn and 8 mile...How long?.. Fifteen minutes all-right good lookin'." Kevin said hanging up his cell phone. Kevin threw on some jogging pants and a hoody. It was windy as hell outside. He threw a fitted cap on and went out the back door, He hopped s couple of fences to get to the next block, se no one would notice him if he came out the front door. When he got to the store he called Solo, Solo told him he was riding down B mile right now, Solo pulled op in a green Cutlass on 22' triple gold Daytone, Kevin hurried up and jumped in. "What up doc? Where yo' truck at?" Solo asked. "That bitch totaled. Somebody shat ay shit up yesterday." Kevin said looking back to make sure nobody was following them. "Straight up, you know who did it?" Solo asked. "Fuck yeah, I know who it was. They had blue rags covering their faces but that shit didn't mean nothing.

It was them hoe ass Blood niggas that stayed down the street from Selina." "So what's up? Solo asked. "First I gotta get my baby moms out that crib, then we can move on em'." Kevin said. He had called Skeebo and told him he was going to be at the shop on Puritan. After he hung up Solo was locking at him weird. "You all-right fam'." Solo asked. "Naw man, these niggas just tried to kill me. I ain't feeling none of this shit, These lil' niggas been giving me problems for the longest. I just didn't do nothing about it because they were kids, but now it's over. They fucked up by letting me live." "Whenever you ready to ride, let me know!" "Naw fem', you got a family. You got a daughter mart. This my beef." "What's yo' beef is my beef!" Solo said. "I appreciate that but you don't have to do nothing but I am." Kevin said. "All-right." Solo said. "I need to get my hands dirty anyway. I ain't had no fun in long time." Kevin said.

When they got there the little homey's was holding the shop down. 'I'm goin' wait here for a minute." Kevin said. "All - right, I gotta see what's been going on cause these lil' niggas nowadays couldn't be trusted." "Yeah you right." Kevin said while waiting in the car. Kevin ended up getting out after he called Skeebo to see where he was. He said he was on I-94. Kevin waited for a couple more hours

until Skeebo pulled up in a blue 2002 Monte Carlo on 20' blades. Whatever he was listening to was banging. I hopped in and we drove off. "So what's up f am'?" Skeeobo asked. It's time to put in work. Somebody shot my truck up yesterday." Skeebo was shocked. "What the fuck! Tell me you know who did it!" Skeebo said stopping at the red light. "Oh don't worry about it, I know exactly who did it. It's goin' be a lot funerals coming up, believe that." Kevin said. "You ain't never lied," Skeebo said.

It had to be like six in the morning. I still was waking up early. I called Ilaria to see how she was doing. We talked for a good minute. She kept asking me when I was coming home. I told her probably next week. Chris was sleep so I didn't get a chance to talk to him. She told me she loved me and to be careful. I told her I loved her and hung up. I got up and hopped in the shower. Wes' kept me out all night. He got me and him cussed out by Monic. She wasn't having it. When I went downstairs Esco was in the back feeding his dogs. I looked in the refrigerator and it wasn't shit in there but beer. "Time to go shopping homey." Esco came in and said. "Yeah that's what it's looking like." I said. "Vou a take me to the grocery store?" Esco asked. "Yeah, let me go get my keys.". I said going to go get my keys. Esco was sitting at the table when I came

back down. When we got in I told him he'd bet not have no pistol in here. "Naw homey I know you on papers." Esco said. "All-right." I said. "A homey it's a lot of shit goin' on and I hope you're not involved in the shit." Esco said. "What the hell you talking about? The shit with my home boy clothing store?' I asked. "Naw, somebody tried to kill Kevin a couple days ago. Thay shot his truck up but he got away. Ward on the streets is a lot of shit is bout to pop off. He knows who did it." Esco said. "Who told you this?" I asked looking confused. "Listen man what I'm tellin' you is true homey. If you got anything to do with it let me know. It's a big coincidence that when you got here somebody just happen to try and kill Kevin." Esco said. "Listen man, I ain't did nothing. That's my word. I would never bring heat to your house." I said getting angry. "I just wanted to know homey, cause it's about to get real serious. Do he know your back in the city?" Esco asked. 'Naww, not that I know of." I said turning into the lot of the grocery market. "All-right let's go shoppin' then. Esco said getting out the truck when I parked.

When we loaded the truck up with the groceries, I asked Esco why he get all that microwave ass shit. "That's what we eat homes." Esco said. "law Mexicans eat heans, rice, peppers, and tortillas." I said laughing. "Ohhh okay. I

have a question for you. Why did you buy all that soy meat and veggie burger crap? Black people eat Chicken, oh let be more specific, fried chicken, water-melon, and cornbread." He and Esco broke out laughing. We shot back to the crib and Esco filled his refrigerator up while I took my groceries upstairs and put them in the small refrigerator. I was kind of tired so I went to sleep.

The shop was closed for a minute. Daron was at his shop in Dearborn chilling with Rah-rah and Big Bo. Daron was kind of mad because they didn't kill Kevin, Now he had to watch over his and Suga back. Deran tried to call Dre but he didn't pick up. "Aye, you think Kevin know who did it?" Big bo asked. "I don't know, maybe you should be asking Rah-rah that," Daron said turning his head to Rah-rah. "We had on blue bandanas. On some real shit, when somebody bussin' at you, you ain't tryna see who it is, you tryna get the fuck on. Right or wrong?" Rah-rah asked. "You right about that." Big Go said. "You never know. Stay alert cause we ain't fuckin' with no young nigga." Daron said. "You heard from K-dog or Roll?" Big bo asked Rah-rah. "Naw, they been layin' low on the east side. Rah-rah said. Suga walked in the store looking mad as hell.. "I need to talk to you." Suga said walking all the way to the back. "Uh-oh, somebody in trouble." Rah-rah said.

'Man shut the fuck up." Daron said while going to the back. "What up?" Daron asked Suga. "What the fuck you mean what's up? You haven't called to check on Diamand nor came to see her. What the hell is your problem?" "Baby I been busy." "Busy tryna see who robbed you or to busy trying to see who shot my cousin?" She asked. "Girl quit it out, you know damn well I care about her." "I can't tell, all you do is stay in the streets. Dre has been up there so many times. You my fiance now. Were not boyfriend and girlfriend no more. I'm carrying your baby. You acting like you still in school. You know I love you but you really on some bull shit." Daron was heated. He wasn't mad Suga, he was mad at Dre. "I'm goin' get it together baby. We gotta communicate more. That's all we need." "No we need more than communication." Suga said. "Yeah." Daron said shaking his head. "Now give me a hug nigga." Suga said smiling. Daron hugged her and kissed her. "Not to tight boy, this boy been kickin' me all day." Suga said. "I love you girl." Daron said. "I love you too." Suga said. "How Diamond doin." Daron asked. "She good, she should be out this week." Suga said. "Call me when you get home." Daron said. Suga walked past Big Bo and Rah-rah. "Yaw better keep my husband out of trouble especially you Biggs." Suga said talking to Big Bo. Daron came back in

the front rubbing his waves. "Awww nigga don't even try it I heard you, 'I Love you baby'. Aww wait to I tell Lou' this." Big Bo said teasing Daron. "Mannnnn get the fuck outta here." Daron said.

Chapter 28

It had been a week since they shot up Kevin truck. Kevin was in his crib chilling with Skeebo, Osama, and Sambo. "Somebody gotta die, a lot of people gotta die. I been havin' my home boy check out everything. He told me niggas still be crankin' out that spot. I wanted to wait 'til it calmed down cause the hook been watchin' strong. So we gotta be careful. Sambo I know you ready to put a hole in everybody but we gotta use our brains. We gotta light they shit up and dip. We need a pick up truck, probably a dodge Ram or something. Fuck that mini van shit niggas hip to that." Kevin said. "Yeah you right." Skeebo said. "So when we goin' do this?" Osama asked. "Soon, but this shit can't go wrong." Kevin said. "All choppas, nothing else. We tryna kill something." Sambo said. "You right about that." Skeebo said. "What about yo' girl crib?" Sambo asked." She good, by the time we do this she'll be living here, so when we leave here, that's what I gotta talk to her about." Kevin said taking the weed out the jar.

Selina was coming from work. She had been a bail bondsman in Oakland county for the last seven years. She was tired and exhausted. She didn't even notice the white Neon that had been following her for the last two days. She

finally made it home. She was almost due." She couldn't believe she was still working. She parked on the street instead of parking in her driveway. When she walked in the house she fell right out on the couch and went to sleep.

Mindy had been following Selina for a couple of days. "This bitch is dead. I can't believe Kevin done put a baby in this bitch. What does she have that I don't? Well he won't have to worry about him being a daddy." Mindy said. Mindy had two cocktails in her back seat. It as just getting dark so it was almost time to eat. She had went to McDonalds and got her something to eat. Mindy had got fat and out of shape. She didn't care how she looked no more. She had seen Selina so many times but Selina never paid her any attention to her because of the weight gain. After she was finished eating she went back to

Selina house. It was going on 10:30. She didn't see any lights on at all. All she seen was the TV light on. It wasn't nobody outside because of the shooting that took place a week ago. She cut her lights off and parked a few houses down. She grabbed the cocktails and walked down to Selinas' house. She lit one of the cocktails and threw it through the front window. She lit the other one and threw it on the roof. The fire was everywhere. Mindy ran as fast as

she could. She made it to her car and sped off. Selina was so tired. She thought it was the crack dealers down the street until she couldn't breath that well. When she woke up, everything was on fire. She panicked. She couldn't die right now. She finally crawled all the way to the back door. She couldn't get it open. She couldn't see nothing from all the smoke. She was now pounding on the door. She heard somebody calling her name but she didn't know where it was coming from. She passed right out.

"Lina, Lina where you at?" He yelled through the smoky house. He had came through the side door. He seen the whole thing but he couldn't chase the chick down because he would of had to leave Selina. He called her again but no answer. "Please be alive Lina." He said while searching the house. He finally found her stretched out on the kitchen floor. He opened the back door and carried her outside. She was heavy as hell. He carried her as far as he could away from the house. He just came home from boot camp so it really wasn't no problem picking Selina up. He performed CPR on her trying to get the smoke out of her lungs. He heard the fire truck sirens going off. He had called soon as he seen the cocktail go through the window. He ran to the front to let them know she was in the back and she needed medical attention. A couple of fireman had

rushed back there while the rest tried to put the fire out. It took a minute for them to put the fire out. He went to the hospital with Selina to see if she was going to be all-right. When they got to the hospital she went straight to emergency. "Are you family?" One of the doctors asked. "No, I'm a close friend." He said. "Well I'm sorry you can't be in here." The doctor said. "Please." He begged. "Okay, just say you're her brother. What is your name sir?" The doctor asked while letting him in. "Terry Crawford. I really appreciate it." Terry said.

A couple hours later Selina was woke. "Excuse me doctor, how's she doing? Terry asked. "You got a trooper, she's doing fine. So is the baby. She should be all-right tomorrow." The doctor said. "Thank you doctor." "No problem, that's what I'm here for.

The next day, Terry was rolling Selina out of the hospital in a wheelchair. "Thank you so much Terry. I probably would of been dead." Selina said. "Don't worry about it, how's your baby?" Terry asked. "He doing fine, they said he inhaled a lot of smoke but he's gonna make it." "That's good to hear. Come on let me help you in the car." Terry grabbed the wheelchair and put it in the car trunk, Terry hopped in his moms caravan and looked at Selina.

"What now?" Selina asked. "Nothing, it's just been along time. "The last time I seen you, you were smaller." Terry said laughing. "Boy shut up, we ain't kids no more Terry." Selina said. "So where do you wanna go, your brothers house?" "No, me and my brother are not on good terms. He still doin' the same shit so I gotta stay away from that. ill your mom have a problem with me stayin' over until my boyfriend comes and pick me up?" Selina asked. "Naw, not at all. You know you're always welcomed." "I really do appreciate it too. How is your mom doing anyway? I try not to go down that way because all those young guys. I know that loud music be driving her crazy." "Yeah, she was writing me complaining about her neighbors every week. But she's actually doin' fine. She's thinking about moving. She told me that they love her, and even though their loud they protect her. So it's kind of a good thing them guys be over their. Me and my brother got that crap started." "Where is lil' B?" "He in juvenile. He'll be out soon." "What did he do?" Selina asked. "He got caught with a gun." "That's not good." "Yeah, you right, hopefully he learns and won't have to go through what I went through." "I hope so too. I just wish they were watching my house." Selina said. It was quiet in the car until we drove down Cherrylawn. "Oh my God! Look at my house." Selina said

busting out in tears. "Stop the car, stop it!" Selina screamed. Terry stopped the van and Selina got out and just stood in front of what use to be her house. She was crying now. "It's going to be all-right, come on let me get you back inside. Terry said getting out. Terry stopped her and looked into her eyes. He still loved her. "Lina everything happens for a reason." She put her head down. "Look at me." Terry said. Selina looked. "If they didn't let me go early early we would have been burying you. You can get another house, you can't get another Selina. Don't beat yourself up okay?" Terry said. "Okay." Selina said feeling much better. "Now let's go Lanetta." Terry said laughing. That was Selina made up name he gave her when she would argue with him. She smiled and got back in the van. When they drove up the driveway, she seen Peaches running around in the backyard. "Is that Peaches?" Selina asked. "Yea, that's Peaches still running around chasing her tail. When they got out Terry was about to grab the wheelchair but Selina told him she was all-right. "It's been so long. I don't even remember how it looked in the inside." Selina said walking up the steps. When she walked in she seen Ms. Crawford sitting in her rocking chair knitting. "Hi MS. Crawford, it's me Lina." "I know who you are. How can I forget a beautiful face like that?" Ms.

Crawford said looking up with her big prescription glasses on. "How have you been Ms Crawford?" Selina asked. "I have been fine, the person I'm worried about is you. I heard what happened. That's a shame. All day I have been praying for you and seems like they worked." Ms. Crawford said. "I really appreciate it, because I do need them." "Make yourself at home." Ms. Crawford said. Terry and Selina went into the kitchen. "So Tb, when did you get out of prison?" Selina asked. Tb was his street name, but he didn't like it at all because it described the old him. "Well first off Ms. Lopez, it's Terry and secondly I got out of prison December 11, 2000. They transferred me from Indiana back to Michigan in January and made me do 90 days in boot camp. So actually I was freed in March." Terry said. "Yeah Ms. Crawford told me you were incarcerated." Selina said. "Why didn't you write?" Terry asked the million dollar question. "I don't know, I was mad. Mad that you left me. That still no excuse. I was dead wrong Terry." She said. Terry was mad but she was right, he did leave when she told him not to go. "Don't worry about it, I was good." Terry said. "Do you have a phone so I can call my ride?" She asked. Terry handed her his cell phone. "Thank you." Terry and Selina use to date. He was the only guy friend she had that her brother use to let come

around. Terry went out of town and ended up locked up for drug trafficking. Selina called Kevin and told him what had happened. He told her he was on his way. After she hung up she caught Terry staring at her. They talked about everything that happened while Terry was gone. She told him about her job and how her family had split up. Terry told her how prison was and how he managed to graduate from boot camp. "You hungry? Ms. Crawford asked while coming into the kitchen. "Yea ma, I'm starving." Terry said. "Boy shut up you always hungry. How about you Lina?" "Yeah, I wouldn't mind. Selina said. After they ate Hamburger and fries, Kevin was out side of the house blowing his horn. "That's my ride." Selina said. "Tell that boy I said he better come inside next time. I don't like all that horn blowing." Ms. Crawford said hugging her. "I'll be sure to tell him when I get in the car. Thank you for having me over Ms. Crawford." "No problem. Just come visit more often. Selina hugged Terry and told him thank you for everything. "Anything for you Lina." Terry said. "I'll make sure to call as soon as I get home." "Yeah right." Terry said laughing following her outside.

Kevin was waiting in his black Harley Davidson F-150 with tinted windows in front of the address Selina gave him. He was hot and he knew it but he didn't care, he lived

for this shit. He blew his horn a couple of times until Selina and some dark skinned nigga came out. That must be the nigga Terry she said helped her. The dark skinned nigga grabbed a wheel chair out of mini van and brought it to the truck. Terry asked Selina where should he put it. "Put it in the back." Selina said. He put it in the back and went to the driver side window. "You Terry?" Kevin asked while not letting his window all the way down. "Yeah." Terry said. "I appreciate everything you've done." Kevin said. "No problem." Terry said. "If you need anything let me know fam'." Kevin said. "All-right, but you don't owe me. But it was good meeting you, uhh? "Kevin, but you can call me Kev'.". Kevin said rolling down the window so Terry could get a good look at his face. "All-right Kev', make sure yaw drive home safely.". Terry said. "We sure will." Kevin said driving off. He looked at Selina. "You all-right?" Kevin asked her. "Yeah I'm all-right." Selina said without looking at him. "It would have been worst but Terry seen everything, so he ran down to the house before the fire got to me." Selina said. "Did he see who did it?" "Yeah, he said he thought it looked like a female, he wasn't sure though." "Straight up?" Kevin asked. "Probably was one of your girlfriends." Selina said. "Hell naw, don't try to blame that on me. I haven't seen that girl in almost a year." Kevin

lied. "Whatever." Selina said. "How's my son doing?" Kevin asked. "Our son." Selina said correcting him. "Girl you know what I mean." "Yeah, I know exactly what you mean." Selina said being sarcastic. "So who's this Terry nigga?" "Do I smell a hint of jealousy?" "Naw I just wanna know. He seem like he aight." "Yeah right." "Naw for real doe." Kevin said. "Dang boy you nosey as hell. He was my boyfriend a long time ago." "How long ago?" Kevin asked. "Oh my God. Boy that was almost ten years ago, ten fuckin' years." Selina said getting upset. Kevin switched the subject. "So you ready to move in?" Kevin asked. "I don't have a choice do I?" Selina asked. "I guess not." Kevin said. "You goin' have somebody go pick my truck up?" "Yeah, don't even worry about it." Kevin said. "So what am I going to do about my job?" Selina asked. "You still can work if you wanted to. How hard is it to just bail somebody out? Kevin asked. "Boy you crazy. My job is harder than what you think it is. It's not that simple." Selina said. "Yeah okay." "Boy shut up, I'm hungry." She said playfully hitting him. "I thought you just ate." Kevin said. "Yeah I did, but being on this freeway making me hungry. Selina said. "Girl you crazy. How the freeway making you hungry?" Kevin asked. "Looking at all the food billboards silly." "What do you want?" Kevin asked. "Rally's." Selina

said. "Why you gotta be so difficult? Rally's, come on Selina please name something else." Kevin said. "Rally's, Rally's, Rally's.". Selina repeated herself like a little kid. All-right, all- right. I get the point. Damn most people a say something common like McDonalds, Burger King, or Wendy's, But Rally's. If you know where a Rally' at let me know." Kevin said. "Oh, don't even trip, I will be looking for a Rally's sign." Selina said. Kevin turned the music up and kept driving until he seen a Rally's.

Everything was straight. I was on my back to Arkansas. I was probably going to be gone by next week. I called Daron to ask him did he want to hang out but he said he was good. I called Wes' to see what was up but he didn't pick up. "A Dre, I gotta go check on my family." Esco yelled up the stairs. "All- right. A, you want me to stroll with you?" I asked. I didn't have nothing to do anyway. "I'm good homey. Good looking homey doe." Esco said. I looked out the front window and I seen Esco El Camino speeding off.

Esco punchad a number in his cell phone. "Hello...Yeah, she still there....What time was this?....Was she all-right?....You know who did it or have any clues?...All-right, keep your eyes and ears open. Amor."

Esco hung up the phone pissed. Esco didn't like anyone fucking with his family. Esco pulled up to his home boy house and got out. His home boy Ortiz was sitting on the porch. Ortiz was Esco mans even though they were under two different sets. Ortiz was a Surenos 13. What's up homey?" Ortiz asked. "You heard what happened?" Esco asked him. "Yeah I heard, she all-right?" Ortiz asked. "Yeah she's good. Where's joker at?" Esco asked. "He's inside with Vito." Esco went inside and seen Joker lying on the couch watching TV while little Vito was running around the house with a blue bandana tied around his face. "A homes, what chu' doin'?" Esco asked the ten year old. "Playin' shoot em' up." He said running to the back. Esco thought Joker was sleep but his eyes were open. "Joker get the hell up." Esco said kicking his leg. Joker got up instantly. "What man, what's up?" Joker said trying to get up. He was at least 350 pounds. "Man why you got Vito round the house with blue bandanas throwing up gang signs?" Esco asked. "Man shouldn't you be askin' Ortiz that? That ain't my son, that's my nephew." Joker said laying back down. "Man you pitiful." Esco said. Joker let out a loud fart and shifted his body. "Awwww man, what the fuck. Man get up." Esco said. "What man, I'm up. I can't lay down?" Joker asked. "You heard what happened

225

to Lili?" Esco asked. Jokers eyes were now opened. "Naw what happened homey?"

Kevin and Selina was laid up in his bed. "Baby you woke?" Kevin asked her. She didn't answer. Kevin got up and picked up the phone. "Hello...Yeah...Don't know who did it, but I believe it was them hoe ass gang bangin' niggas...Yeah today it goes down...They goin' be out, they be out every night. Selina had a new blue Jeep Cherokee parked on her Cherrylawn. That could be the getaway car. Come park one of your cars over here so when yaw drop the Jeep off, yaw a have a whip here....Yaw gotta come pick up the keys.....That was easy. You remember the Caldian chick Mindy...I told her me and Selina broke up and I told her where she lived...Yea, but the bitch is locked up cause of the finger prints on the glass bottles....Yeah two birds with one stone. What time yaw goin' be over here?...I'm goin' be here. The keys goin' be in the mailbox...All-right make it clean." Kevin hung up the phone and went back to sleep.

Chapter 29

"That was Kev' right there." Skeebo said. "It's bout to go down." Osama said. "You know it's some bloods so we out to kill." Skeebo said. "We goin' kill anyway." Sambo said laughing. "Grab the choppas so we can go pick up the keys to the getaway car." Skeebo said. They grabbed the choppas from the basement. "Gloves bro', make sure you got cho' gloves loading them bullets. Wipe the choppas down too because I'm thinking about leaving em'." Skeebo said. "Aww man, what type a shit you on?" Sambo asked. "Listen, we ain't driving one of our cars back we driving a hot ass blue Jeep Cherokee. I mean it's legit, but yaw know the hook target all Chrylers and Dodges. See in the hood the hook different, in the 'Dy niggas steal cars everyday and that's a common ass car to steal. Now you see where I'm coming from." Skeebo asked Sambo. "Yeah I feel that." Sambo said. "We can get some more choppas, but nigga we can't get no lawyer to get us off when we got the murder weapons in the car." Skeebo said. "True, true." Osama said shaking his head up and down. "Yaw ready?" Skeebo asked. They both said yeah. They grabbed the choppas and hopped in Sambo '96' Impala.

When they pulled up to Kevin crib, Skeebo told Sambo to grab the keys out the Mailbox. He got out and grabbed the keys and hopped back in the car. Skeebo drove off.. "Aw man, I forgot that we had to leave a car at Kev's house. Fuck it, we don't have time to waist." Skeebo said. "What chu' talking about?" Sambo asked. "I'll explain it later fam'." Skeebo said. It took exactly three hours to get to the 'D'. Sambo and Osama was sleep. "A, yaw won't something to eat?" Skeebo asked them. They didn't respond. Skeebo was the second oldest but he acted like he was the oldest. He pulled up in the Coney island drive thru. "A wake up. What chu' you want to cat?" Skeebo tapped. the passenger seat. "What man, a nigga tired." Osama said waking up and yawning. "Get me a order of chili cheese fries with extra cheese." Osama said with his eyes closed. "What chu' want?" Skeebo asked looking in the back. "Get me a 10 piece wing ding dinner." Sambo said. "I'm ready to order. Can I have a order of chili cheese fries, two wing ding 10 piece dinner and three large sprites." Skeebo said to the intercom. "Your total is $11.79. Please drive ahead." The female voice said. Skeebo drove to the next window. The chick sounded bad through the intercom but when Skeebo pulled up she was big as hell. "$11.79 sir." She said smiling showing her black gums. Skeebo gave her the

money and she gave him back his change. The food was ready quick as hell.. "Man why we ain't go in? We don't never eat in the car." Sambo said grabbing his food. "Man you wanna go inside, fuck it, we go inside then." Skeebo said parking the whip. They got out and went inside the Coney Island and sat down. "Man you been cryin' a lot, I hope you ain't goin' soft on us." Osama said to Sambo. "Never dat' bro', I'm still the same, prolly cause I'm growin' up." Sambo said. "Whaaat, Sambo growing up?" Skeebo asked. "Is something wrong with that?" Skeebo asked. "You know what I think it is, it's that bitch you been fuckin' wit." Osama said. "Fuck naw." Sambo said. "Yea that's what it is. It's that stanky whore." Skeebo said. All three broke out in laughter. "Man fuck ya niggas dog." Sambo said. After they were finished, it was time to put in work. Skeebo drove around to find a stolly. "Naa, the hook be over here tuff so we gotta do this shit right. We goin' go get a mini van, I'm goin' drive, yaw shoot.". Skeebo said. "I thought Kev' said niggas be on that?" Osama asked. "Yeah but Kevin not here. Yaw know how we do it." Osama and Sambo both nodded their heads." Now we goin' park the cars, yours and the stolly. I'm goin' walk up the block. She live right on the corner so I won't have to walk past the niggas. When I come back with the Jeep we park it

and go do our thang. Now we gotta find a Caravan. That shouldn't be hard though." Skeebo said. They ended up finding a purple one on 7 mile and Meyers at the K-mart on the corner. Osama was the coldest, he was in an out. He made sure he covered his face cause they didn't wanna risk any chances getting caught. They had parked about six blocks away from Selinas'. Skeebo had on a red hoody with some black jeans. He wanted to fit right in with everybody else even though he couldn't stand the slob ass niggas. He was now walking down the block and seen a crowd standing in front of a house in the middle of the block. He was hitting the alarm to Selinas' Jeep Cherokee. He hopped in and hit a u-turn in a driveway and drove towards 8 mile. He didn't wanna ride past the niggas because they might have stopped him. When he pulled up in the gas station Sambo and Osama was parked in the Impala. "Yaw ready?" Skeebo asked. "Yeah, they out there?" Osama asked. "Yop, deep as hell too." Skeebo said. "Man take that hoe ass hoody off.". Sambo said. "I had to wear it to look like I was off the block." Skeebo said taking off the red hoody. Skeebo hopped back in the Cherokee and followed Sambo and Osama to the Caravan. They had parked it in the alley behind a construction company, not to far from Cherrylawn. They hopped in in all black. Skeebo

hopped in the driver seat and Osama and Sambo got in back. The choppas was already loaded. They drove down Cherrylawn and seen a crowd of niggas in the middle of the street playing basketball. "Man it's kids out there," Osama said. "Naw, that's father down, we good." Skeebo said. Skeebo parked in the driveway. They wasn't even paying attention to the Caravan. Osama was in the passenger seat and Sambo was in the back sliding the door just little bit. "A you saw that?" Rell asked Tb. "Yeah, you talking about that dude with the red hoody?" Tb asked. "Yeah, ain't that Selina truck he hopping in?" Tb asked. "Yeah, I seen the alarm click off so it's probably somebody she know." Tb said. "Fuck it." Freaky Rell said. "Yaw wanna go hoop?" K-dog asked. "Fuck naw, it's cold as hell." Freaky Rell said. "Well I'm bout to go hoop. I'm a holla." K-Dog said walking towards the basketball rim in the middle of the street. "That nigga always wanna hoop but don't even know how. That's crazy ain't it?" Freaky Rell asked Tb. "Yeah, but he be tryin', some dudes don't do nothing but smoke weed all day." Tb said. "Nigga what chu' sayin'?" "If the shoe fit, put it on." "Man get the fuck on." Freaky said. Rah-rah came out the spot with this chick. "That dude be havin' a female in the spot everyday." Tb said. "What can I say, when you doin' yo' thang the hoes goin' come."

231

Freaky Rell said. "Man ain't nobody trying to mess with no hood rats." Tb said. "So you think you just goin' come home and get a bitch with money? You might as well come back to the block. When you got this, you can have any bitch in the world." Freaky Rell said pulling out a fat knot. "I'm through with that life. They already got almost ten years out of me, I'm good. It's plenty of ways to get money." Tb said. "Suit cha' self." Freaky Rell said putting the knot back in his pocket. Soon as Rell put the knot in his pocket he noticed a Caravan driving towards them. Before he could even see it, shots just rang out. Tb hit the ground. Rell pulled out the .40 and started shooting back. Rah- rah tried to run but he was shot in the back. The female got knocked through the front window. Rell was still standing when the shots stopped and the caravan was gone. When he looked down his blue jeans was burgundy. Rell passed out. Tb didn't get hit. The first place he ran to was his mom. Ms. Crawford was next door and he knew bullets had went through his house. He was calling his mom. "Ma where you at?!" He yelled. "Terry is that you?" "Yeah ma', it's me where are you?" Tb asked. "I'm in the basement." She said. "Are you all-right?" Tb asked hugging her. "Veah I'm fine. I was more worried about you." She said. "How did you get down here so quick?" Tb asked. "Boy you know I ran track

in high school. Fast for an old woman? She asked. "Aww man I gotta go check on Rell and nem'. Tb said running back upstairs. He ran outside and he seen K-dog trying to help Rell up. "What the fuck happened?!" K-Dog yelled. "Man I don't know. I just heard shots and I ran." Tb said with his hands on top of his head. It was more people out there then Tb thought. It was at least five people hit, Tb didn't even notice the niggas on the side of the spot. Th ran up on the porch. Rah- rah was still breathing but it was a lot of blood gone, The young chick was dead. After the police and the ambulance came, K-dog had called Daron and told him what happened. Daron was heated. Rah-rah and Rell was in critical condition and probably wouldn't make it. The other three niggas that was on the side of the house were in the hospital but they were all-right.

"Damn, that bitch ass nigga shot me." Sambo said. "You goin' be all-right just hang on." Skeebo said. "This shit burnin'." Sambo said. "Where you hit at?" "My fuckin' stomach!" Sambo yelled. "You gotta talk to him Osama." "What the fuck do I suppose to say?"! "That's yo' bro', how the fuck you don't know what to say?!" Skeebo yelled. Skeebo finally got to the impala and the Cherokee. "Tie that shit up so it can slow down the blood." Skeebo said. They put Sambo in the back seat of the Impala and Osama

hopped in the driver seat and Skeebo hopped in the Cherokee and sped off. Sambos' blood was all in the caravan. They couldn't go to the hospital, if they did they would get caught. Skeebo pulled over on the freeway to check on Sambo. Sambo was dead. "Bitch, damn my nigga gone!" Osama said. "He in a better place." Skeebo said. "Man that nigga ain't in no better place. That nigga suppose to be here with us Skee." Osama said. "I know, it's nothing we can do about it." Skeebo said. Skeebo hopped back in the Cherokee and drove off. Osama followed him. "Damn how am I going to explain this to his moms?" Skeebo asked his self. He was fucked up. He wanted out the game and he knew Osama wanted something different. Osama wanted revenge but that's how all this shit had happened. Revenge. Skeebo didn't wanna call Kevin yet so he didn't. He was going to holla at Osama to see if he wanted to let all this shit go and leave town, because fucking with Kev' was going to have us in some bullshit. We were goin end up dead or in prison. Skeebo just hoped that Osama was feeling the same. They drove back to Benton Harbor as quick as they could. Skeebo pulled over again. "Listen man, you gotta clean all this shit, all the finger prints gotta be gone. We gotta leave em' like this." Skeebo said. "Hell naw bro'. Not like this." Osama said.

"For real man or this shit goin' trace back to us, all that shit. The club shit, and probably that shit with Daron store." Skeebo said. All-right man." Osama said. They still had their hoodies on so no one would see them. Skeebo helped Osama clean the car. They put Sambo in the driver seat and left hm there him the car running. They hopped in the Cherokee and drove off. "Listen man, I'm ready to leave this shit alone. I'm ready to settle down with a bitch and pursue this rap shit. Ain't no good coming out of this. We got enough dough to just leave, so what's up?" Skeebo asked. "I'm down Skee, fuck this shit." Osana said. "We can't tell Kevin, we just gotta leave." Skeebo said. "All-right." Osama said. Skeebo drove to his town house and told Osama to follow him in the Monte. Osama followed him to Kevins' house. Skeebo left the keys in the car and hopped in the car with Osama. "Should we tell Kevin about Sambo?" Osama asked. "Yeah we got to." Skeebo said. "Damn '0', I can't believe he gone. After the funeral we out, no looking back." Skeebo said. A week later Osama and Skeebo were sitting next to Ms. Brown. Everybody had on their R.I.P Carl Brown AKA Sambo shirts. Almost the whole hood was there. Kevin even showed up. After the funeral Kevin came and kicked it with Osama and Skeebo. "Yaw straight?" He asked. "Yeah we good." Osama said.

"Yaw don't need no money do yaw?" Kevin asked. "Naw we good, we were just goin' throw his moms some money." Skeebo said. Come to find out Skeebo had a daughter on the way. He didn't even tell Osama or Skeebo. We threw his girl a couple of stacks and took her house and cell number down. They also threw his moms some money. She was like their moms too. Skeebo and Osama sold the Cutlass and gave most of the money to Ms. Brown and Sambos' baby mama La'Sha. When they hopped in Skeebo Monte they were ready to get the hell out of Michigan. "So where we headed?" Osama asked. "To da' south, Atlanta, GA boil" Skeebo said peeling out. "What's down south?" Osama asked. "Music bro'." "You sure?" Osama asked. Skeebo just looked at him and put his eyes back on the road. This one for Sambo. I promise we goin' get on. Skeebo thought to his self. "Damn I miss that nigga." Skeebo said. "Me to bro', Osama said. "Don't worry bro', we goin' be straight. We just gotta grind cause ain't no record deal just goin' fall out the sky." Skeebo said.

Chapter 30

Everybody was at Rah-rahs funeral fucked up. Freaky Rell was still in the hospital fighting for his life. Rah-rah just turned 21 and was on his way back to college. Big Bo and Lil' Lou was sick. I didn't even know the nigga. I just came on the strength cause it was Bo and Lous' cousin. Plus Daron asked me to come. I went to the interment and that was it. I didn't go to the hall for dinner, I wasn't feeling the vibe. I told Daron to call me and I left, Shit was all fucked up. It was time for me to go back to the south. I called Wes' and told him to come holla at me.

When me and Wes' met up, he had on some Gucci Airforce ones. "Damn, when them come out?" I asked. "They not coming out," Wes said. "Yeah fam', I'm goin' be leaving soon. It's to much shit happening. Somebody robbed Darons' store, shot up Kevins' car, somebody just killed Darons' home boy." I said. "Yeah I heard. I knew lil' Rah-rah. I went to Cody high school with him. That was one silly ass nigga." Wes said. "I ain't know dude so I can't speak on him." I said. "So when you coming back?" Wes' asked. "Man, I don't know, the question is when you coming down south?" I asked. "Man ain't no tellin'. It's just to hot down there. Wes' said. "What's that you

237

listening to? I asked. Oh, that's then 'Rockbottom' niggas. Then niggas hot for real. Ona of em' from Hp.", Wes' said. "Straight up?" "You can get it, I fuck wit em' like that, I could get another one." Wes' said going into his Caprice. "Good looking fam'." "Yeah, it ain't shit," Wes' said. "Yeah I'm goin' make sure I call you and tell you when I'm leaving so I can drop the truck off." I said. "Where you headed now?" Wes asked, "To go holla at Esco." All-right fam', keep yo head up.". Wes' said. "Yop, you know what it is." I said shaking his hand. I hopped in the truck and I started thinking about that nigga Rell. It was fucked up, but that's the life he was out there living. When I got to Esco crib I seen his car parked in the front. parked in the driveway. When I got out it was a bunch of Latinos out there I mean a lot. They were looking at me like I was crazy. When I walked inside it was guns everywhere. "What's up homey?" Esco asked. "Shit, what up wit chu'?" I asked. Esco sat the Ak-47 down and got up and pulled me to the kitchen. "Somebody fire bombed my little sister house, so something gotta shake homey." Esca said. I could see the fire in his eyes. "A Esco." Somebody. yelled from the front "Not now homey!" Esco yelled back. "It's important homey." "What?!" Esco asked the young Latino dude. The young Latino looked at me and then ha

238

whispered ln Escos' ear. Esco looked at me while he whispered to him. I didn't know what the fuck was going on. "All-right, good looking homey." Esco said. "What's up?" "They got the person who did it. It was a female. She's locked up for Arson and two attempted murders. We're gonna bond her out and see what's up. I don't care how much the bond is," Esco said. "Is your sister straight?". I asked. "Yeah, I haven't talked to her yet but my homeboy said she's good.". Esco said. "That' a good. I wanted to let you know I'm bout to be goin' back to Arkansas in a minute. Probably in next few days." I said. "You sure?" Esco asked. "Yeah, I gotta go check on my wife and plus it's a lot of shit happening and I:ain't tryna see that hoe as county again. Feel me?" "Yeah I do homey." "You don't need nothing? I asked. "Naw homey I got this shit taken care of." Esco said.

Diamond was out the hospital and the shop was back open. Daron knew Tb was trying to be legit so he hired him to help Suga while Diamond recovered. K-dog was working with Big Bo' in Dearborn. Rell was still in the hospital. He was getting better.

Daron was till trying to find out who robbed him. Suga was still mad at him. She was now 4 months pregnant. Daron

couldn't wait to be a father. He never told dre about them trying to kill his brother. Dre wouldn't mind anyway. Daran thought to his self. When Daron got to the hospital, he seen K-dog in the waiting room. "What up fam', all is well." K-dog said. "All mighty." Daron said shaking up with him. "Rell aight'?" Daron asked. "Yeah he good, actually he doin' real good." K-dog said. "That's good. When can we see him?" Daron asked him. "Shit, we should be able to go up in a minute." K-dog said looking at his Cartier watch. "Mr. Lockman, Mr. Thomas has just auaken." The nurse said. "Could you add Hicks too." Daron asked. "I believe there's a Hicks already on there. Let me check." The nurse said. It took a second for her to check. "Ummm Daron Hicks?" She asked. "Veah, that's me." Daron said getting up. "Could I see some identification please?" She asked. Daron showed her his state ID. "Okay here's your visitor passes." She said handing them the clip on tags. They clipped them on there shirts and got on the elevator. They got off on the floor the nurse said he was on. When they got to his room it was bright as hell. rell had a tube through his nose and mouth. His eyes were open and he was watching TV. K-dog was sick. This was his ace. He was mad because he wasn't there. He felt like he betrayed his best friend. They both sat down and was tellin' him

what had happened to Rah-rah. He couldn't talk but he could hear them.

Kevin and Selina was at the mall buying clothes for her and the baby." "I gotta start all over." Selina said. "Don't worry about it, you goin' have everything you want." Kevin said with his arm around her shoulders. She felt so secure with her man. They had so many bags it was unbelievable. "Baby I love you so much." Kevin said squeezing her tighter. "I love you too." Selina said. After they were finished shopping, they went out to eat.' "Why we don't never go eat in the hood? You scared or embarrassed to be seen with me?" Selina asked. "Naw, why you say that?" He asked. "Because every time we do something it's far as hell away from the city." Selina said. "we can go anywhere you want. I just want you to have the best." "I told you, I'm not-a materialistic chick, I'm just a regular girl who ended up fortunate. I don't care about none of this. As long as you love me and treat me with respect." Selina said. "You know I love you to death. I know you don't care about what I got, that's why I'm with you Selina." Kevin said. They finished up there meal and went home. "You need anything bay?" Selina asked. "Where you going?" Kevin asked. "I'm going to go pick up a few things for the house." Selina said. "I thought we grabbed everything?" Kevin asked. "Personal

things for me big head." She said. "Well just grab me some chicken fingers and some wing dings from the market for me." Kevin said. "All-right baby." Selina said opening and closing the door. She got in her Cherokee and drove to the grocery market.

"So how do you know Selina?" Esco asked the girl that was tied up. "I told you I don't know a Selina, why are you doing this to me?" Mindy yelled. Esco smacked her and told her to tone her voice down. "Grab it." Esco told Ortiz. Ortiz came back with the blow torch. "Oh my God, what are you gonna do "with that?" Mindy asked stuttering. "First, I'm goin' burn those pretty feet and make my way up to where the sun don't shine." Esco said. "I'll tell, I'll tell, I swear to God." Mindy yelled. "I'm waiting." Esco said. "I know Selina through Kevin. He told me he broke up with her and told me to fire bomb her house.se that's what I did." Mindy cried out. "Fuckin' liar." Esco cut the torch on and burnt her foot for a second. Mindy screamed to the top of her lungs. "I'm telling the truth. I swear to God." Mindy said crying.

I heard a bunch a screams in the house so I went downstairs. It was coming from the basement. I hollered down to see if everything was all-right. "Come on down

homey." Esco yelled back up the steps. When I walked down the steps I seen Esco holding a blow torch and a chick tied up in s chair. She had to be mixed with something. She was crying so hard. Her face was blood shot red. "What's up homey?" Esco asked me. "Shit, I thought something was wrong, but I see everything good." I said walking back up the stairs. "No homey, come back down." Esco said. "You sure?" I asked. "Yeah homey." He said. I didn't really want to go but I did anyway. When I came down I seen the huge burn on the mixed chick foot. "This is what happens when you mess with family. You're my family, he my family." Esco said pointing the guy standing next him. "I'm your family, those motherfuckas upstairs are family. This bitch here is our enemy. She has no respect for neither one of us. Hand me the pistol." Esco said to the dude standing next to him. The girl started crying begging for her life. "Please I'm not lying." She cried. Those were her last words. Esco had put three slugs in her head from the nine millimeter with the silencer. "Get this shit clean." Esco told Ortiz. Esco put his arm around me and we went upstairs. "Anybody ever cross as you and you let them get away be looking forward to getting crossed again by the same motherfucka." Esco said still

holding the pistol. "I feel that." I said. "So you leavin' tomorrow huh?" Esco asked.

"Yeah I'm gone fam'." I said. "Make sura you call me when you get down there." Esco said. "Yop." I said going back upstairs. I was searching through the refrigerator because I was hungry as fuck. I fried two veggie burgers on the George Forman grill and called it a day. The next day, I was on my way out the door. Esco was up as usual feeding his pit bulls. He locked them up before-I came out. "So you about to be gone?" Esco asked. "Yeah, I appreciate everything too Esco. I left some groceries up there to for you." I said. "Good looking. Oh about that shit yesterday in the basement." "Don't worry about it." I said cutting him off. "Family is first. When someone tries to harm my family, you tryna harm me. You got me?" Esco asked. "Veah most def'. I said. "I left some loot up there for you too." I said. "Man you know I ain't takin' that shit. That's why you left it upstairs. You're slick for that." Esco said. "Yeah, I just couldn't leave yo crib without giving you something." I said. "Well I guess it's goin' go to Rosci and Sheeba." Esco said looking at his dogs. "Make sure' you be safe on your way back." Esco said. "You know I will. You just make sure you stay out that county." I said shaking his hand. I grabbed my bags and put them in the back and

chucked the deuce. I hopped in the truck and drove off. I had called Carla und told her I was going back to Arkansas. She told me she loved me and her and Zetroc will be down there in the summer. After I got off the phone I called Daron but he didn't answer. I called Aunty Vicki next. "I know she up." I said out loud putting the phone to my ear. "Hello...Hay ma...I'm fine and you?....I was calling to tell you I was headed back to Arkansas...Yeah I gotta leave...You know she mad. I been gone for a while so I'm goin' surprise her...All-right ma, ah ma could you tell Daron I love him and to stay out of trouble... All-right thank you. I love you....Bye bye" I hung up my cell phone and headed towards Wes' house. I called his cell phone but he didn't pick up. I tried it again and I got a answer. "Hello...This Dre...Wes' there?...Yeah I'm on my way to drop the truck off....All-right fam'," This nigga girl was nutty as hell. She thought I was a chick calling trying to change their voice. That girl was goin' kill Wes' 17 she found out he was cheating on her. Damn I couldn't, wait to get home. It took me a minute to gat to Wes' crib because it was raining. When I got there Wes' was sitting on the porch, he had two bags with him. He grabbed the bags and ran to the truck and got in. "Damn it took you forever," Wes' said getting in. "Nigga it's raining cats and dogs." I

said. "Man my bitch trippin'. She was trying to sound like me when you called. She talkin' bout I be puttin' niggas names in my phone instead of female names. She crazy fam'. We had a big argument." Wes' said. "Yeah, her voice was deep as hell." .I said laughing. "I ain't tripping causa I'm bout to go back home and fuck the shit out of her." Wes' said. "What's in them bags nigga?" I asked. "Oh this is for you and your girl," Wes said. Wes' pulled out a pair of Gucci Air-force ones and a New York Knicks Frazier throwback jersey dress for Ilaria. I ain't forget about lil' man either. He pulled out some Gucci Chuck Taylors. "This should be their size. I got it from them when yaw had that party." Wes' said putting the stuff back. "You sneaky as hell." I said. "Nigga I knew you wanted some so I got em' for you."

We finally made it to the airport. It had stopped raining. I grabbed my bags out the truck and sat them on the roof. "Damn, it's goin' be whack as hell. You know I don't fuck with nobody." Wes' said. "Same here. "I said. I gave Wes' $400.00 for letting me rent the truck. "Man I told you I ain't want nothing. This ain't no rental, this my shit. I was just waiting for the summer time. I knew you were goin' take care of it." Wes' said.

I was fucked up, "Man take this money." I said. Wes' didn't refuse it the second time. He took it and put it in his pocket. "I'm out fam'." I said grabbing my bags. "All-right." Wes said hugging me. "Take care fam'." Wes' said. "You already know." I said. The flight went straight. I was on my way home to my family. It. took almost forty-five minutes to get home. When I got out the cab I seen Ilaria lexus in the driveway. Soon as I walked in I fell out on the couch. I was so tired. Ilaria was probably at work and Chris was over Kims' house. I had called Ilaria before T was here so she would know because she didn't really like surprises. I made me a couple of peanut butter and jelly sandwiches and drunk some cold chocolate milk cause that plane food was horrible. I ended up dozing off after I ate and took a shoer. Esco was on the hunt for Kevin. He had to go. It didn't matter what it took. What if he would of killed Selina. Selina Lopez was his baby sister. His only sister. That's what the initial S.L stood for. He was riding around asking questions seeing if anybody had seen Kavin. He had all the homey's looking for him. He wanted Kevin alive though. Solo was at work making sure everything was flowing right. He seen a black Navigator pull up. Two Mexicans hopped out, but one walked up to Solo. "Can I help you?" Solo asked. "Yeah, I want my truck cleaned

inside and out." The Mexican said. Kevin had built the carwash so when you're setting your car cleaned you sit inside. All-right that will be $20 plus $5 because it's a truck." Solo said. "All-right." The Mexican said handing him a fifty dollar bill. Solo gave him his change and the Mexican waved over to his homeboy and told him to give them the keys. The other Mexican walked over to Solo and handed him the keys and they walked inside the car wash. "A moody." Solo yelled. "What up?" Moody yelled back. "Tell Rog, Ben, Forty to come holla at me and you and Boogie could clean that truck over there. When they came out Solo had gave Boogie the keys to clean the truck. "A right. I don't know what's up with them Mexicans but watch em, don't look suspicious doe. Yau got cho' mags?" Solo asked. Solo had bought all of them .380s out of their checks. It was a must they all had one. "Yeah." All of them said at once. "Tell Mitchen the same. Hurry up." Solo said, Mitchen was solos' home boy since middle school. "Hello...Yeah he ain't here...We getting the truck cleaned right now...All-right homey...Ortiz said getting off the phone. "What Esco talkin' bout?" Filleto asked. "He pissed, he said don't even ask about Kevin." Ortiz said. Ortiz seen the three black dudes come back in. Two of them played a arcade game and the other one went to the

back. It took about twenty minutes for them to clean the truck. When they left, they all came out to see if anything was going to happen but the Mexicans kept moving.

"Damn I can't wait to see your uncle." Ilaria said looking back at Chris. "Me too." Chris said with a big grin on his face. Ilaria had called his cell phone but he didn't pick up. She tried the house phone but she got no answer. She knew he was home cause he had called her. It was drizzling a little bit so she wasn't speeding. Lord knows Dre would of been mad as hell if she got a scratch on his truck. When she pulled up, her Lexus was still parked in the driveway. She parked right behind it. She had got Chris out of his car seat and went inside. "Dreeee, you here?" She asked opening up the door and putting Chris down. She went to their bedroom and seen Dre stretched out with his boxers on. "Damn, look at you." She said. She climbed on top of him. "Did you miss momma?" Ilaria asked kissing his lips softly. "Yea I missed you." I said with his eyes still closed. "I missed you too baby." She said kissing his lips again. "Where's Chris?" I asked. "In the front room." Ilaria said. I was now cuffing her ass. She had kissed me some more but she added a little tongue. "Hold on baby." Ilertia said getting up and leaving the room. I got up and put some hoop shorts on. My dick was on hard so I had moved it up

so my shorts could hold it in one place so it wouldn't be poking through my shorts. Ilaria was in the front with Chris taking off his coat. "Watch him for a minute while I go to the bathroom." Ilaria said. "What's up uncle Dre?" Chris asked. "Nothing, just been missing you." I said hugging him. Chris was telling me all about his new friend Olivia. I let him talk his self right to sleep. I waited for Ilaria to come out. I heard the shower running. So I walked in. "You aight'?" Dre asked. "Yea yea I'm all-right." Ilaria said. "Want me to come in there with you?" I asked. "Naw I'm all- right." Ilarie said. I left out and finished watching sports center. When Ileria came out she hurried up and walked past me and went to the room. Something was wrong so I followed her. When I walked in the room she was naked. She tried to cover herself up like I had never seen her naked before. "Baby what's wrong?" I asked. She had dropped the cover and showed me her stomach. It was poking out more. "You don't like it do you?" Ilaria asked sounding insecure. "Like what?" I asked. "My body." Ilaria said, "That's what this is about? Me not liking your body?" She put her head down. I walked over to her naked body and hugged her. "I love you death. I don't care how you look, you hear ma Ilaria?" I asked. "Yes." She said with her head still down. "Look at me baby." I said. She looked at

me and I kissed her on the forehead, then her lips. I then made my way down her neck down to her large breast. I kissed each of her nipples. I got down on my knees and put my ear up to her stomach. "I think I hear something. I think I heard somebody say 'mommy you're not fat'." I said making Ilaria smile. "Boy you crazy." "I know, so let me make love to you." I said kissing her between her legs. I loved the way she smelt. She knew I how I liked it too, not a lot of hairs and not to little. I feasted on her until she climaxed. "You taste so good baby." I said. "Do I really?" She asked while her hand rubbed the top of my head. "Yea baby." I gently laid her down and kissed her all over beautiful body. We wasn't fucking, we were making love. We made love for at last a hour. We had worked up a good sweat. We were drained, we couldn't even get up to get in the shower. We went to sleep holding each other sweaty body. I had woke up in the middle of the night. It was a horrible nightmare. I was glad I didn't wake Ilaria up though I got out the bed and checked on Chris. He was still sleep. I drank a glass of water and laid back down. Somebody had had car accident but I didn't see who it was in the car. I ended up back to sleep after a few minutes trying to remember who it was.

Chapter 31

Selina was almost due. Kevin couldn't believe he was going to be a father. Selina was now officially living with Kevin now. "A bay I gotta make a run right quick." Kevin said. "You going to the city?" She asked. "Naw, I'll be right back.". Kevin 'said. "All-right, I love you." Selina said. "Love you too." Kevin said. Kevin had seen Stephanie in some tight daisy dukes watering the grass. She had seen him and waved. Kevin waved back. She had turned around and bent over trying to untangle the knot out of the water hose. Her ass cheeks were showing more now. She was teasing him. He hadn't fucked her since he fixed her stove. He hopped in the Cherokee and went to the gas station to get his favorite candy, 'Mike and Ikes'. When he came out he had seen a state trooper car sitting in the parking lot. He didn't pay it no mind. When he got in and drove off, they followed him. He didn't know what was going on. They ended up flicking him. Kevin pulled over. They hopped out with their pistols pointed in his direction. "Cut your car off and remove your keys from the ignition!" One of the troopers said. Kevin did what the trooper demanded. "Now throw your keys out the window and put both of your hands out the window!" The trooper Kevin did everything the trooper said. Since one was said. black Kevin thought he

was good but now he realized that that didn't matter. "Open the door with you left hand slowly." The trooper said. Kevin got out the truck. "Keep 'your hands up." Kevin was now out the truck with his hands up. Another State trooper pulled up. "Turr around and back up towards us." The black state trooper said. When Kevin finally reached the trooper one of them slammed him against the patrol car. They threw him cuffs. He was in the back seat of the squad car while they searched Selina truck. "What the fuck is going on?" Kevin yelled. The black officer came to the squad car. "Mr.Clark right?" The black officer asked. "Yeah, what's the problem sir?" Kevin asked. "Your car was spotted at a murder scene. Blue Jeep Cherokee. You fit the description. A guy by name Carl Brown shot and left in his vehicle. Do you have idea on what's going on?" The black officer asked. "No sir. This is my fiance truck. She just moved here not to long ago." Kevin, said. "Nothing." The white officer said looking through the truck. "Do I need to call my lawyer?" Kevin asked. "No, there's noticed for that but I will be in contact with you if anything comes up." The black state trooper said. They took him out the cuffs and the black state trooper gave him his card and told him if he had any information call him. Kevin jumped in the truck and sped off. He was heated. Skeebo and Osama

never told him what had happened. Kevin threw the card out the window and made his way back home. When he got home he didn't tell Selina nothing, he just went to the back room and grabbed Selinas' cell phone and tried to call Skeebo, but when he didn't pick up he tried Osamas,' number, but nothing. "'Baby that's you?" Selina asked. Yeah bay, it's me.". Kevin said. "These bitch ass niggas tried to get me caught up." Kevin said to his self. Something had to shake. Kevin called his, lawyer and explained to him everything that happened with the State Police. His lawyer had told him not to worry about it and he would take care of it. Kevin stayed in the house for the past few weeks because Selina was due any day. Kevin was smoking a blunt while Selina was talking on the phone. "Baby my water broke!" Selina screamed. Kevin dropped the blunt and it burned a little hole in his shirt but he hurried up and knocked it off and stomped it out on his carpet. Kevin ran in the front room and the carpet was soak and wet. Kevin helped her to her Jeep since it was parked on the street. He drove to the local hospital as fast as he could. "Baby hurry he's kicking the hell out of me!" Selina yelled at Kevin. "All-right baby. If I' go any faster we goin' crash!" He said panicking. Kevin pulled in the emergency parking lot. When he stopped he rushed out the

truck to the passenger side to help Selina out. "Breathe baby, breaths.". Kevin said helping her out. Sir you can't park there." One of the Security guards said pulling up in his security car. Kevin just ignored him and left the truck running with the drivers door still open. Seconds later Selina was on a gurney headed towards emergency. Kevin was running with her holding her hand saying it was going to be all-right.

"What up doe, where you at?" K-dog asked Daron over his cell phone. "All-right I'm bout to go slide by there." K-dog hung his phone and continued to drive to Highland Park. The doctors had told him Rell was still doing good but he needed to stay a little while longer. It was almost May and Rell had been gone for minute and that's what it felt like for K-dog.

Darron was at his Grandfather barber shop waiting for K-dog. Daron seen K-dog pull up in his box Chevy Caprice. When he walked in he was looking fucked up. "All-mighty." K-dog said shaking Darons' hand. "All is well." Daron said back." Boy what I tell yaw about all that gang banging stuff?" Darons' grand dad Pete asked. He was old, real old and he was still cutting hair. "Awww pops, come on." Daron said. "Your grandmother wouldn't like it so you

need to stop." Pete said putting the lavender on his hands. "You right." Daron said. "You can't speak young man?" Pete asked K-dog. "Oh, what's up pops?" K-dog asked snapping out from daydreaming. "Nothing much, just trying to keep my grandson out of trouble." Pete said. "All-right pops we goin' go to the back and shoot some pool." Daron said. "Don't be back there smoking no weed." Pete said. Daron just ignored him and kept walking. "I know you hear me Daron?" Pete asked. "I hear you pops!" Daron said getting irritated. Pete was Darons' fathers father. He hated that Daron was gang banging. "So what's up?" Daron asked while grabbing the pool sticks. "Man you ain't find out who did that shit?" K- dog asked while racking the pool balls up. "Man I ain't worrying about that shit, everything goin' fall right into place." Daron said breaking the balls. "Man fuck that, Rell in the hospital and shit while we out here bullshitin'." K-dog said. "Man what the fuck you want me to do? Huh? What the fuck can we do? I don't know who did this shit and best believe nigga I wanna kill those niggas just as bad as you do guy." Daron said getting upset by K-dogs' comment. "Yeah you right. We just buried Rah- rah so I'm fucked up. I been drinking and smoking these feeling away." K-dog said. "So have I nigga. I done smoked so much weed, it don't make no sense. But that

don't mean I'm goin' go out and kill every mothafucka I see. Feel me?" Daron asked K- dog. "True true." K-dog said nodding his head. "That nigga' L' want me to slide by the shop later on. I on't know how Big Bo' and Lil' Lou feeling right now about Rah-rah, so like around five o'clock I'm goin' holla at them too." "Shit, I'm bout to go check on Rell moms and see how she doin'. I'll be by there doe, you know her house right around the corner from the shop. You should stop by. You 'know she a be glad to see you." K-dog said putting the pool sticks up. "I on't know man. You know I be busy as hell. I might come through. If I don't show I call over "there." Daron said. "All-right, all-mighty." K-dog said. "All is well." Daron said back. Daron and K-dog left the back room. "All-right pops." K-dog said to Pete. "All-right Kartl, stay out of trouble." Pete said. K-dog hopped in is whip and drove off.

Kevin was holding his new born son. "He has you eyes baby." Selina told him. "I know, he has my nose too." Kevin said. what are gonna name him?". Kevin asked. He wanted to automatically say his name is Kevin. "How does Kamani sound? Selina asked. "I don't know bay, how about Kevin? Kevin asked. Selina smiled. "Kevin Kamoni Clark Jr." Selina said. I smiled and kissed her on her forehead. Kevin felt good. He finally was a father and he

was with the woman he loved. Everything was going good for him.

Two days later Kevin Kamoni Clark Jr. was at home. 9 pounds and 6 ounces. KJ had everything and more. It was nothing he didn't have. Solo, his girl Neicey and his daughter Brieana were visiting. Solo and Kevin chopped it up a little while Selina, Neicey, KJ and Brieana were upstairs. "I heard what happened to Sambo. That was fucked up." Solo said while pouring some kool- aid. "Yeah, I was fucked up. I taught him how to hustle, took care of him like he was mines." Kevin said. "Some Latinos came up to the shop not to long ago, prolly like a week and half ago. they were looking for somebody. They got their truck cleaned and dipped out." Solo said. "What kind of truck was it?" Kevin asked. "It was a black Navigator, the Lincoln truck." Solo said. Kevin already knew who it was but he didn't tell Solo. He just wanted to know why Esco was looking for him. He probably was looking for Selina to congratulate her. What the hell did he want? That was the big question. "Don't even worry about it, I'll take care of it." Kevin said. "You sure?" Solo asked. "Yeah I'm good, don't even trip" Kevin said. "Yeah I'm thinking about moving to Tennessee to take care of my moms." Solo said sitting down. "So you dipping on me huh?" "Yeah I talked

to Mitch about it, he was like do you, you only get one momma." Solo said. "You right about that." Kevin said thinking about Mary. "So you a pops now huh?" Solo said laughing. "Yeah, you know how that feels." Kevin said. "Yeah, a real job, especially with a girl so you kind of lucky." Solo said. "I'm thinking about leaving too fam'. It's to much, no matter how matter how far you away from the 'D', you always wanna come back." Kevin said lighting the blunt.. "I feel dat." "What yaw doin' down here?" Selina said coming down the steps. "Don't try to hide it, I can smell it." She said talking about the strong scent. "Girl ain't nobody doin' nothing." Kevin said handing the blunt to Solo so she couldn't see it. "You full of shit Kevin and so are you Mike." Selina said putting the clothes in the dryer. "And I know you heard the washing machine stop." Selina said. "My bad bay." Kevin said. "My bad bay." Solo mumbled repeating him. "Man shut up fool." Kevin said to Mike. "What chu' say boy?" Selina asked peaking her head out the laundry room. "Girl you hearing thangs." "Yeah all-right." Selina said putting her hand on her hip and shaking her head up and down. "Just don't let that smell reach upstairs. That's all I ask." Selina said walking up the stairs. "All-right baby." Kevin said but she probably didn't hear him. "So where you thinking about going?" Solo asked. "I

259

don't know some where far from here. I ain't tryna go down south though. I'm thinking about Nevada." Kevin said lighting the blunt up again. "Oh yeah?" Solo asked. "Yeah I'm tired of Michigan." Kevin said. "When you plan on leaving?" Solo asked. "I don't know, soon doe. I gotta holla at Selina about it." "I'm trying to leave before the winter." Solo said. "Naw I wasn't talking that soon." Kevin cut em' off. "Shit, when den' nigga?" Solo asked. "Probably next year. I on't know." Kevin said looking confused. "Ah baby, you ready?" Neicey yelled down the steps. "Yeah give me a couple of more minutes." Solo yelled back. "You know when Neicey get started it's a wrap so you already know what time it is." Solo said getting up. "I'm goin' get at chu' fam', make sure you hit me up to let me know when you leaving.". Kevin said shaking up with Solo. "You already know you ain't nothing but a call away." Solo said hitting the blunt one more time. "You a fool nigga." Kevin said. "Come on Mike.". Neicey yelled again. "She goin' kill yo' ass." Kevin said. "Not before Selina kill yo ass." Solo said running upstairs. The basement was quiet as hell. All Kevin thought about was Esco. Another problem to worry about. First Dre, then Daron, now Esco. "Baby you all-right down there?" Selina yelled. "Yeah, I'm good bay, just catchin' up on the news."

Kevin said. "All-right, let me know if you need anything." Selina said. "Yop." Kevin continued to flick through the channels. Kevin was really thinking about moving out of Michigan before it was to late. He put the blunt out and watched Martin until he was knocked out on the couch.

Couple of weeks later Rell was out the Hospital. He had lost mad weight. They had threw him a big party but he wasn't feeling it. He was tired of all that fast living now that Rah-rah was gone. He hopped in his Monte and drove to Rah-rah grave site. He was fucked up. "Whoever did this goin' pay." Rell said under his breathe. His phone started to ring. It was K-dog. "Yeah.....Almighty.....Yeah I'm good......At Rah-rahs grave site....Yop...Love you to nigga."。 K-dog was the only one who really cared. Rell knew it too. Daron was to busy trying to find out who robbed him. He couldn't be mad. All this happened right after Kevin truck got shot up. This was all Darons' beef and he didn't even care Kevin knew exactly who did it. Than blue rags didn't mean shit. It was a wrap for Kevin. Daughter, girl, whatever, whoever, with him. Rell thought to him self. Rell hopped in his whip and peeled off. K-dog wanted him to meet him up at the Coney Island on 6 mile and Davidson. It took him a minute to get there but when he did he didn't see K-dog caprice up there. It kind of

worried Rell. Soon as he walked in he seen K-dog pull up. Rell ordered when K-dog walked in. "What up doe?" Rell asked shaking up with K-dog. "Nothing, just fucked up about Rah-rah." Rell said. "Yeah, I talked to his moms not to long ago. I couldn't even look her in the eyes." K-dog said. "She know we had Rah-rah out there on some bullshit. That's why I couldn't look her in the eyes." Rell said. I been thinking about all this shit. All this shit started with Daron and Dre. We ain't have nothing to do with this shit. All this Escalated from them niggas. Even though Daron our bro', he been real flip floppy. That nigga turned on his on brother, what makes you think he won't turn on us if we don't ride or do something he don't like?" Rell asked. "I mean I feel like that to but I don't think he'll turn on us bro'. I have noticed a lil' change in him but not like you saying. Where, where you gettin' at with this?" K-dog asked stuttering. "Listen I ain't sayin' fuck Daron, but just play the side line and you'll see. I ain't goin' tell you nothing wrong bro'." Rell said getting up grabbing his food. "You ain't order me nothing?" K-dog asked. "Hell naw nigga, yo' big ass can talk, you better get cho' ass up and order you something." Rell said laughing eating his fries. "You ain't shit." K-dog said getting up and ordering him a cheese burger Deluxe. "That's right, you ain't no

262

baby." Rell said stuffing his face. K-dog threw up his middle finger. "So what chu' bout to get into?" K-dog asked sitting down. "I don't know, it's a lot of shit I gotta catch up on. That party last night got me tired as hell. I might have a baby mama in a couple of months." They both started laughing loud as hell. "Shit me too." K-dog said laughing even harder. After they were finished eating they went their separate ways. Rell just hoped that K-dog listened.

It was a lot of shit on the floor and Daron wasn't telling us. Rell was goin' find out and if Daron had anything to do with Rah-rah getting killed he was goin' pay just like Kevin was going pay.

Chapter 32

I had one more year on parole and I was through with this shit. I wanted to hurry up and get it over with cause my Po been tripping about me not having a job so I guess I'm going to have to get in the shop and work. He been letting me slide but I think he fed up with my shit. I guess it was a good thing since Ilaria was pregnant, she could chill at the crib while me, Chandra and Mya ran the shop. "Ilaria is very lucky." Mya said. "Why you say that?" I asked while folding up the new stock of tee- shirts. "Cause ain't to many like you." Chandra cut in. "Like me? I'm just a average person just doing what's right." I said. "You're lucky too cause Ilaria can't keep your name out her mouth." Mya said. "Oh yeah? What's this about cause yaw up to something?" I asked. "Chandra gotta boyfriend and she's in love." Mya blurted out. Chandra gave her a look to try and get her to shut up. "She be on the phone all night with him and momma don't know but she said he's the one." Mya said. Chandra shoved her in the arm giving her the sign saying that's enough. Eventhough Chandra was brown skinned her cheeks were still turning red. "So Ms. Chandra gotta boyfriend?" I asked. Chandra was embarrassed. I didn't know why, she was pretty, very pretty. I could tell she was very insecure. It's going to be real bad when she

find out that she's pretty and she could have any nigga she wanted. Damn women were dangerous and it was our fault for making them like that. I could tell that Mya knew she was the shit. For someone to tell Mya she was bad is like telling her her name was Mya. Chandra just wasn't use to the attention. I had to talk to her quick before one of these little niggas got into her head. I just left the topic alone. "So how's Olivia doing?" I asked. She all-right. She's about to start a program that's for kindergartners." Mya said rubbing her arm from the shove Chandra delivered a couple of minutes ago. "Yeah, Ilaria was saying something about that but I was busy talking to my officer." "So after you get finished working here what do you plan to do?" Chandra asked. "Shouldn't I be asking you that question Ms. Richardson?" "Why do you and Ilaria do that? Always answer a question with a question. That is so annoying." Chandra said folding her arms. "Do what?" I asked "See that's, uhhhhh never mind." Chandra said getting fed up. "So are you gonna Answer my question?" I asked. "I don't know, I like to talk to people." Chandra said looking like she was uncomfortable. "Talk like how? Motivational speaker, psychologist, psychiatrist, teacher, news reporter, meteorologist, I can go on and on." "All-right that's enough.. I sure don't want to be a teacher." "I don't blame

you." Mya cut in laughing. "I know you ain't talking, being a stripper could take you far, oh my bad I mean e entertainer." Chandra snapped back. "Awww come on, that ain't nice." I told Chandra. "She started it!" Chandra yelled. "Just because you're a dancer doesn't mean you're labeled as a stripper smart ass." Mya said. "All-right that's enough we got customers." I cut in. After being with Chandra and Mya for half of the day I was exhausted. I fell right on the couch soon as I came in the door. All I could hear was Chris calling my name telling me to get up but I was so tired.

Chapter 33

"You find em'? Joker asked Esco. "Naw homey.. It's been a month since I last heard about Lina. I got one of my homey's checkin' up on her though." Esco said. "A toss me one of them Coronas out the fridge." Joker said looking at fish boy through the kitchen. Fish boy grabbed two tossed one to Joker and guzzled down the other one. "You need to slow down homey." Esco told Fish boy. "You wasting ya' breath. Ortiz said while loading up the clips. "So when you tryna do this?" Joker asked Esco while grabbing the Mac II off the couch. "I'm' in no rush, we wait. When we rush, things go wrong. Linas' all-right so we have nothing to worry about. The dirt has been done. I don't know what the reason was for, but Kevin will pay. Lina could have been killed and my nephew. I hate that she even had a baby with that piece of shit. Lina means the world to me and I know yaw can say the same. I also know that I don't wanna hurt my sister anymore then I already have. If we kill Kevin her son won't have a father. I know Lina would be crushed if something happened to him. We gotta be smart. Word on the street is Dres' brother is beefing with Kevin so we might not have to do nothing. But if it's taking to long then we move." 'Esco took a sip of his beer and sat it back down. "I don't wanna start a war, I'm trying to end it

before it goes that far. I don't want none of the homey's hurt.". Esco said. "I feel that." Joker said. "So how long do we wait?" Ortiz asked. "It might be a month, 3 months, shit it might be years from now." Esco said.

"Damn it feels good to be out." Rell said looking out the window riding with K-dog. "Yeah it look like you lost 100 lbs nigga." K-dog said laughing. "Man shut da' fuck up." Rall said playing. "Damn man I can't believe lil' Rah-rah gone bro'." Rell said. "Yeah I'm fucked up still and it's been over a month." K-dog said pulling up in white Castle. They both got out of the Caprice shinning with Cartiers on. K-dog had bought Rell a platinum chain with a iced out 5 star pendant. "Damn bro', it feels good to be out." Rell said again. "Man this like the eleventh time you said that shit." K-dog said. When they walked in all eyes were on them. "Gotta piss like a mothafucka. A yaw gotta bathroom?" Rell asked one of the employees. One of the male employees gave him a key and Rell went to rest room. K-dog ordered two number 3s and a number 4. Rell came back out shaking the water off his hands. "Damn yaw ain't got no paper towels back there?". Rell asked while handing the key back. "I'll be sure to put some back there sir." The male employee said. People was laughing in the back round. When they got their food they were on their way out

until a gang of niggas in all black blocked the door so they couldn't come out. When K- dog and Rell stepped to the side to let them in, they didn't come in, instead they circled K-dog caprice. "Man these lil' niggas don't even know." K-dog said reaching for his pistol on his hip. "Chill out bro', we good, maybe these lil' niggas ain't got nothing to do." Rell said. K-dog looked at Rell with a question mark on his head. "Man it's 2001 man them lil' niggas tryna take our shit. On everything bro'. Nigga you been in the hospital to long or something. You got a case of anesthesia nigga?" K-dog asked Rell. "Do you want me to call the police?" The male employee asked. "That ain't necessary." K-dog said putting his hand up. "You right bro'. That's my fault. Rell said. "If they want it, then I'm goin' give it to em'." K-dog said putting his glasses in his pocket. Rell followed right behind him. K- dog was six foot one 220 lbs and Rell was five ten and 150 lbs. Rell had lost 30 lbs in the hospital. They both been locked up so they still had that strength from the joint. "They goin' get it then." Rell said. When they walked out it was five niggas outside in hoodies. K-dog knew they were some young niggas and him Rell would of slaughtered the little niggas but K-dog wasn't in the mood for hand throwing and he knew Rell wasn't in no condition to fight. "Yaw gotta problem?" K-

dog asked while approaching his car where the five little niggas were. They ignored K-dog. K-dog looked at Rell and laughed. When K-dog turned around he pulled out the .357 out and Rell pulled out a p.90. The little niggas put their hands. "We good man, we on't want no problems." One of the young niggas said. Rell kept looking. It was people all in the windows. "Get the fuck on!" K-dog yelled. Before K-dog finished his sentence the little niggas scattered in every direction. K-dog knew if he got caught with another burner he would be back in joint. They hopped in the Caprice and peeled off towards the freeway.

When they pulled up to Darons shop, his car was parked right in the front. Rell and K-dog got out looking like they just robbed a bank. When they walked in the store it was semi packed as always. "What up doe?" Daron asked K-dog and Rell. K-Dog and Rell just walked straight to the back. Daron followed behind them. Lil' Lou and 'L' just watched. When Daron got back there he seen K-dog and Rell putting the heaters up. "Man, what the fuck goin' on?" Daron asked getting irritated. "Man these lil' niggas tried to rob us!" Rell blurted out. "What?!" Daron asked in the same tone. "We on't know if the lil niggas had pistols or not. We pulled the burners out and they ran. We ain't let no shots off doe." K-dog said. "Where yaw was at?" Daron

asked. "White Castle on Woodward by the BLVD." Rell said. "Camera catch yaw?" Daron asked., "Most likely." Rell said. "Damn it's always something. Yaw ain't see the lil' niggas faces?" Daron asked. "Nope." Rall said. "Yaw good, don't even worry about it. I know they goin' come for you k-dog cause you did that two flat. So they goin' try and get you wit felonious assault, but if these lil' niggas never show up you should be good." Daron said. "What chu' mean about I should be good?" K- dog asked looking worried. "Just like I said, if the camera got chu' you, den' you know what time it is. K-dog. You know you goin' have a dog ass lawyer so don't trip bro'." Daron said. K- dog was pissed, he knew he was going back to the joint. Rell was good, he probably was looking at probation. Rell wasn't the type to complain so he was quiet the whole time. "We just gotta wait and see." Daron said walking out. Daron was fed up with all this shit. They should have killed that bitch ass nigga Kevin. When Daron came from the back 'L' and Lil' Lou was looking at him. "What up?" 'L' asked. "Shit. I'll holla at chaw' later on, we got business to take of." Daron said checking out the young females who crowded the store. Every time he thought everything was going wrong, a pretty face, fat ass and small waist always seemed to brighten up his day. K-dog and Rell walked out

in different clothes. Daron didn't even give them any contact. They were still fam', but fam' had to be dealt with. This shit had to change. Daron thought to his self.

After Kevin got out the shower ready to head to the 'D'. "Bay you all-right in there?" Selina asked. "Yeah bay, I'm on my way to Detroit to check on my shit, you wanna ride with me?" Kevin asked while drying off his body. "I'm all-right, you just be safe okay?" "You know I am." Kevin said. It was hot outside so Kevin threw some shorts on with a white tee and his Prada sandals. He gave Selina and Jr. a kiss and left out and hopped in his Lexus. He seen a red drop top Mercedez Benz in his rear view mirror. he couldn't tell who it was by the large hat and the dark shades. All he knew was that she wasn't black. When he stopped at the light, the red drop pulled up on the side of him. His tent hid him from the familiar face. It was Stephanie. Kevin rode down his window. "So, you have permanent company?" Stephanie said. "Yeah, life goes on Steph." Kevin said shortening her name. "Are you happy Mr. Clark?" She asked. Cars were now moving and horns were blowing. "Sure I am." Kevin said pulling off making a right turn leaving Stephanie in her drop. He didn't want to give up on her but he knew she would only be trouble and

that was something he had enough of. Where would he find another Selina?

When he was in the 'D' it was still looked the same. Nothing but the same shit. After he saved up enough money he was out. He thought about moving to Florida. Selina would like that and He would enjoy it even more Kevin chirped Solo on his Nextel.

"What up? Where you at?" "I'm with my Bm." Solo chirped back. "When you got time?" "Give me about an hour." Solo said chirping back. "All-right." Kevin said. "Might as well go to the Key." Kevin said. When he got to the strip club, it wasn't to many cars parked in the parking lot. He parked the Lexus valet and went inside. Wasn't to many people in there because it was still early. He wasn't in the mood to throw no money anyway, he just wanted a drink. "The usual Kev?" the young female bartender asked. "Yeah Cherry." "You look exhausted." Cherry said pouring him a shot of 1800. "law, I'm good. Thanks for being concerned." Kevin said. He always tipped Cherry good even when she had her days. Kevin watched the strippers for a minute until Solo called and said he was on his way. Kevin went outside to wait on him. Solo pulled up in his green Monte. He parked his shit in valet too. He still had

his chain Kevin gave him when they first opened up the car ash on Puritan. They shook hands and went inside. "So what's up Kevin?" Solo asked. "Man ain't shit up." Kevin said getting another drink. "Man you ain't call me down here for nothing." Solo said. "How you feel about taking over the car wash?" Kevin asked Solo. "What?!" Solo asked sounding surprised. "Yeah I'm gone man. I need you look after all the businesses end in return you can have the car wash." Kevin said. "Is you drunk? Cherry what the hell you give my mans?" Solo asked Cherry. "Nothing, he just came in looking crazy." Cherry said. "You serious ain't chu'?" Solo asked him. "Veah man, but this business shit serious, you can't slack fam'? Niggas take advantage of that. I know where I'm going to." Kevin leaned over and said in Solo ear. Solo mouthed 'Nevada'. "Naw man." He leaned over again and whispered 'Miami'. Solo heard him loud and clear and he smelt the Tequila on his breath. "You can't let nobody know where I'm at." Kevin said. "You got my word fam'." "How Neicey and my god daughter doing?" Kevin asked. "They straight, just dropped them off at the crib." Solo said. "You still thinking bout movin' to Tennessee?" Kevin asked. "Shit I on't know, by you delivering this news to me I might move mom dukes up

here with me." Solo said. "So what's up, you goin' take the offer?' Kevin asked.

Chapter 34

Zaria was due in a month. She was huge. I was so happy I was going to be a father. "What are you thinking about Drc?" Zaria asked. "Nothing bay, just happy as hell. "Chris your birthday is coming up. What do you wanna do?" Zaria asked. "I don't know." Chris said. "Do you have any friends in your class that you want to come to the house?" "Yep." Chris said. "Well you make sure you let uncle Chris know se he can tell their parents." Zaria said. "Okay." Chris said. Chris was enrolled in the summer program with Olivia. He was doing good. I made sure I kept him busy. It was a wrap for video games everyday. I was thinking about going to Detroit before the summer was over. I had to first get with Zaria about it. "What do you think about going back to Detroit to go visit?" I asked. "I don't mind. I prefer to have the baby first then go." Zaria said. "That's cool. I know the family would want to see the baby." I said. "Have you heard from Daron?" She asked. "Nope, but I know that Suga is due real soon." I said. "I gotta call her and I have to call Tiffany and see what's up with her. I know her and Sunny would happy to see me now." Zaria said. "I want to go to mama Kim house." Chris said. "We gotta call her and see if she's busy Chris." I told him.

A month later Suga was having her first child. Daron was right beside her through the whole thing. "Come on baby push. He's right there." Daron said. Suga was screaming to the top of her lungs. She seen the doctor pulling her new born and she almost fainted until Daron started squeezing her hand. The baby came out crying and Suga was now a mother. "Look at him bay. He looks just like you." Daron said. "I got real strong genes." Suga said laughing. She held her baby close to her wanting to never let go. Darnell Hicks was born September 4th. "Are you going to be a father Daron?" She asked him. "Baby what kind of question is that? Of course I am. I love you so much Chelle it don't make no sense.

Daron was at the crib chilling with 'L', big Bo, and III Lou'. "Damn you a dad now bro'." 'L' said. "Yeah, you know Suga goin' be trippin' bout me being over yo' crib." Daron said. "I already know. No more pussy for you." 'L' said laughing, "Man shut the fuck up. I do what the hell I wanna do." Daron said. Big bo started nodding his head agreeing with Daron. Suga was upstairs with her baby boy. She picked up the phone-and called "Man I don't know fam', give me some time. This something I gotta talk to Neicey about." Solo said. "Let me know as soon as possible cause I'm on my way up out this bitch." Kevin said.

"Gotcha, I'm bout to go holla at Neicey right now. I'm goin' be calling within these next few days." Solo said. "Aight' fam'." Kevin said. "Yop. Solo said getting up and leaving Kevin in the strip club. Kevin knew he had to go before something happened. He couldn't afford to lose everything. He hated his life but he enjoyed it. He had to much on his plate and it was time to dump that shit in the garbage. Kevin stayed a little while longer and he dipped out. He thought about not having Osama and Skeebo with him. He needed to recruit asap. Solo had told him about a guy named M.A. that he just hired at the car wash. If he was going to take somebody with him down south it was going to be somebody Solo trusted.

Zaria. "Hey girl...Thank you, who told you?.. ⋯I haven't talked to her yet but I know she wanna see her grandson......Yeah, When yaw coming?.... I hope so cause girl I miss you...All-right I'll talk to you soon." Suga hung up her phone and finished breast feeding Daron Jr. "A bay I'm bout to go pick up Rell. Do you or Jr. need anything?" Daron asked. "No, I'm all-right baby. Just stay out of trouble." Suga said. Daron hopped in the Tahoe with big bo', lil Lou', and 'L'. They drove to the 'D' to go holla at Rell and K-dog. Daron hasn't seen them in a while. They been rolling on the east side so he haven't been kicking it with them like that. "Yaw ain't heard nothing about Kevin?" Daron asked. "Hell naw." Everybody, said at once. "That nigga been hiding cause I ain't seen em' at none of his car washes." Daron said. "We'll find em' cause his pride is to high to hide." Big Bo' said. "You right about that." Daron said.

Kevin was riding through Detroit. He was heading towards Solo crib on Linwood. Solo had told him about a young nigga that been putting in work. Kevin was thinking about putting him down. When he pulled up in Solos' driveway, Solo and the young nigga came out the house. The little nigga looked familiar but Kevin couldn't put a name on him. When they got in they smelt like a pound of weed.

279

"Damn yaw ain't save none of that shit?" Kevin asked. "Nigga you know damn well I brought some." Solo said. "So whose the lil' homey?" Kevin asked. "This Pee-wee." Solo said. "What up Joe? "Pee-wee asked. "You from Chicago?" Kevin asked. "I use to live in the Chi' but I moved to Indiana a couple of years after I was born." Pee-wee said." I heard a lot about you. I heard you be in Inkster and shit." Kevin said. "Yeah I gotta lil' spot over there." Pae-wee said. "Inkster huh? I know a few guys from that way." Kevin said. "Oh yeah?" Pee-wee asked. "Solo told me a lot about you. He said you were about yo' paper and that's what I need on the team." Kevin said. "True, cause if it ain't bout the paper I'm good." Pee-wee said. "Fam' is first Pee-wee. Remember that." Kevin said. "You right, but sometimes fam' don't be right." Pee-wee said. Kevin kind of took offense because of the situation he was in with Dre. "We not goin' worry bout that to much right now. We goin' go to All-stars and celebrate. Welcome to the family." Kevin said shaking Pee-wees' hand.

Rell and K-dog were riding in the box chevy going to pick up Tb from work. When they pulled up Tb was coming out with a couple of bags. "Damn nigga, everytime I come get cho' you, you bringing out bags." Rell said. "Man I can't look good?" Tb asked. "Shit I ain't knocking your hustle at

all. I wanna see you shinning like I'm shinning." K-dog said flashing his wrist showing off the ice in his Movado watch. "Man yaw got some nerves. Yaw goin' sell dope all yaw life?" Tb asked. "Yop." K-dog said pulling off. They were going to Northland Mall to pick up a few things from city slickers. "This what Daron need in his store, Mauris." Rell said. "Man nobody not trying to buy that expensive stuff. You buy like four pair of those and you got a car in your shoe closet." Tb said. "What kind of car you driving?" K- dog asked and Rell busted out laughing. "Man yaw can clown me all yaw want. 'm getting my shit together the right way." Tb said. That's cool. Not me though. Let me get these orange ones in a size 10 please." Rell said to the employee. He brought them out two minutes later. "I don't need to try em' on." Rell said pulling out his knot. "Your total is $537.45 sir." The cashier said. Rell peeled six one hundred dollar bills out his not and handed them to the cashier. "You good Tb?" Rell asked him. "Yeah man I'm good. I don't need nothing." Tb said. "I can't tell." K-dog said laughing. "Man forget yaw." Tb said laughing with them. They ended up leaving the mall and riding down 8 mile. They stopped at the light and K-dog noticed a Harley Davidson F-150 in the parking lot of All-stars. "A what kind of truck you said you saw oh girl in?" K-dog asked.

"Who you talking about?" Tb asked. "The Latino chick whose house was burnt down." K-dog said. "One of those Harley trucks." Tb said. "A bro' I bet that's that nigga nigga Kevin truck right there." K-dog said. "Man you know how many trucks it is like that?" Rell asked. The light turned green and K-dog pulled off. "Man I bet that's him." K-dog said again. "Man whatever yaw do, yaw can drop me off straight up." Tb said. "Man shut the hell up with all that scary shit. I don't need another co-defendant anyway." K-dog said. "Ain't nobody scared, I'm just smart." Tb said. "Yeah smart and scared." Rell said.

Kevin, Solo and Pee-wee was on their way inside the strip club. It was just getting dark. "Damn this bitch goin' be jumping." Pee-wee said. "You got cho strap with you?" Kevin asked Pee-wee. "Hell yeah I got it." Pee-wee said. "You ever been to a strip club?" Kevin asked him. "Nope. I ain't shit but sixteen." Pee-wee said. "Man you bullshittin'." Kevin said. "Hell naw he ain't." Solo cut in and said. They stepped in and Kevin and Solo showed their ID and Pee-wee just stood there. "He with us.". Kevin said giving the bouncer two hundred dollars. He let them in without searching them. The club was Just getting packed. Some of everybody was in there. "A lil' mama, this my lil' mans. Why don't you show him a good time." Solo said to

one of the dancers. Pee-wee tongue was hanging out his mouth. The chick was bad as hell. When she walked over to him she bent over and whispered, "don't worry I won't bite." She turned around and started giving him a lap dance. Solo and Kevin was laughing hard as hail. "Look at his face fam'." Solo said. Pee-wee was hard as a brick. The dancer was even giggling. After she was done Kevin tipped her good and she left. "Damn lil' homey, you act like you ain't never had no pussy." Kevin said. "Not no grown pussy. Shit I only fuck with hoes my age." Pee-wee satd. "Well we goin' end all that tonight." Solo said. Pee-wee had a big grin on his face. They bought drinks all night and had almost all the dancers around them. Kevin was going to put the little homey down with the team.

Shit, yaw ready? Kevin asked Solo and Pee-wee. "Yeah I'm good." Solo said. Pee-wee was just looking around like he was lost. "Pee-wee." Kevin called his name again. "Yeah yeah what's up?" Pee-wee said fumbling out his words. "You ready?" Kevin asked him again. "Yeah I'm ready. They got up and left a nice tip on the table.

Chapter 35

K-dog pulled up in Tb driveway and they all hopped out. Tb asked were they good and they both said yeah at the same time. k-dog and Rell ran in the spot next door to Tb house. They grabbed the burners and hopped back in the Chevy. "You ain't grab the hoodies?" K-dog asked Rell. "Hell naw you was supposed to grab em'." Rell said. "Man you on some bullshit." K-dog said getting out. He came back five minutes later with the hoodies. "We goin' do this shit right nigga." Rell said. "No mistakes." K-dog said. "Load that Mac II up nigga." Rell said. "Nigga I know already, you just hurry up and worry about catching this nigga before he leave." K-dog said. "If I miss that nigga coming out Jesus ain't die on a cross." "Nigga you a fool." K-dog said grabbing the Mac-90. Both guns were loaded and they were ready. They finally got to All-stars and the truck was still there in the parking lot. "Man I hope this him." K-dog said. "Fuck hoping. This gotta be him." Rell said. They parked the Chevy om Strathmoor 'a block after Hubbell. All-stars sat right on the corner of Hubbell. "We bout to lace this nigga bro'." K-dog said. They hopped out with the machine guns and their hoodies on. They waited two cars away from the truck. "I see em', I see em'." Rell

said. "We got this nigga now. He won't dodge this one." K-dog said.

Kevin, solo, and Pee-wee came out the strip club laughing. "Man you was like a lil' kid at a candy store." Solo said. "Man get the fuck outta here." Pee-wee said. "He good, that was his first time bro'.". Kevin said pushing his alarm on his truck, Soon as Kevin opened the door all he heard was, "Got cho' bitch ass na." The whole parking lot lit up. Kevin knew he was dead and it wasn't nothing he could do about it. Solo and Pee-wee dodged all the bullets they could. They both had their pistols out but it was to many shots coming. "Fuck that." Pee-wee said. He stood up and started shooting back but he stood no chance. It seemed like the shots came quicker. "God damn." Pee-wee yelled out. They didn't hear Kevin voice at all. When the shots stopped they looked under the truck and Kevin was lying on his stomach. "Kev', Kevin." Solo whispered but he got no response. Pee-wee hopped up with the nine and looked around. Once he seen everything was clear he ran to the other side of the truck. Before he made it to the other side he noticed he was hit in the arm. It burned like hell but his mission was to get to Keyin. Solo was right behind him. People were now coming out of the strip club. When one of the strippers seen Kevin on the ground she screamed to the

top of her lungs and ran back Inside the building. "Somebody call the ambulance." Solo heard somebody yell. They turned Kevin over on his back. He still was breathing but It was so much blood on the ground, Solo Just knew he wasn't going to make It. Pee-wee was now walking back and forth with the pistol still In his hand. "I can't believe this shit. We got caught slipping fam'. What the fuck we goin' do man?" Pee-wee asked. "We can't do shit but wait for help." Solo said. They heard the sirens but they Just knew It was to late. "Put that pistol up fam', the hook a be here any minute. You good?" Solo asked. "Hell naw I ain't good. I'm heated nigga." Pee-wee said. When the ambulance showed up they strapped Kevin up to the gurney and put him inside the ambulance truck. The F-150 was fucked up. Solo had to call Neicy to come pick him and Pee-wee up. The police questioned them but they had nothing to say. The detective gave Solo and Pee-wee a card so they could contact him If they remembered anything. Neicy pulled up in her Durango. She hopped out so quick and hugged Solo. "Are you all-right baby?" She asked Solo. "Yeah baby I'm good, but it's looking bad for Kevin." Solo said. "We gotta get to the hospital Solo." Pee-wee said. "He right bay." Solo said. They hopped in the truck and headed to the hospital.

"We got his bitch ass." Rell said taking off his hoody. "Man if he live after that nigga the devil." K-dog said. "He outta there." Rell said. "I hope so cause we could of kept shooting that nigga." K-dog said. "Man you need to lose some weight. It took you forever to get back to the whip." Rell said. "Man shut the hell up. I ain't tryna hear that shit." K-dog said. "My bad I think I might have struck a nerve." Rell said. "Man whatever. Did you see his face when he seen us though?" K-dog asked Rell. "Hell yeah! seen his face. That nigga looked like he shit his pants." Rell said laughing. "A bro, we ain't tellin' nobody what happened, not even Daron. it'll bring to much heat to us. You know he plugged and niggas a come for us that he' don't even fuck with just to be cool with em'." Rell said. "I feel that bro'." K-dog said. "We good now, so roll that weed up." Rell said. "Where the blunts at?" K-dog asked. "Man you mean to tell me that you don't got no blunts?" Rell asked. "Man where the keys at so I can shoot to the store?" K-dog asked. "They in the kitchen on the counter." Rell said. K- dog grabbed the keys and went out the side door. The store was right on the corner so he didn't have to drive far. He hopped in the Chevy and drove to the liquor store on 8 mile. When he got on 8 mile he seen red and blue lights flashing from All-stars. He parked and hopped

out. He seen a couple of his blood homey's in front of the store rolling. "Blood love." K-dog said. They greeted him back. K-dog went in and bought the blunts. When he came out his little home boys were gone. He seen the Oakland County sheriffs pulling up in the parking lot. K-dog didn't pay them no mind. They looked his way and parked their car. This wasn't their jurisdiction so K-dog wasn't tripping. He made sure not to cross 8 mile. He hopped in his whip and drove off checking his rear view mirror. He seen that they were 'still in the parking lot. They probably were there because of the little homey's. He parked the whip and walked into the house. Before he walked in he made sure that the hook was no where to be found. "You get the blunts?" Rell asked. "Yeah nigga. I got em', now you roll up." K-dog said taking off his coat. "This that fire too." Rell said breaking down the weed. Rell lit the blunt hit it a couple of times and passed it. K-dog took his hits and was passing it back. "That shit hittin' nigga." K-dog said. "I know, I got it from Shameka." Rell said. "Thick ass Shameka?" K-dog asked. "Yop, the one with the butterfly tattoo." Rell and K-dog said it at the same time. "This day couldn't get no better." Rell said exhaling the smoke.

The next day Zaria was getting ready to go to work. She heard the phone ringing so she stopped everything to go

pick it up. "Hello....Yeah hold on girl. Dre, Carla on the phone." She yelled downstairs. "Hold on bay, here I come." I said running up the stairs. I had some old hoop sorts on with a tore tank top. "What chu' been doing, fixing on cars?" Zaria asked. "Naw, I was downstairs cleaning up the basement: Unpacking all those boxes." I said reaching for the phone. "Hello....What?!......Hold on, hold on Carla. Are you sure it was him?".... I can't come up there, Zarias' due any day now.... I'll see but I can't make no promises...I love you too." I hung up the phone. "What's up bay?" Zaria asked. "Kevin got shot bad and it's not looking good at all." I said. "Is that a good thing or a bad thing?" She asked. "Honestly baby I don't know. He's done so much shit to the family. He's still my brother Zaria. Carla wants me to come see him. You know he has a son and if he don't make it I want to be apart of my nephews life." I said. "Well I can understand that. Whatever happens I'm with it cause you're my baby." Zaria said. "I don't know how long he's going to be in the hospital but I do want to go see him. I mean that's the least I could do. He might even explain to me why he did the things he did." I said. "Well I'm going with you and so is Chris." Zaria said. "Well we can get our tickets today and head out." I said. "What are we waiting for then." Zaria asked.

"Oh my God, this can't be happening. Not my baby." Seline said rushing into the hospital. "Where is he, where is he?" She screamed. "Calm down ma'am." One of the security guards said. "Listen I just wanna see my husband. Where is he?" She screamed again. "Listen you're going to get arrested if you continue to cause a scene." The security guard said. "Get the hell off of me." Selina said snatching her arm away. "Hold on wait." A voice Selina has heard before. Selina turned around and seen Carla running towards her. "Wait, that's my sister." Carla said. The security guard released her and Selina took running towards Carla and she embraced her. "How is he?" Selina asked. "It's not looking good at all." Carla said while still hugging her. Selina broke out in tears. It's goin' to be all right." Carla said squeezing her tighter. "I need to see him please." Selina said. "Come on." Carla said grabbing her hand and leading her to the room. "What am I going to do now Carla? I told him, I told him. He never listened to me." Selina cried out. "Girl Kevin didn't listen to nobody." Carla said. When they got to the room Neicy stood up and ran towards Selina to hug her. "Girl I'm so sorry." Neicy said. "Why, he knew these guys were out to get him." Selina said. "He's been shot eight times. He has lost a lot of blood. We have him on a breathing machine right now. We're

trying our best." The doctor said. "Oh my God. This can't be happening. Solo couldn't even look Selina in the face. He just put his head in his lap. Could I please see him." Selina asked. "Are you an immediate family member?" The doctor asked. "Yes, I'm his wife." Selina cried out. "All right just you though." He took her inside the room. Kevin was breathing through tubes. She had never seen him like this. She wanted to lie next to him but she knew she couldn't. she tightly grabbed his hand and whispered everything is going to be okay.

Kevin could hear everything. He couldn't move a muscle in his body. He wanted to squeeze her hand back so bad but he couldn't. He loved her so much. All the evil things he'd done he wished he could erase them. Something felt strange and something was grabbing hold to him and it wasn't Selina. "He's going into shock." The doctor yelled. "Somebody get some help." The doctor yelled again. Selina was crying even harder now. She was still standing by his bedside until more doctors rushed in and she had to leave. "He's fading away, grab the machine." The doctor yelled. One of the nurses escorted Selina out of the room. Selina looked back and they were yelling "CHARGE and CLEAR". She seen his chest jumping up and down. The doctor came back out taking off his gloves. "I'm sorry, he

didn't make it." The doctor said. Solo left out the hospital. He couldn't take it. Selina burst out in tears screaming. Carla ran to her hugging her. "Come here girl." Carla said. Carla had to call Dre and tell him what happened. Dre didn't believe her at first but he heard everybody in the background.

"Dre are you all right?" Zaria asked. "Yeah bey, I'm all right. Just can't believe he's gone. Never got a chance to ask him why." I said rubbing my head while driving. We have to go up there now baby. I said. "I know baby." Zaria said. I could now live my new life without looking over my shoulder. It was me and Carla now. I heard the phone ringing again.

"Hello……What?......Where are you now?......All right I love you too." I said. "What's going on bay?" Zaria asked. "The FEDS just ran up in Darons' house." I said. "Oh shit." Zaria said.

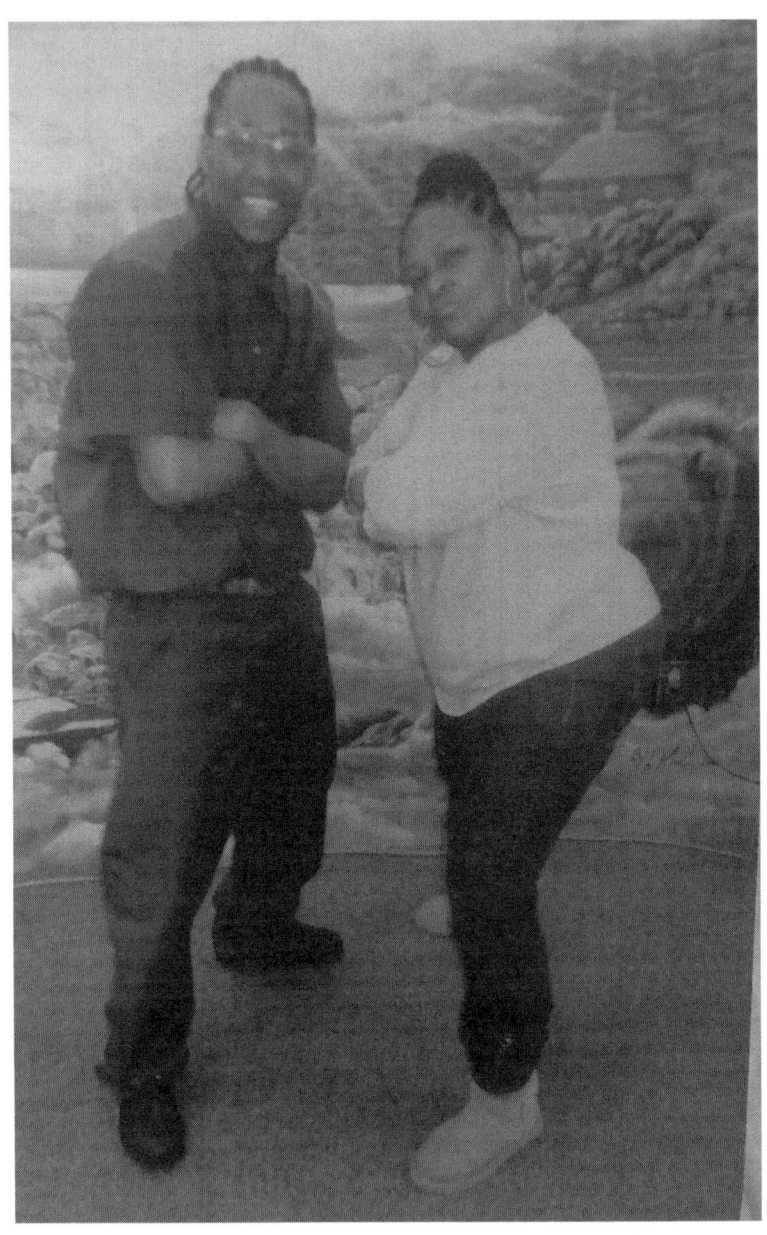

Made in the USA
Columbia, SC
27 March 2023

14408339R00161